"A BRISK, SAVVY NUMBER."
—*Kirkus Review*

"AMOS WALKER IS BACK ON THE JOB—AND THAT'S WELCOME NEWS FOR FANS OF HIGH-OCTANE DETECTION."
—*People*

"THE WALKER BOOKS ARE AMONG THE MOST ENJOYABLE BEING WRITTEN TODAY IN THE CLASSIC PRIVATE-EYE FIELD . . . impressively crafted, at once sentimental and cynical."
—*San Francisco Examiner*

"AMOS WALKER IS DAUNTLESS, INCORRUPTIBLE, AND UNDERPAID . . . JUST WHAT A PRIVATE EYE SHOULD BE."
—*Newsday*

"OTHER WRITERS DO IT WELL. ESTLEMAN DOES IT BEST."
—*Armchair Detective*

By Loren D. Estleman

LOREN D. ESTLEMAN

THE WITCH FINDER

WARNER BOOKS

A Time Warner Company

WARNER BOOKS EDITION

Cover design by Rachel McClain
Hand lettering by David Gatti
Photo by Jim Allor

Warner Books, Inc.
1271 Avenue of the Americas
New York, NY 10020

Visit our Web site at
www.warnerbooks.com

 A Time Warner Company

Printed in the United States of America

Originally published in hardcover by The Mysterious Press.
First Paperback Printing: September 1999

10 9 8 7 6 5 4 3 2

For the cousins:
Marlene and Gene,
Janet,
Buck (in fondest memory),
Randy, Jason, Jan, Lindy, and Bobbie;
and for Aunt Irene

Never chase a lie. Let it alone, and it will run itself to death.

—Lyman Beecher

THE WITCH FINDER

One

THERE ARE MORNINGS, just after dawn on unseasonably hot June days when every breath you draw is filtered through forty pounds of wet laundry, that you welcome the clear cold icicle of the telephone bell ringing.

You sit on the edge of your bed for a while waiting for the overcast to clear, uncertain whether you were preparing to rise or retire, then the ringing comes again, an hour behind the first, and you get up and squish out into the living room where the air from the open window chills you in your damp underwear, and the second ring is just ending. Everything you hear and see and do is at quarter-speed. It's a kind of brownout of the brain.

"Is that Amos Walker?"

A man's voice, ageless and tweedy, with Big Ben chiming on the consonants. I'd tapped into an episode of *Upstairs, Downstairs*.

"It was last night. I can't answer for it now." I sounded like a low-revolution drill even to myself. "What time is it on my side of the Atlantic?"

"Shortly after six. Did I wake you?"

"Hold the line, please."

Hearing the birds now—they were singing at normal speed, which in my present condition sounded like a chorus of slipping fan belts—I found a box of matches and a butt longer than an inch in the ashtray on the telephone stand and lit up. The smoke chased the bees out of my head. "Okay, I checked the bed and I'm not still in it. Who am I speaking to?"

"My name is Stuart Lund. I'm an attorney."

"Not a barrister or a solicitor?"

One of those screwy computer scales you hear on the telephone played in the pause on his end. "No, I'm a naturalized American citizen and have been for fifteen years. I'm prepared to offer you a retainer in the amount of one thousand dollars if you'll agree to meet me this morning here in my suite at the Airport Marriott."

"Which airport?"

"Detroit Metropolitan, of course. Did you think I was calling from England?"

"The accent threw me off."

"Indeed. I wasn't aware I still had one."

"You don't need one if you're going to use words like *indeed*," I said. "Okay, make the offer."

"I believe I just made it."

"You said you were prepared to. I thought you people were more careful with the language than us born Yankees." The filter ignited. I punched out the butt. The stench of scorched rubber hung on the stagnant air. "Pardon the impertinence, Mr. Lund. Also the effrontery. I'm experiencing a power surge. My standard retainer is fifteen hundred."

"There will be a substantially larger sum involved if I decide to employ your services as an enquiry agent. The thousand is merely for coming out. It's yours whether or not we agree to do business."

"Are you acting on behalf of a client?"

"More accurately, in compliance with a client's wishes. I'm representing the estate of Jay Bell Furlong."

"Jay Bell Furlong the architect?"

"The same. Can I expect you?"

"I haven't read or seen the news since last night. Has he died?"

"As of my last call to Los Angeles five minutes ago, no. Although my use of the term *estate* is technically premature, as his executor I'm under instructions to waste no time. Which is precisely what I seem to be doing." His tone acquired a measured amount of impatience, as if he'd raised one of a series of internal floodgates an inch.

"I'll be there in less than an hour, Mr. Lund."

He gave me the number of the suite and broke the connection.

I showered, toweled off, and shaved, feeling fresh sweat prickling out of the open pores as I stood in the cross-draft between the window and the bathroom doorway. Dressing, I selected a blue shirt, dark blue knitted tie, the tan summer-weight, and brown mesh shoes, on the theory that if I looked cool I might at least make someone else feel cool and maybe he'd return the favor. I combed my hair and reconnoitered the gray. The beard beneath the skin was as blue-black as ever, but my temples were beginning to resemble the Comstock Lode.

There was no time for breakfast, even if I were in the habit. I swigged orange juice straight from the carton, overcame the urge to climb into the refrigerator with it when I put it back, and went out to the garage. I drove with all the windows down and the wind lifting my combed hair, which the hell with it. When that model of Cutlass roared off the line, air conditioning was for Rolls Royce.

My clientele had taken a stylish turn. At eighty and change, Jay Bell Furlong was the last of the legendary school of American architects who had cast away the posts and lintels and marble scrollwork of the Old World. They had substituted horizontal lines for vertical, invented the concept of harmony with the environment, and fought a desperate and ultimately losing battle against the Xeroxed glass, girder, and reinforced-concrete designs rolling out of the cost-effective East. Theirs was the last dying bellow of art in a field seized by accountants and the low bid. For a heartbeat their bold innovations had swept a continent. Now Louis Sullivan was forgotten, Frank Lloyd Wright was dead, and Furlong was about to be, rigged as he was with tubes and insulated wire in the cancer ward at Cedars of Lebanon Hospital in Los Angeles, the elephants' graveyard of forgotten movie stars, one-hit rockers, and disgraced presidents. The media deathwatch had been going on for a week. Furlong's rallies and relapses made the Eleven O'Clock Report as regularly as the box scores.

What his attorney was doing in Detroit, where impressive architecture was looked upon as an empty lot in the making, was foggy.

As I swung into the short-term lot at the airport, a leviathan of a 757 shrieked overhead at a steep angle, sucking its wheels into its belly and dragging its shadow over the car like a coronation train. The sky the jet was headed for didn't look any more inviting than the ground. A low dirty cloudbank had been stalled over the metropolitan area for days, trapping the kind of temperatures and humidity normally associated with the Philippines. Old people die like goldfish in that weather, also high school juniors at fast-food restaurants with hundred-dollar sneakers and short tempers.

The lobby air hit me like a bucket of ice water after the

convector of the pavement. That particular Marriott may be the only hotel in the world built directly onto an airport terminal. Certainly it's the only one this side of Beirut where you have to pass through a metal detector to check in or visit. I said something on that order to the guard at the gate, who scowled and tipped his head toward a sign that informed me my First Amendment rights were suspended on the premises. I told him what I thought of that, but by then I was two floors up in the elevator.

Stuart Lund came in at six-two and three hundred pounds in gray silk tailoring with a large head of wavy yellow hair, blue eyes like wax drippings, and a black chevron-shaped moustache he hadn't bothered to bleach. He was about fifty. After opening the door to his suite, he shifted a mahogany cane with a cast-silver crook to his left hand and offered me his right. "You're punctual. Very admirable."

I stepped past him into a large room that would have been cheerful if the drapes weren't drawn, with fat armchairs and a free-standing refrigerator under lock and key. A television on a swivel was tuned in to CNN with the sound very low. Lund asked me to sit and approached the refrigerator, leaning a little on the cane.

"I never shall get over the way they see to one's creature comforts in this country's hotels. I'm sinfully well stocked. It's early, but I understand all you detectives are seasoned imbibers."

"That's fiction," I said. "Make mine a Bloody Mary."

"One of the more fascinating queens." He used the key, married the contents of a toy vodka bottle and a miniature can of tomato juice in a barrel glass, and brought it over. "I apologize for not joining you. The lag," he explained, lowering himself into a chair that for anyone else would have been a loveseat.

"Did you fall off the ramp?"

He lifted his eyebrows, then glanced down at the cane. "Gout, I'm afraid. The complaint of colonial governors and certain kings of France. I'm under physician's instructions to lose a hundred pounds, but I'm in revolt. People who have been fat all their lives and suddenly become thin are pathetic to see, like polar bears wasting away in the wrong climate. The stick belonged to an ancestor: Sir Hudson Lowe, Governor of St. Helena and Bonaparte's gaoler for the last six years of the Corsican's life." He pronounced the word the same as *jailer*, but he wouldn't have spelled it that way.

"My grandfather rode shotgun on a beer truck."

He wiggled his moustache, then hooked the cane on the arm of the loveseat and produced a fold of paper from an inside breast pocket.

The check bore Jay Bell Furlong's name and address in the upper left corner. Lund had signed his own name. I pocketed it. "Power of attorney?"

"The privilege did not come cheap. I've been Jay's legal adviser, secretary, business manager, confidant, and frequently his whipping post ever since he brought me here from Gloucester. He disengaged me from a firm of solicitors that represented William Pitt, and which another ancestor of mine helped establish. It was quite the family scandal at the time; although I daresay dear old Uncle Nigel's decision to attend a meeting of the House of Lords in a chiffon evening dress and diamonds has supplanted it."

"Was it before or after six?"

He worried his moustache with a row of small perfect teeth. No English dentist was responsible for those. "Do you know, I never asked. I hope the old boy hadn't cast off *all* his breeding."

Now that I was there his impatience seemed to have ebbed. I picked up the pace. "Who gave you my name?"

"A colleague, Arthur Rooney. He hadn't many flattering things to say, but what wasn't good was irrelevant. I'm chiefly interested in your ability to maintain a confidence."

"I've been to jail over it four times." I spelled it *jail*. "That's public record. No sense telling you how much it's cost me in ace bandages. That isn't."

He weighed me. The waxy eyes looked as if they would retain thumbprints. "Do you know the historical definition of the term *witchfinder*?"

"I do if it's anything like witch *hunter*."

"They're not the same. Not quite. The Puritans of your— excuse me, *our*—New England colonies employed hunters to rid them of witches. The hunters in their turn engaged witchfinders to gather evidence against them, or rather to manufacture it. I'm not at all convinced that there weren't such things as witches, but I do question the statistics of the time."

He rested a hand on the crook of his cane, clouding the shiny silver with his personal humidity. "In the country of my birth we were quick to condemn the Pilgrims for fleeing England in search of religious freedom only to impose a far more repressive creed upon themselves. But they behaved as they did out of a sincere belief in the forces of good and evil, Christ the Redeemer and Lucifer the Tempter. The witchfinders did not share that belief. They were paid commissions on the witches they managed to expose; not an incomprehensible arrangement when you consider the state of colonial finances, but it was scarcely fertile ground for verdicts of innocence. The tests these finders conducted upon the wretches who stood before them accused were barbaric. Those who survived were judged guilty and hanged."

"Burned, I thought."

He shook a finger at me.

"You really should know at least as much about your native country's past as a newcomer. They burned werewolves. They hanged witches."

I looked down at the glass in my hand. He looked too comfortable to get up and fix me another, and at the rate he was going I would touch bottom long before he reached his point. But he'd hired the audience along with the hall. Behind him on CNN, a brief tape biography of Jay Bell Furlong ended and the camera cut to a reporter standing on the sidewalk in front of Cedars of Lebanon Hospital. You know it's a slow news week when builders log more air time than destroyers.

"When witches passed out of fashion," Lund went on, "the finders lost their comfortable posts, but not forever. In a culpable society there will always be employment for the bearers of false witness. They're less flamboyant now, more difficult to identify. They no longer hang out shingles and they've burned their black cowls. That's why I called you. Your assignment is to find the witchfinder."

"Speak American, Windy. You're wearing the man out."

This was a new voice in the auditorium. The door to the suite's adjoining bedroom had opened. The famous Furlong bone structure was on the screen, and as I craned my head around I thought at first those Lincolnesque features had burned into my retinas, moving with my eyes. The man the nation's press waited to photograph on his horizontal way to the Los Angeles County Morgue was standing in a hotel doorway in Detroit with a drink in his hand.

Two

FOR A GHOST-IN-WAITING, Furlong looked healthy. As narrow as Stuart Lund was wide and almost as tall, he had on one of his trademark pale yellow suits over a pink silk shirt with the collar open, no necktie, and held a tall glass with a couple of ice cubes floating in clear liquid. His hair was white and fine enough to sift sugar through, his complexion brown not so much from the California sun as from natural pigmentation—he was descended from Greek stonecutters on his mother's side, according to *Who's Who*—and he had a face like a flying buttress: all planes and angles and prowlike nose with blue veins showing under the tight skin across the bridge. The impression overall was that of his buildings, soaring strength laid on top of tensile steel.

The details belonged to a different blueprint. His collar sagged slightly and the drape of his trousers was off, as if his body were shrinking away from his clothes. The hard glitter far back in the deep sockets of his eyes looked more desperate than determined. He was not just leaning against the door frame; it was supporting him entirely.

Lund put weight on his cane. "Jay, you should be resting. I was going to bring Mr. Walker in to see you in a few minutes."

"Don't be the mother-cow, Windy. I'll be resting soon enough, and forever." He straightened, found his balance, and came into the room to take my hand in a hard, bony grip. "Thanks for coming, Walker. Rooney told us a lot of good things about you." The glitter now was determination. That settled the point. He was dying.

"A lot of bad things too, I guess."

"They said much worse about my designs for most of my career. Then suddenly I was sixty and a national treasure. I got a medal from the president and a week on *Hollywood Squares*. Live long enough and you become respectable. Die early and you get to be a legend." He glanced at the television. Annoyance crawled under the muscles of his face. "Switch that damn thing off, will you, Windy? Listening to your own obituary gets old fast."

Lund was on his feet now. He trundled over and punched the POWER button.

I said, "Every news story I was ever part of sounded like something else when it reached the air. But I never knew them to miss quite this wide."

"That's my fault," Furlong said, "although I had help. We're so health-obsessed these days it's really amazing how far we'll go on the word of a couple of doctors who like to see themselves surrounded by microphones. We're in danger of elevating them to the station of high priests, when what we ought to do is replace the caduceus with the Jolly Roger."

"Spoken like a patient." I ignored the look that bought me. "What's it costing you?"

"A new maternity wing at Cedars. My design. Someone else will have to see it through, though."

He swayed. Lund took his arm and steered him toward the loveseat. The thinness of the architect's ankles showed when he sat down. They were bare, and the bones stuck out like socket wrenches.

He gulped down half the contents of his glass and set it on the table at his elbow. An orange flush glimmered on his cheeks and went away. "It isn't so much a lie as an accelerated truth," he said. "My condition is inoperable and since I refuse to submit to chemotherapy and radiation I've been given four weeks. It should be enough."

"To find the witchfinder?" I sat down on the adjacent couch and drank my Mary.

"Stuart will dramatize. That's how he got his nickname."

"You're the only one who ever called me Windy." The attorney shifted his cane and raised one foot, looking like a chubby flamingo.

Furlong glanced around, wrinkling the tight skin of his nose. "I might as well be in the intensive care ward as here. I labored fifty years to restore warmth and character to the piles of stone and glass we're condemned to live in and work in. What a waste of a life. People must want to crawl around in test tubes or we wouldn't have the buildings we have. We used to make fun, we smug young geniuses, of those neoclassical, Neo-Gothic, Neo-Renaissance horrors Albert Kahn plopped down all over this city in the twenties. Everything was *neo* with him, nothing original or startling or intrinsically American. But he loved what he did, drank it and breathed it and fucked it, saw it through from drafting board to dedication. He didn't just spit up a six-pack of silos like that abortion on Jefferson and go home. These new Turks have never even held a piece of charcoal, wouldn't dirty their hands on it. They program their goddamn *faux* ceiling beams and triple-paned windows into the computer and let IBM do the rest. Is it any wonder there's no blood in their work?"

He sat back suddenly, as if a string had snapped. "Well, I won't have to look at it much longer."

But he wasn't through. The glitter fixed itself on me. "I started here, did you know that? Took a degree in engineering from the Detroit Institute of Technology in thirty-three, worst goddamn year in the century to try to start a career. I worked my ass off with the WPA as an apprentice mason for three years, thirty a week and glad to get it. Before I ever drew my first groined arch I'd built a dozen with my own hands, hoisted the pieces one by one up a sixteen-foot ladder. I was so musclebound I could barely close my fist around a Number Two Ticonderoga. My first wife married me for those muscles. When they went away so did she. No refills, Windy. The stuff goes a lot further than it used to."

Lund, who had come forward to take Furlong's glass when he drained it, put it on top of the little refrigerator.

"The Depression hung on here and I went West and invented California Modern, not that anybody ever gave me the credit, nor would I want it, considering what they did to it. Well, you can read about what else I did in back numbers of *Architectural Digest*. I never saw Detroit again until eight years ago, when the business retired out from under me and I accepted a job as guest lecturer at Wayne State. 'He draws! He speaks! He wears yellow on the cover of *GQ*! Come See the Living Fossil Before It's Too Late!'" He balled his fists on his knees, bone on bone. "Anyway it paid better than the WPA, and I got to fool myself into thinking I was still part of things. Also that's where I met Lily."

I finished my drink, sat back, and crossed my legs. We were drifting into my waters now. There was usually a Lily.

"She was a graduate student," Furlong said, "and, yes, she was young enough to be my granddaughter. Beautiful woman. Lovely skin. Lousy architect, but a first-rate artist.

She dropped by my office between classes to show me her portfolio. We went out for coffee. We went out for dinner. We had breakfast. I bought her a ring. That's the chronology. The time span doesn't matter."

He paused to recharge his cells. The story was taking as much out of him as several flights of stairs.

"I'm not the imbecile you're starting to think me," he said. "I was a grandfather then—a *great*-grandfather now—with three wrecked marriages and a score of silly affairs at my back, and sex is just candy, you can have enough for a lifetime early if you're greedy enough at the start. I was. And love is a chimera, not nearly as tangible nor as pressing as bursitis after a certain age. Of course I felt something. Of course Lily was in love: with the idea of being married to Jay Bell Furlong, as well as to his line of credit and controlling interest in Furlong, Belder, and Associates, with offices in New York, L.A., Detroit, and Tokyo. And as Windy might say, it was a good job she was.

"It makes more sense than falling in love with an incandescent smile and masses of hair, things that will go to porcelain and naked scalp soon enough. When I *had* those things I had better taste than to choose a partner with so little foresight. You have to respect a woman first because respect is likely to be all you wind up with at the finish. I respected Lily."

"This is the part where I find it difficult to squeeze back the tears." Lund rubbed the ball of a meaty thumb over a flaw in the silver on his cane.

"Stuart's a romantic. It's the reason he never remarried after his own divorce."

"It most certainly is not. I'm a homosexual."

"Who isn't these days?" Furlong's color came and went. "All right, damn it, I'll say it. I was lonely. I was and am a monument, with a footing as deep as the tallest of my buildings. I could pick up a telephone and order the Hollywood goddess of my choice as my escort for the evening—I could make her my wife—but she wouldn't be the company Lily Talbot was. She was intelligent and stimulating. She took sides, not always mine, and forced me to reconsider my position on everything. A companion like that is damn rare where I am. A man needs someone he can talk to without having to hire a tutor to brief her first."

"Excuse me, Mr. Furlong," I said. "I'm nobody's choice for judge. I'm guessing you didn't marry."

The architect opened one of his fists. Lund shifted his cargo to his tender foot like a clerk laying out Fabergé eggs and gave me something from a manila folder on the table. It was a five-by-seven photograph, a crisp professional-looking black-and-white shot like you hardly ever see in our Kodachrome society, of a couple in a naked condition amid rumpled bedding. The woman was dark-haired, with good bones and an athletic body. The man was fair and flabby. The photographer had caught them in the act of breaking an embrace, the woman starting to turn her head, not yet looking directly at the camera, the man staring full into the flash. A reflection of the bulb showed in each of his shiny pupils.

I returned the picture. "I can see why you became attracted."

"The picture came by mail to my office at Wayne State in a brown envelope without a return address," Furlong said. "U.S. Postal Service mark, addressed with a typewriter. They weren't all in museums then. I still have the envelope if you want to see it."

"I left my junior fingerprint kit in my other pants."

"Understand, it wasn't the sleeping around that bothered me. Only an ass expects sexual integrity under those circumstances. It was her partner I objected to. The young man's name is Lynn Arsenault. At the time the photo was taken he was a junior partner in Imminent Visions."

"Furlong and Belder's principal competitor," Lund explained.

"To hell with that, it's misleading. This isn't about free enterprise. Imminent Visions was founded by a man named Vernon Whiting. The son of a bitch is dead now, and the worms can have him if they can keep him down. He was my apprentice. I taught him how to use a protractor and then he went around telling everyone I stole one of his designs. He told it enough times and in enough places it's entered the lore of this profession. By the end I think he believed it himself. When I saw that picture of Lily with Arsenault, I was convinced Whiting arranged for her to romance me in order to steal some of my own designs; revenge for a wrong I never did him.

"Well, I broke off the relationship. I didn't trust myself even to speak to Lily. The tabloids would have lapped up a public scene. I had Stuart send her a letter on Furlong and Belder stationery, gave notice at Wayne State, and went—fled—back to L.A. The only cowardly act in my adult life. I'm telling you all this to give you some idea of how I felt when I found out the picture is a fake."

"It's a good one," I said. "I didn't spot it."

"You'd need a glass and some training. I had both but didn't bother to use them. I fired that pup Arsenault from my firm the year before when I found out he was spying for Whiting. It all fit together, so I never questioned the picture. Then last month I was sorting through some things, getting my affairs in order, when I found the original of the photograph they used of Lily. The damn thing was taken of us together at a charity dinner at the Pontchartrain, an Associated

Press photo. I'd clipped it and never looked at it again. I didn't recognize it, the expression and angle of her face, in the composite. Some genius I am. Another, please, Windy." He gestured toward the empty glass on the refrigerator.

Lund hesitated. "Are you certain?"

"I think you'll agree the condition of my liver is someone else's concern."

The attorney upended a dwarf bottle of gin into the glass, added ice, and passed it over the back of the loveseat. The stain on Furlong's cheeks when he drank lasted as long as breath on a mirror.

"The question is," he said, "who faked the picture and who sent it to me? Find out."

"Who stood to gain from a breakup?"

"My heirs. Naturally I'd have bequeathed the bulk of my estate to my widow and distributed what was left among the others. If I didn't, the State of California would have, and not the way I'd have chosen. For an old man, the list is fairly short."

I got out my notebook and pen while he took another hit from his glass.

"My son John, who has spent every penny I've given him on various crackpot schemes, including video telephones and solar houses in Seattle, where it rains two hundred days out of the year. My charming first wife Karen, his mother. She tried to run me down in my driveway the morning of the day I left her, and I've no reason to believe she's mellowed in thirty years. Oh, and my kid brother Larry, who I haven't seen or spoken to since nineteen forty-seven. I assume he's retired from the post office by now if he's still living. Assorted other relatives. I had Stuart prepare a file."

Lund picked up the manila folder from the table and handed it to me. It contained the photograph and a word-processed typescript double-spaced on heavy bond secured with brass fasteners. The first name after the paragraph on Lynn Arsenault was Oswald Belder.

I looked up. "Your partner?"

"He inherits the business. I can't believe he's mixed up in this. Ozzie's the conscience of the firm. I'd trust him with anything but this mission. He'd have tried to talk me out of it. And he might have succeeded."

I paged through the dossier. Despite his disclaimer, it seemed like a lot of suspects for one lifetime. "Most of these addresses are out of state. I'll have to farm some of it out. You might get faster results with a larger agency. Say, two people."

Furlong smiled for the first time. It made his face look like the label on a bottle of iodine.

"You didn't think I dreamed up this deathwatch ploy for my personal amusement, did you? It was the best way to get the news around. Most of the heirs have already made contact with Windy. Some of them are already in town for the reading of the will. The rest are on their way. The English gentleman will give you the details."

"Why Detroit? Los Angeles is crawling with private operators."

"In my condition you put a lot of thought into where you go, because the odds are that's where you'll spend eternity. Detroit is home. I was born here. This is where I found my direction and it's where I intend to be buried." He'd quit smiling. "Also I'm fairly certain Lily wouldn't come out to the Coast even if I promised her an interview with the ghost of Diego Rivera. She runs an art gallery here. That's the second part of the assignment, Walker. I want you to talk to her. I need to apologize to her while there's still time."

"It could take a while."

"You've got four weeks. Less than that, if I'm any judge of doctors. The checkbook, please, Mr. Lund. I'll draw this one up myself."

He'd made that simple act sound like a job for heavy equipment. Which it was, for him; by the time he'd signed his name, a plain signature as legible as the name of the bank engraved in block capitals across the top, he was sweating in that air-conditioned room.

"What happens when I find the witchfinder?"

"I'll have the satisfaction of looking into the eyes of a coward."

Three

HE TORE THE CHECK LOOSE and held it up. Stuart Lund looked at it and gave it to me. It was made out in the amount of seventy-five hundred dollars.

"That should get you started," Furlong said. "Now I'll rest."

Lund helped him to his feet and through the door to the bedroom. It was a lot of weight for one very old cane to support; but as the architect had said, they built things better then.

When the lawyer returned I filled several more notebook pages with information on the incoming relations. I left him resting his sore foot on an ottoman and went straight to my bank. When a man who tells you he's terminally ill cuts you a check you don't stop for lunch.

With a comfortable eight thousand, five hundred dollars lying between me and a reservation at the Cardboard Hilton, I paid some bills, pocketed a couple of hundred to walk around on, and treated myself to a stuffed breast of chicken in a restaurant on West Congress, complete with flatware and tablecloths. Between bread and coffee and the main course I carried my notebook to the pay telephone by the restrooms and made an appointment for that afternoon with Oswald Belder, Furlong's business partner. Most of the relatives on the list had not yet arrived in town.

Next I tried Lily Talbot's art gallery. A female voice with wintergreen laid in over the cornpone told me Miz Talbot wasn't expected in until tomorrow. I said I'd call back. Solvency breeds patience.

The world headquarters of Furlong, Belder, & Associates shimmered in heat waves like isinglass curtains, an urban mirage. It was a retired warehouse on the lip of what they call Bricktown now, converted in the Furlong manner into wide bands of pink stucco with continuous tinted windows slitted in like wraparound glasses. An endangered species, warehouses. I don't know where we're going to store all our stuff when the last of them has gone to indirect lighting and swank magazines in the lobby.

Receptionists on two floors directed me to a waiting room the size of a softball field, lined with striped carpets and pressed-tin paneling. Watercolors in black steel frames represented original Furlong designs in ideal settings with plenty of space and garnishes of pruned shrubbery. Another ideal setting, an S-shaped curl of molded plastic aspiring to be a desk, sheltered a burnished black work of art inside its curves. She wore cornrows and dangling earrings that refracted light. The top two buttons of her teal silk blouse were unfastened, below which shadows beckoned. As I approached she reinterred a beige telephone receiver in its form-fitting standard and asked if she could help me.

"I thought you weren't supposed to wear diamonds during the day," I said.

She touched an earring. Her smile was cool in an oval face that didn't seem to have any pores. "They're cut crystal. It's hard to ask for a raise when you're wearing precious stones, Mister"—her lashes swooped down over her appointment book, then back up—"Walker?"

"That is I. He in?"

She lifted the receiver, passed along my name, and hung up. "Mr. Belder's office is at the end of the hall." She tilted her head toward an opening without a door. The earrings swung and sparkled.

"Thanks, Crystal."

"Damaris is the name."

The band of tinted glass across the back of Belder's office looked out on the river and Hiram Walker's distillery—no relation—on the Canadian side. The room was nearly as large as the reception area, painted powder blue, with a deep navy shag carpet and recessed shelves containing oversize pictorial books on architectural subjects and scale models of buildings and stairways. An easel behind the desk held up a detailed sketch of the Pentagon; only the block legend in the corner identified it as a shopping center. Belder—or the man occupying his swivel—sat profile to the door with his elbows on his knees and his chin in his hands, glowering at the sketch. He was a long sack of assorted bones in a blue suit cut to his peculiar shape, wearing thick glasses in aluminum frames. He smeared his glistening black hair straight across his scalp from a part above his left ear. The skin at his left temple was spotted like old cheese and he seemed to be worrying at a set of teeth that didn't fit him nearly as well as the suit.

He spoke without stirring or looking away from the easel. "Do you know anything about drafting?"

"Not a thing," I said.

"I'm trying to figure out what's wrong with it. It's like one of those pictures in a magazine where you spot the errors and win a cruise. I never made it up the gangway."

"It looks like a good place to buy a thousand-dollar screwdriver."

He lifted his chin. "Say that again."

"All it needs is a flag and a row of staff cars parked in front."

"That's it." He straightened and clapped both palms on his knees. "It won't do to remind consumers how much of their withholding is being spent on the military. No more three-martini lunches for the boys in market research." He swiveled and stood. "Pleased to make your acquaintance, Walker. You may have saved us some ugly press."

He wasn't as tall as he looked sitting, but his knees bent slightly, and anyway, anyone was bound to seem short after a meeting with Jay Bell Furlong and his attorney. Belder had a long sad face blurred with years and what might have been drink, and pocked all over like the Sphinx. My information said he was ten years younger than his partner, but he looked older and a lot less well. His was the type that always acted as pallbearer for more robust friends.

"You probably would have caught it yourself."

"Maybe not. Sometimes it takes a stranger walking through a door." He waited until I was sitting before he resumed his own perch. "You're working for Stuart Lund, you said. Is he in town?"

"Briefly. He doesn't want to be away from L.A. too long." Furlong's actual condition and presence in Detroit were the secrets of the day.

"Yes." The sad face got sadder. "I wanted to go there as soon as I heard, but my doctor says with my blood pressure I might as well arrange for a hearse to pick me up at the airport. He's young enough to think that a bad thing. I sent a telegram. No flowers. Jay had—has—definite opinions about pretty things that die and shed petals all over his interiors."

"His opinion of you is just as definite. Lund says he considers you the conscience of Furlong and Belder."

"Jay often said that. Once, many years ago, when the company was overextended, I talked him out of signing a deal with a manufacturer who wanted to put his name on a line of prefabricated houses. I convinced him there are some things you just don't sell. Well, the manufacturer found someone else, went *Fortune* Five Hundred, and we had to close down our offices in London and San Francisco. But an office is just desks and a water cooler in the corner. A man's name carries the value he himself places upon it."

He got up, turned a blank sheet down over the drawing on the easel, and sat back down with a little exhalation that smelled like cherries. "I sometimes think of repeating that old gesture, but we're a corporation now. You can't be a conscience to a committee. However, you haven't come to listen to an old man cry in his expensive imported beer."

I didn't jump on the cue. I asked him if I could smoke. He used the intercom and a moment later the black vision I had seen in the reception room glittered in, laid a ruby-colored glass ashtray on the corner of the desk, and shimmered away. She crowded six feet in her modest two-inch heels. Furlong's hiring practices weren't exactly consistent with his love of the horizontal.

Belder interpreted my thoughts. "A half-century-old joke. Frank Lloyd Wright, Jay's mentor, was a short man. That's why his ceilings are so low. Jay got a perverse pleasure, whenever Wright came to visit the old office, out of watching him look up at the clerks from the mail room. I wouldn't ever accuse my senior partner of overlooking talent and skill in favor of stature, but his little rebel conceit has become second nature in Personnel. I doubt they even realize it when their eyes drift first thing to the physical description in the employment application."

I set flame to a Winston and sledded the match down the tray's glossy side. "Stuart Lund hired me to track down all the heirs to Furlong's estate," I lied. "The reading of the will is to take place here in town as soon as the last of them makes it in."

"Sounds like an easy enough job. People undertake the most arduous journeys whenever a rich relation's health fails."

"Not so arduous in your case. You're already here."

He nodded. On him it looked like palsy. "I inherit the business and its headaches. But I already have those. I've *been* Furlong, Belder, and Associates ever since Jay decided that just being Jay Bell Furlong was occupation enough. Perhaps it is. In my extremity I've come to the happy realization that mediocrity has its advantages. I have little to live up to. But to correct you, I've nothing to do with any will. We drew up a mutual agreement when we formed the partnership. Whichever of us predeceases the other, the survivor claims full interest."

"Which, in dollars and cents, comes to—what?"

There was no guile in that funereal face. Either that, or there was nothing but. The expression that moved across it said he was going to answer the question, truthfully and to the last decimal point. The one that came right behind it said nothing. He folded his long, spotted hands on the place where his blotter would have been if he had one. "Lund would have that information," he said. "Are you really working for him?"

"He's staying at the Airport Marriott." I gave him the suite number. "You can call him and ask."

"I think I will." He got on the intercom and asked Damaris in reception to dial the number. When Lund was on the telephone the pair talked for two minutes. Belder's end of the conversation said the attorney had no surprises for him. He cradled the receiver.

"I'm satisfied. I think Stuart watches old Ray Milland movies to brush up on his accent. There's a lot of espionage in this business, and that's as close to an apology as you'll hear from me."

"It's closer than you need. I gave up slapping people with gauntlets years ago."

"In that case, please don't insult me with this story about locating Jay's heirs. Some of the younger members of the board of directors are trying to force me into retirement on grounds of senility. They won't succeed."

I smoked the rest of my cigarette. By the time I twisted it out in the ruby tray I'd made a decision. I took the photograph Lund had given me out of my inside breast pocket and laid it face up on the desk. He looked down at it without moving his head, let his eyes register a full stop, then looked back at me. "I've seen this before. Jay showed it to me the day it came."

"What did you think?"

"I thought she had a beautiful body. I was eight years younger than I am now." Something that would have been a tragic expression on any other face, but which on his passed for a smile, pulled at the corners of his mouth. "If you want me to say I was shocked, I'll have to disappoint you. When a man who has passed his threescore and ten takes up with a girl in her twenties, he's a fool to think he can satisfy all her needs."

"It doesn't sound like you thought much of her."

"I didn't think much *about* her. I met her only once, when Jay brought her to the office to show her the operation. She didn't chew gum and she asked intelligent questions. Beyond that I couldn't judge her. And wouldn't if I could. I met my wife modeling nude for a life drawing course I attended in nineteen thirty-nine. When we went out she told me she'd appeared in a two-reeler 'exposé' set in a nudist camp; a silly little teaser, but it postponed my proposing to her for six months. Six months I never got back. She died five years ago and never once gave me cause for embarrassment. I wish she could have said the same about me. What are you getting at, Walker?"

"The picture's phony. Furlong only found it out recently. Someone who didn't want them to marry rigged it up."

He sat back. "Poor Jay."

"Poor Jay wants to know which one of his beneficiaries fitted the frame while he's still capable of knowing anything. That's the job. So now you know more than you've told me. Maybe I ought to ditch this line and look for something in advertising."

"If he changes the will in his advanced condition the family will break it."

"I don't know what his plans are when he has the information. That much Lund didn't confide in me. Do you know who the man is in the picture?"

"I recognized him then and I still know him. I saw him just two months ago at the Builders Trade Show in Novi. When this was taken he was only a junior partner in Imminent Visions. Now he's CEO."

"I guess women's lib accomplished something after all," I said. "You no longer have to be female to sleep your way to the top."

"Ah, but he didn't. Isn't that your point?"

I picked up the picture and returned it to my pocket. "Perceptions change, even if people don't. These days the appearance of impropriety is evidence enough to convict. Witchfinding is becoming more respectable all the time."

"I'm afraid I don't follow you."

"History. Phooey. If Lily Talbot had married Furlong and inherited the best part of his estate, where did that leave your partnership agreement?"

"There would be no change. As I said, the agreement was exclusive to the terms of his will. Is this the third degree?" He tried to appear wry. He only managed to look like a recently bereaved bassett.

"As the widow she'd have been in a strong position to overturn the agreement in court. Or she might have persuaded Furlong to do it himself while he was still alive."

"I hadn't thought of that."

It was my turn to sit back. "I believe you. I was just trying to make you sore. Do you get sore?"

"Not over money. Never over that." He refolded his hands. Hands like those—long, yellow, and webbed between the fingers—were made for folding. "Maybe I can help. I've met most of Jay's friends, enemies, lovers, and family over the past fifty years. I think I'd enjoy playing detective."

"Who do you like for it?"

"Just off the top of my head, Karen Furlong."

"The first wife?"

"The three that followed all signed prenuptial contracts limiting them to flat settlements in their respective divorces. Karen's been bleeding Jay for alimony for thirty-five years, and as the mother of his only surviving son she's not the type to stand by and watch any part of his inheritance go to a latecomer like Lily. Manufacturing an incriminating photo would not be beneath her."

"I guess you two don't exchange Christmas cards."

"She's the most morally repulsive person I've ever known. The great tragedy of that split—the only tragedy, to my mind—was that Jay lost his influence over his son. Under his mother's thumb John has wasted his life trying to emulate his father's success through a series of enterprises that were doomed to disaster because Karen can't abide the thought of that boy—well, *man,* and a middle-aged one at that—making anything of himself outside her largesse. One way or another she's seen to it that whatever he attempts turns to sawdust and splinters. No," he said, rotating his head from side to side, "we don't exchange Christmas cards."

"But you stay in touch."

"Jay's association with Stuart Lund began many years after the divorce. It's been my enviable task since the beginning to draw Karen's checks on the Furlong and Belder account. Fortunately it's John who comes to pick them up. He keeps me informed and never seems to realize just how much he's telling me about his relationship with his mother."

I doodled a dog wearing a hairbow on a page of my notebook. "What do you know about Furlong's brother Larry?"

"Absolutely nothing. I never met him. I don't think Jay's seen him since the forties. He was a postmaster or something out in the country last I heard. I'm sure that's over now. He must be close to eighty. Jay hardly ever mentioned him."

"Vernon Whiting?"

"Dead."

"That's it?"

"It is where he's concerned. Not for Jay. He didn't lose his temper often, but the mere mention of Whiting's name did it every time. What did Lund tell you about him?"

"Just that he accused Furlong of plagiarizing one of his designs."

"Poppycock."

"Poppycock?"

"It's what people expect me to say when I mean bullshit. On

his best day, Whiting never came up with a concept to compare with a Furlong castoff. He built Imminent Visions on that myth. I replaced him here, so I didn't meet him until later, when we started attending shows. Whenever one of them entered a room the other would leave. If anyone had a grievance in that affair, it was Jay. I expect they'll have it out in hell."

"Why hell for Furlong?"

The wry bassett returned. "He wouldn't last a week in paradise. St. Peter would send him down for trying to redesign the pearly gates."

"Any other nominees?"

"None I like as much as Karen. Heavy irony on the word *like*. She's pretty hard to see around."

I put away the notebook and stood.

"Thanks, Mr. Belder. I don't usually get this much candor all at once."

He kept his seat. "Prejudice is a more appropriate term. When you get to be my age, a good many of the things they'd condemn you for any other time suddenly become virtues. It's small enough compensation for prostate failure."

"Live long enough and you become respectable." I said it automatically.

His head jerked up like an old eagle's. "Where did you hear that?"

"Lund. He attributed it to Furlong."

"Oh." He nodded his palsied nod. "That was Jay's favorite maxim for years. For a moment I thought—but that would be impossible, wouldn't it? Poor Jay. Well, good luck. I'd ask you to give my best to Karen out of simple good manners, but the best is lost on women like her."

I grasped his weak old hand and got out of there before I spilled the name of my favorite teddy bear.

Four

"FURLONG RESIDENCE."

"FURLONG RESIDENCE."

Another female on the other end of another telephone. This one had a Middle Eastern accent. There are more of those in the metropolitan area than in all the remakes of *Beau Geste* put together.

"Mrs. Furlong, please." I lit a cigarette and watched the smoke hang on the motionless air. I miss booths. The telephone had its own built-in shade, leaving me outside to face the heat and noxious gases on East Jefferson. A red 1965 Mustang convertible mumbled past, followed by a 1915 Ford depot hack, a 1950 Hudson Hornet, and a Tucker; on their way to a road rally to celebrate the centenary of the automobile. There was always some kind of motoring anniversary coming up, and Detroit never missed one. It was the only thing good that had happened to the city since Cadillac came ashore to dump the water out of his boots.

"Who is speaking?"

"My name is Amos Walker. I'm an investigator hired by Mr. Furlong's attorney to—"

"Is he dead?"

This was a new voice, a contralto without age or nationality and precious little gender.

"Mrs. Furlong?" Araby was confused.

"I've got it, Khalida. You can hang up." After the click: "This is Karen Furlong. Are you calling to report Jay's death?"

"No, he's still alive," I said.

Air blew out through a pair of nostrils. "The son of a bitch was always on his way somewhere else all the time we were married. Why did he have to pick now to hang around? What did you say your name was?"

I said it again. "Stuart Lund has hired me to interview the beneficiaries of Mr. Furlong's will. It's a routine investigation connected with the reading. Are you free anytime today?"

"I suppose so, if it will speed up the process. Four o'-clock."

"Will John Bell Furlong also be available at that time?"

"Yes, yes. My son's always available. Don't be late. I have the decorator coming at five."

I hung up on the dial tone and walked the block and a half to where I'd left the car. By the time I got there I was squelching inside my clothes. At Rivard a big cop was directing traffic around a stalled Bonneville with steam rolling out from under its hood. The cop had sweated through his light blue uniform shirt and his face had the look of pavement buckled in the heat. I didn't ask him if he was intending to celebrate the invention of the automobile.

I had thirty minutes to kill and the office was nearby, so I parked in the abandoned service station across the street from my building, gave the derelict who lived in the empty bay a dollar not to slash my tires, and went up. The stairwell smelled of kippers. There hadn't been any food in the building since the stove manufacturer who built it converted it from apartments in 1911, but on stagnant days the ghosts of old meals prowled the hallways.

The only things waiting in my waiting room were the voting-age *Field & Stream*s on the coffee table. I'd left the table fan, a refugee from the Eisenhower administration, oscillating on the window sill in the think pit; a homey odor of burning bearings greeted me when I opened the door. A pigeon feather jigged around in the current when I closed it, paused on top of the telephone, then fluttered off again when the fan swung back that direction. I wondered where it got its energy.

In the little water closet, installed as an afterthought by an exasperated contractor when the fad for indoor plumbing didn't pass, I stripped to the waist, splashed my face and chest and under my arms, used the thin towel, and applied a generous layer of talcum. I broke a fresh shirt out of the black iron safe and sat down behind the desk without fastening the buttons. I contemplated the picture on the wall of Custer having it out with the Sioux. He looked hot. I decided to shop for one of Peary at the Pole.

The feather came back and landed on the telephone a second time. I took the hint and called Barry Stackpole.

I'd met Barry in a shell crater in the jungle. Since then he'd lost a leg and two fingers, acquired a silver plate in his skull—all this stateside—written a couple of books, and established his reputation as the Detroit *News*'s expert on organized crime. Now he had shucked off the dead cocoon of print journalism and joined the enemy. He'd been nominated for a couple of Emmys as the producer of a weekly crime watch segment at one of the cable stations in town, losing both times to a Cajun cooking show out of Louisiana.

A future TV anchorwoman with a thirty-seven-word vocabulary put me through to Barry's office.

"How are things in the Magic Kingdom?" I asked him when we'd run out of insults.

"It beats thinking. I had lunch with the station owner yesterday. I found myself using words like *skew* and *demographics* without feeling like a complete horse's ass. Which means, of course, I am one."

"Breeding shows."

"Funny guy. We may go syndicated this fall, if Channel Fifty doesn't move *The Brady Bunch* into our time slot and knock us out of the book. How about you? I hear AIDS is working wonders for the keyhole business. All those husbands and wives and significant whatevers wondering what the better half may be bringing home from the office besides the bacon."

"My job's secure until they get that humanity thing worked out," I said. "What do you know these days about pictures that don't move?"

"An old girlfriend comes to mind."

"Now you're getting corny. I'm looking for someone who can trace a faked photo to the artist."

"Blackmail case?"

"Nothing a big-time muckraker like you would be interested in. For the record, it's a honey of a job. The Rembrandt who did it must have a reputation."

"I don't know. I watched a kid here at the station who couldn't spell CNN morph up a picture of the current Ayatollah chomping on a Big Mac that would spark a new revolution in Iran. The equipment was strictly Radio Shack."

"This one goes back eight years. Computers hadn't quite made dark rooms obsolete."

"Sure I can't do anything with this? I need something for the fall sweeps."

"I'll let you have it if it jumps that way." If Furlong's doctors were anywhere near right, he wouldn't be around to see the show.

"Throw in two bottles of H-and-H and I'll see what's under my silver plate."

I paused. "I guess AA was just a lark."

"No, I'm back with the program to stay. I've got sponsors to ply. Be glad I'm not with one of the networks. There it's kilos."

"Two pints."

"Fifths."

"One fifth," I said.

"That's less than two pints."

"I flunked Weights and Measures."

"Two pints," he said. "And the story."

"I repeat, if it jumps that way. You know this drill, Barry."

"Randy Quarrels is your man."

I wrote down the name. "Photographer for the *News*, right?"

"He ran the staff until he snuck a picture of the chief of police snoozing on his office sofa on Law Enforcement Day. The chief pulled a string at the paper and hung Randy on the end of it. These days he's holding down a portrait studio in Birmingham."

"Ritzy."

"If you call Jonas Salk working a counter in a drugstore ritzy. Randy's eye is wasted on rich little spit-ups who won't smile at the clownie. If anyone can track your picture to its source it's him." He gave me a telephone number. Barry's head is a directory; he'd be an idiot savant if he didn't have an IQ of 180.

I thanked him. We traded vile comments on our respective lineages and I worked the riser and dialed.

"Cassandra Photo."

It was a relief for once to get a male voice first thing. This one was an interesting combination of shallow youth and the flat bone-weariness of disillusioned age. You hear it in cops who are no longer rookies and reporters with no hope of ever mounting to the editorial staff. I asked if I was speaking to Randy Quarrels.

"Well, I'm not Cassandra."

There was no humor in the reply. I introduced myself, said I'd gotten his name and number from Barry Stackpole, and told him what I needed.

"Positive or negative?" he asked.

"Positive."

"Depends on the quality of the print. Bring it around. The best guys have their own style. If it's one I know it won't take long."

"How long if it isn't?"

"Not much longer if it's as good as you say. There aren't that many aces in this deck."

"How late are you open?"

"I close at five sharp."

"Can you spot me an extra half hour? I have to be in Farmington Hills at four."

"I'll have to charge you double the usual sitting."

"That's okay. I wasn't planning on retiring this year."

Pause. "Yeah, you know Barry, all right." The connection went away.

Karen Furlong's house was a half-timber job with gables and shake shingles, six thousand square feet if it was a cabana, overlooking the rest of Oakland County from the top of a shared private drive winding up from Orchard Lake Road. It wouldn't have made much of an impression on the dozen or so half-million-dollar structures it was tucked in with. I parked in front of a horseshoe-shaped front porch, straightened my tie, and rang the bell. Poppies and impatiens spilled over the sides of a two-wheeled carriage with red spoke wheels encamped on the pampered lawn.

The door opened between the ding and the dong. I identified myself to a golden-olive face above a maid's black uniform trimmed with white lace and she let me in. The entrance hall was a vertical shaft rearing straight up for thirty feet to a leaded-glass skylight that divided the sun into colored slices on the ebonized wood at our feet. She curtsied in that fluid way of societies where the women wear veils and went off to find the mistress of the house. It didn't seem like enough for her to do given the setting. For the first time in years I was sorry I'd stopped wearing a hat.

I killed time trying to make eye contact with a fierce old buzzard in a frame crusted over with gilt Cupids, the room's only decoration. He wore a wing collar, iron-gray handlebars, and the general air of a man who preferred to mess around with moustache wax and studs. He was clutching a rolled document as if it contained directions to the Lost Dutchman.

"Fascinating old gargoyle, isn't he?"

The man who had appeared at my side was my height but forty pounds heavier, most of it around his waistband. He had on a cream-colored knitted polo shirt with an animal embroidered above the pocket, loose tan cotton slacks with pleats, and cordovan loafers, artfully scuffed. Underclassmen's clothes, with a butch cut to match; but there was plenty of gray in it, and salt and pepper in the whiskers his razor had missed between chins. He was late forties, maybe fifty, but his eyes hadn't gotten the news. They were as bright as uncirculated dimes.

"Mother commissioned the painting last year. They mixed dirt in with the varnish to make it look old. I forget just which one of my ancestors it's supposed to represent, but I understand he stole a railroad. They named a bridge after him in New York. All Jesse James got was a bullet in the head. John Furlong." He turned and extended a hand the size of a flipper. "Are you the detective? I'm sure you're not the decorator."

I told him my name and gave him back his hand. Like his face it was as pink and soft as salmon flesh. I searched the face for signs of his famous father and came up empty. There was nothing more to connect him to the ferocious party in the painting. Chromosomes will do that sometimes.

"You move quietly, Mr. Furlong. I never heard you coming up on me."

"Mother's hearing is preternatural. You learn to sneak around if you're going to have any sort of freedom."

There was a pause that needed filling. "I'm sorry about your father."

"Thank you. I rang him up just last month to cut him in on a little syndicate I'm putting together. Naturally I wouldn't have disturbed him if I'd suspected he was in poor health. I imagine that's why he decided to pass up the opportunity." The dimes brightened. "You wouldn't happen to have some capital lying around you don't know what to do with, by any chance?"

"I wouldn't call it capital. More like lower case."

"Oh. A shame. It's a crackerjack idea, and all mine. I borrowed against my trust fund to buy a stable of racehorses, but they all turned out to be related and there was something wrong with the bloodline. They faint when they get excited. The least little shock and they drop like laundry."

"Tough break."

"I thought so, too. Then I rented this old movie starring Gary Cooper. The Bengal Lancer Something."

"Lives of a Bengal Lancer."

"Have you seen it?" The dimes glowed.

"I like old movies."

"Well, then, you know there are a lot of battle scenes with cannons bursting and horses falling and things. The studios were terribly irresponsible about how they made horses fall back then. They used tripwires. Dozens of animals broke their legs and had to be destroyed. It was barbaric."

"Now they just dump helicopters on the underage actors."

"Yes." He wasn't listening. "These days they hire trainers to teach the horses to fall on command. I started thinking about that, how I could rent these fainting horses of mine to Hollywood productions and make a fortune. I don't even remember how the movie ended, I was so full of this wonderful idea."

"At least."

"That's the definition of true genius, you know: the ability to identify a liability, analyze it, and convert it into an asset."

"I thought it was an infinite capacity for taking pains."

"That's another. There are several. The trouble is I don't have any contacts in the industry. That's why I hoped Father could help, I mean being out there and known by everyone. If I'm going to make any sort of impression there I have to check into the most expensive hotel in town and throw money around. Also the horses are stabled in New Jersey and transporting them across the country will be complicated, especially since—"

"They'll be falling down in ten states."

"Right. So any way you look at it I need more money than I've ever had to make more money than I've ever dreamed."

"Ain't that the way, though?"

"Ain't it indeed." He looked glum as roadkill.

"Ever have this problem before?"

"Almost constantly. But not to this degree."

"Know anything about photography?"

He thought about that one. Thinking about things would always be a problem for him unless they appeared in the flare of the spastic lightbulb that lived inside his skull, like a cartoon character's. It would be pretty dim in there between flashes. If it was an act, he'd had it down cold a long time before I came.

He was still struggling when Karen Furlong joined us from the next room. At a glance I could see that here was someone who was related to the predatory-looking gent in the oil painting.

Five

SHE STOPPED JUST INSIDE pistol range, hands locked together under her bosom. She was either performing the Heimlich maneuver upon herself or getting set to pounce on high C. Whichever she chose you had to look at her.

She wasn't tall—the first planet in the Furlong galaxy I had met that wasn't—but the elevation of her chin, the rise of the lacquered blue-gray hair above her widow's peak, and the sweep of her floor-length dress, deep green and frogged with gold at the shoulders, all conspired to create the impression of height. Her eyes were as gray and as hard as whetstones. She had a broad, brainy forehead, but below the heavily rouged cheeks her face narrowed sharply like an old-fashioned keyhole. She was a well-curved seventy.

"Mr. Walker? I see you've met John." It was the contralto of the telephone, smooth, ageless, with every hint of regional origin lathed away.

"We've been discussing investments."

"Yes. It's how he breaks the ice."

The maid appeared behind her. Mrs. Furlong knew she was there without turning. It wasn't prescience. The maid would always be there.

"We'll have coffee in the garden." Hands locked, she walked right past both of us and through an arch on the opposite side of the room. The maid followed. John and I fell in behind.

Two rooms, a grand piano on a marble floor, and several hundred thousand dollars' worth of antiques later, we stepped through French doors onto a terrace done in terra cotta tile with flagged paths radiating out between topiary and banks of flowers. The colors were as bright as construction paper and the mingled scents were inebriating, like boiled perfume. Bees hummed ecstatically among the blossoms. A plane tree many years older than the house, but which hadn't necessarily grown in that spot, cast black shade over the area where the coffee things were laid out on a glass table surrounded by ice cream chairs. There were white bell-shaped cups upside-down on saucers, a silver decanter, and pressed linen napkins in silver rings. The maid upended the cups and poured.

"I'll do the rest, Khalida."

The maid dipped one knee and went inside.

John held a chair for his mother, who unlocked her hands and sat. "Black, Mr. Walker? You don't impress me as the cream and sugar type." She balanced a cup on its saucer. It was brim full.

I said black was fine and accepted the offering. Men who didn't monkey with their coffee were men you could trust. I could see I was going to disappoint her.

John took one of the cups and tipped in four cubes of sugar and a third of the container of cream and stirred until the liquid matched the color of his shirt. I couldn't believe they were family.

"This is a pretty garden, Mrs. Furlong. Do you do the work yourself?" No picture formed of her on her knees weeding the geranium bed.

"Just the dahlias. I allow no one else to touch them. They've taken first prize the last two years at the Detroit Flower Show. Dahlias are difficult to raise, like John."

John gave no indication of having heard the last part. "If Mother wins again this year she gets to keep the trophy."

"I prefer to keep things." She sipped coffee. It was a bitter blend that appeared to have no effect on her. "I don't suppose you have any news of Jay's condition since you and I spoke."

"No, he's still dying."

She exhaled. "Impossible man."

"I know there's not much affection between you and your ex-husband," I said. "Still, you must have mixed feelings about this. There's an inheritance for John, but when Mr. Furlong dies the alimony checks stop coming."

"I've done all right with my money, mostly by never investing it with my son. I'm not suffering. I intend to see that John gets what's coming to him." She set her cup in its saucer with a click. "You're very blunt, Mr. Walker. I am too. What is this nonsense about interviewing the heirs?"

"I've got to get a better story. So far this one isn't fooling anybody." I took the picture out of my pocket and put it on the table.

She glanced at it, then turned it over quickly while John was still attempting to focus. She actually colored. That was a surprise.

"I heard about this filth at the time it happened," she said. "What do you hope to accomplish by showing it around?"

"The picture never happened," I said. "It's a composite. Someone fixed it up to get Furlong to break his engagement to Lily Talbot. Stuart Lund retained me to find out which heir is responsible."

"So naturally you came here first."

"Actually it's my second stop. I'm working my way down a long list."

She was watching me closely. In that place of many colors her eyes reflected only granite. "Ridiculous. No one does anything purely at random. I'll guess your first stop. Oswald Belder."

"He's on the list too," I noncommitted.

"He told you to come see me."

I sipped coffee.

"I despised him from the start," she said. "That's why Jay arranged things so I'd have to go to him for my payments. He knew I didn't want to wait for the mails. It amused him to think of me being forced to look at that miserable hound dog face once a month for the rest of my life. I outsmarted him, though. He didn't count on my sending John in my place."

"I like Uncle Oz," John said.

She didn't look at him. "Ozzie Belder was worse than any mistress any wife ever had to compete with for her husband's affections. He stole Jay from me, he and the business; stole him as surely as some office tramp with black panties and her brains in her vagina."

This time her son colored, stoplight red from his polo collar to the roots of his crewcut. "Honestly, Mother."

"Be quiet. This doesn't concern you. I loved Jay when he couldn't get his designs past the office boy at the shoddiest contracting company in town. I packed his lunchpail when he went to work as a hod carrier and helped him out of his clothes when he came home covered with white dust and too tired to take off his boots. I sank every penny my parents left me into a year's lease on his first office and all its furniture, including the drafting board. It was the two of us all the way to the top, that's how we planned it. Well, we never discussed what was to happen afterward."

"Ozzie," I said.

"Ozzie. Everything changed the day he came on board. From then on I was the toy wife Jay took down off the shelf at the end of the day and wound up to cook his dinner and share his bed. At the office—the office I paid for—they treated me like a visitor. When Furlong, Belder, and Associates threw a party at the old Book Cadillac to celebrate its first overseas contract and it came time for Jay to toast the person most responsible for the firm's success, it was Ozzie he raised his glass to. I knew then it was over. I was six weeks' pregnant with John at the time. Ask Ozzie what it's like to carry a baby you know will be the child of divorced parents. If I framed anyone with a smutty picture it would be him, not Jay. That's if I thought anyone would believe he could ever get it up without a balloon frame to keep it there."

"*Please,* Mother." There were greenish streaks in the red of John's face. He was upstaging the daffodils.

"Framing Belder wouldn't guarantee your son's inheritance," I said.

She gave me the granite stare. After a moment she turned over the picture, took a second look, and skated it back my way. "I never met her. I only knew her face from the newspapers. Photographers can't resist a rich old goat with a sleek young thing. I didn't care by then, of course, but I never believed they'd ever marry. If it wasn't a picture it would be something else."

I looked at it again before putting it away. "What was wrong with her?"

"Nothing would be. Nothing less than perfection would do for the great Jay Bell Furlong, at least in public. It's what was wrong with Jay. He wore those flashy yellow suits on the street, but at home it was old sweaters and tennis shoes with holes in the toes. Oh, he enjoyed parading around with a pretty girl one third his age when people were watching. Artists are like that, never mind what they say about the quest for inner truth. In his case it was a different story after the last flashbulb faded. Look at the other two women he married. I was dowdy enough in those days, overweight and with no idea of how to dress, but they were worse. You don't have to put on airs with a homely unfashionable woman. That's what he looked for in a spouse: the opportunity to stop being Jay Bell Furlong for eight hours at a stretch. He wouldn't have gotten that from this Lily person."

"Maybe he changed."

"People don't change. You know that at least as well as I, Mr. Detective. They just become more like they were at the start."

I drank some coffee. It tasted less bitter now. "I was asking John if he knew anything about photography when you came in."

"He doesn't."

"I can answer the question myself, Mother."

I gave him the sympathetic face.

"I invested some money once with a fellow from a film lab who claimed he'd invented an affordable holographic camera," he said. "You know, so people on vacation could take three-dimensional pictures of Aunt Edna standing in front of the Eiffel Tower. He spent a couple of days showing me around the lab. I still remember some of what I learned."

"What became of the camera?"

His eyes lost some of their shine. "After figuring in advertising and distribution it retailed at eighty-seven thousand five hundred dollars."

"You've known my son less than a half hour, but as I said, you're a detective." Karen Furlong was smiling, not a sight to remember with the lights off. "Do you think he's capable of fooling his father with a falsified picture on the basis of a couple of days' training? Or a couple of years?"

"It wouldn't take him that long to find out where to go to have it done." I finished my coffee. "Thanks for your time, Mrs. Furlong. I'm just going down the list, like I said."

"Who's next?"

"That depends on who's in town. A couple of the grandchildren are coming in, and I don't have an address on Mr. Furlong's brother Larry. I don't suppose you've heard from him lately."

"Not since shortly after the wedding. He and Jay had a fight about something, I never knew what. An old friend in Royal Oak sent me a clipping from one of the *Observer* papers some years ago, a human-interest piece about a postmaster who was retiring after fifty years with the civil service. It was Larry. I thought about sending it on to Jay, but only for a moment. I'm not in the business of arranging reunions."

"Do you remember which community he was postmaster in?"

She shook her head. "It must have been somewhere in Oakland County or it wouldn't have been in the *Observer.* I threw out the clipping."

I thanked her again and rose. John got up with me. "I'll see you to the door," he said.

"Mr. Walker knows the way, John. He's a detective. Come rub Mother's neck. There's a draft." She closed her eyes and tipped her head right and left. It was ninety out and there wasn't a breath of air stirring.

"Good luck with the horses." I shook one of the big soft hands.

"Thanks. Say! Maybe I could sell them for research. If there's something in their blood that can cure insomnia"— the lightbulb faded—"no, I'd be better off to stick with the movies. See, sometimes the ideas come so fast I don't know which one is the best one."

"The burden of genius."

"I suppose. Sometimes I wonder if it's worth it." He stepped behind his mother's chair and began kneading the muscles at the base of her neck with his spatulated fingers. I told her good-bye, but her eyes were still closed and she wasn't listening. The effort of holding back the age from her face seemed to have drained her. When she relaxed her muscles, the years pooled in pockets of shadow.

Six

A HOLE HAD OPENED in the overcast above the northern suburbs, allowing white sunlight through like a spill of molten steel. I drove with my jacket off and my shirtcuffs turned back, and jerked my arm inside when it touched hot metal. For the rest of the day I wore a red welt like a brand across the flesh of my forearm. The weatherman on the radio predicted ninety-eight tomorrow.

More and more cars were displaying the special commemorative license plate observing the first hundred years of the automobile, an uninspiring rectangle with the background and characters reversed, blue on white. You had to get right up on the rear bumper to see the washed-out lines of a spindly horseless carriage stamped in the center. Henry Ford would have smelted down the entire run to make another Model T.

I fought homebound traffic all the way north to Birmingham. The ozone was blue with monoxide. I rolled up my window. Another century of that and we'll all have snorkels growing out of the top of our heads.

Cassandra Photo operated out of the second floor of a yellow brick building with a formal-wear emporium at street level and wrought-iron curlicues to draw the admiring eye away from the bars on the windows. A hairstyling salon called Le Cut shared the strip on one side, with a gift shop selling fourteen-karat pencil cups and Waterford bedpans on the other. Grosse Pointe is old auto money, stacked and stored in ten-thousand-dollar bricks in climate-controlled vaults with the furs. Birmingham is platinum cards carried in quick-draw holsters. The credit came from downtown Detroit banks the cardholders hadn't visited since Nixon.

I parked between a silver BMW and a red Corvette that came up to my knees and went in through an air-locked compartment containing the stairs to the second floor. The chill air inside reminded me I'd left my jacket in the car, but I merely rolled down my cuffs and buttoned them on the way up. Formality is the first casualty of summer.

You can tell a lot about a building by its stairs. There are stairs between green-painted plaster walls fretted with graffiti and paved with rubber speckled with cigarette burns like suppurating sores, lighted (when they are lighted at all) by dusty fifteen-watt bulbs that illuminate only themselves and the shrunken pupils of the human animals that live in their shadows; glossy black-painted iron stairs cast in lacy patterns, rising like smoke through the middle of clean bright rooms full of new merchandise around brass firemen's poles with polished handrails; broad gilded sweeping stairs for the customers of expensively renovated theaters as opposed to narrow cramped Skoal-smelling stairs in the back for the help; creaky stairs layered six inches deep with the odors of meals cooked and consumed and forgotten by people who have passed beyond need of food; quiet cushioned stairs for discreet upholstered people who read the stock market and shipping reports and count their cholesterol; clean, pine-smelling stairs in new buildings full of their future; dirty shuddery garbage-stinking stairs in old buildings emptied by their past; stairs that serve as bathrooms; stairs that serve no purpose at all; cold echoing penitentiary stairs painted gray; crowded chattering schoolhouse stairs too trafficked to paint; stairs to go up but not down, stairs to go down but not up, stairs on the inside to take you to something, stairs on the outside to take you away from something else. They are the ferries of civilization on the cusp of the millennium, and more than any other part of the structures they inhabit they reflect the attitudes and life histories of the people who use them. Any reliable detectives' handbook should include a chapter on stairs.

The one I was climbing was carpeted in maroon plush with an Oriental design and had a smooth oak handrail attached to a wall wainscoted in the old manner, although the building wasn't fifteen years old; unlike their counterparts in Detroit, the Birmingham city fathers become nervous whenever a piece of construction approaches the age of consent. Every time I go there I see a building that wasn't there the last time, although I never see one going up or its predecessor coming down. They do it at night with infrared glasses and pneumatic hammers wrapped in chinchilla to avoid disturbing the residents. The local tax base would keep the Third World in prayer rugs and brown rice through the end of the century.

The door to the photo shop stood open. One of those two-tone paint jobs designed to create a psychological demilitarized zone between the two parts of commerce divided the room into equal sections, blue for the customer, white for the vendor. Like photographers' studios everywhere, the walls were covered with pictures in frames, but that's as far as the comparison carried. There were no laughing children, no Golden Anniversary couples or glowing brides and grooms, no dogs, no sunsets. Instead there was a tight color shot of Alan Trammell sliding headfirst into base that made you want to spit out gravel, and next to it a close-up of a distracted and scowling local high-placed member of the Malevolent Brotherhood of Bent-Nosed Sicilians with whom I had once had a run-in, and of whom no known photograph existed, or so it said in his FBI jacket. The Feds are prouder of their photo files than they are of having shot Dillinger.

That wasn't the best of it, though. The cleanup spot went to a blowup the size of a bedsheet. The camera had caught a Big Cat in the middle of a pounce, at an angle that put nothing behind it but empty blue sky. Red spots glinted in both of its tawny eyes and its curved fangs were ivory-colored against the pure white of its coat. Its body was twisted half around, the hinges of its spread jaws exposed in a silent scream of rage or agony or both. It seemed to echo in the stillness of that room.

"Fucking sherpa I brought along to keep me from falling off the mountain shot the poor bastard just as I tripped the shutter."

I turned to look at the man seated on a stool on the other side of the glass counter. He was using a precision screwdriver on an ordinary Minolta cradled between his thighs.

"Why?" I asked.

"He *said* he was saving my life."

"Was he?"

"This world's got photographers coming out of its ass. What we don't have enough of is Tibetan snow leopards. My life was worth that picture."

"Could be he didn't see it that way. Maybe he sees more leopards than photographers."

"All I know is he skinned it and traded the hide for a new snowmobile."

"What was a *News* photographer doing taking pictures of cats in the Himalayas?"

"I was freelancing for the *National Geographic*. They were all set to put it on the cover when the fucking *Exxon Valdez* ran aground."

He swung the camera up onto the counter by its strap and slid off the stool. It didn't bring his head up more than a couple of inches. He was a squat solid thirty, moon-faced, with ditchwater-colored hair twisted into a ponytail at the nape of his neck, and wore a gray T-shirt bearing the stenciled legend PROPERTY OF JACKSON PRISON: DO NOT REMOVE UNDER PENALTY OF FREEDOM. "Walker? I'm Randy Quarrels." He took my hand in the crossed-palm clasp I hadn't experienced in twenty years. His short thick fingers were as strong as C-clamps.

"It's a long hike from Tibet to a storefront in Birmingham, Michigan," I said.

"Well, freelancing's just another word for bare-assed and out of work. There's something to be said for steady employment. The word is bullshit."

"I wouldn't know. I'm strictly hand to mouth."

"You bring it?"

I schoonered the doctored photograph across the top of the counter.

He stopped it—he had fast hands, ideal for shooting leopards—looked at it, held it up to the light and squinted, then turned and carried it toward the back, grunting for me to join him. I swung up the gate and followed. Below the T-shirt he had on khaki shorts with safari pockets and sandals. His legs were covered with old healed-over scars, from thorns or claws I couldn't tell.

A half-partition masked the working part of the studio and doubled as a background screen on the other side. It was painted deep blue to absorb light and flatter the subject. A stool for posing stood in front of it facing a Nikon perched on a tripod. Lights, a reflecting umbrella, and assorted props stood and leaned and lay about like soldiers off the line. What looked like a genuine human skull grinned from the lap of a department-store mannequin without arms, dressed for the beach. An old steelcase Nikon, larger than the one on the tripod, wallowed in a morass of nylon straps on an oak desk that looked as if it had done time in a service station. Bare metal showed through chips in the black enamel. That would be the camera he carried up snow-capped peaks to photograph endangered species. His kind of photographer belonged on the same list.

He transferred a stack of trade magazines from the desk to the floor, snapped on a gooseneck lamp, and placed the picture in the center of the circle of light. For some time he bent over it, peering through a glass like a jeweler's loupe, placed directly on top of the photograph. He grunted once more and straightened.

"The girl's head came from somewhere else. The skin tones are close, but you won't get an exact match one time in a million; too many variables. This is a very nice job. Whoever did it air-brushed the join so well you'd think it was a crease in the skin if you didn't know what to look for. You came to the one guy in southeastern Michigan who knows what to look for."

"You can skip the commercial. I'm sold. What about the guy?"

"Oh, it's all him. He was in bed with nine-tenths of some-one."

"That puts him in on the frame."

"Either that or he's just about the coolest son of a bitch who ever did a candid in his birthday suit. When did you say this was done?"

"I didn't, but it was about eight years ago."

"Well, one of your possibilities is dead, but last I heard his son was still running the family studio in Flint. I can think of two others who are this good with an airbrush. I'll make a list, but you'll have to look them up yourself. I'm not the telephone company."

I said swell. He made it out on a scratch pad with a happy face in the corner with a bleeding wound in its forehead, tore off the sheet, and traded it for a hundred of Jay Bell Furlong's dollars. As I was leaving I told him to watch out for snow leopards.

"They're pussycats. It's the fucking solid citizens you have to watch out for. They won't be rare in my lifetime."

Seven

IT WAS PAST quitting time, but I was still going, like a battery commercial.

I stopped back at the office to look up the names Quarrels had given me. Two were listed in the metropolitan area, which was a break, and Information had the number of the studio in Flint. But with any luck and thanks again to the squat Indiana Jones from Birmingham, I might not need any of them. I called Imminent Visions in Allen Park hoping for an appointment with Lynn Arsenault, the genuine half of the picture that had shot down Lily Talbot, and got a recording informing me the offices were open from 8:00 A.M. to 5:00 P.M. Monday through Friday. Not to be outdone because of a mere six-figure difference in annual revenues, I closed up and went home.

The teenager next door had bought a street rod, a blaze-orange '69 Roadrunner with a jacked-up rear end and twin scoops punched into the hood. For forty-five minutes every morning and every evening for three days he had been gunning the big 389 in his parents' driveway, cleaning the carburetor for cruise night Saturday night on Jefferson. He'd rammed a broomstick up each of the twin glass-packs to clear out all those pesky baffles, just in case they couldn't hear it in Toronto. I had considered and discarded several plans, the best of which involved going over there under the first new moon and slipping a Clark bar into the gas tank.

Hamtramck was a quiet town back when there were Polish names on all the mailboxes, clean and safe and well-tended; even the trash cans in the alleys sparkled. Then the last administration had condemned its historic section to make room for a General Motors plant, shipping in vandals and arsonists by the carload when the residents were slow to evacuate. They evacuated, the thugs remained. Now the place is just more of Detroit and you don't leave the windows open when you go away if you want to come back to your furniture. By the time I'd flung up all the sashes that weren't painted shut I had sweated right through the summerweight. I hung it in front of a window to air, stood under a cold shower for five minutes, and put on a thin cotton robe. The suit was still there when I came out, evidence that either the neighborhood was improving or my taste in clothes wasn't. I put the oven on the lowest reasonable setting, slid in a tray of frozen drumsticks and peas, opened a beer, and sat in front of the fan in the living room to watch the news.

It was the same thing on all the local channels: a dozen recent Debate Club graduates representing all three sexes and most of the acknowledged racial and ethnic persuasions trying to do the work of one competent reporter. The city cops had chased a speeding driver into a station wagon containing a family of three, another preschooler had been killed in the crossfire between warring youth drug gangs, and the ACLU had won another district court victory in its campaign to stamp out Christianity. The national news was more of the same, with a better wardrobe. The ghoul shift outside Jay Bell Furlong's room at Cedars of Lebanon was in its third week and the news reader stationed on the sidewalk in front of the hospital was running out of quotes from James Russell Lowell. He plainly wanted to be off covering something that required a trenchcoat. I flipped around until I found a rerun of *M*A*S*H*.

The telephone rang during a commercial for PMS, or maybe it was con.

"Inaction News desk."

"Walker?"

Stuart Lund's public-school accent was thickening with the dusk. Head colds are that way too.

"Not much to report, Mr. Lund. I talked to Oswald Belder and Karen and John Furlong, also to someone who knows a thing or twelve about faking photographs." I gave him what I could without checking my notes for fashion details.

"You seem to be running in place," he said. "We've known all along Arsenault had to be involved."

"The first day of an investigation is mostly catch-up. I'll talk to Arsenault tomorrow."

"He'll just deny everything."

"If he didn't, you wouldn't need me. Demolishing alibis is part of the service."

"Will you use force?"

I rapped the mouthpiece twice with the rim of the beer can. "Brass knuckles. They spit out the truth with their teeth."

"I don't suppose I'll ever be a true American. I never know when I'm being gulled."

"Don't be too hard on yourself. I still don't understand steak-and-kidney pie." I set down the beer. It was getting warm anyway; which was another thing about the English I didn't understand. "The truth is I'm getting a little old to throw people down staircases. Fortunately, a big bag of novelties and notions comes with the license. One of them usually clicks before the opening-round bell."

"Just don't break his jaw so he can't talk."

"Now who's being gulled?"

"I once defended an Irish rebel who blew up a busful of English schoolchildren. Violent details are not foreign to my experience."

"Mine neither. But if it's muscle you're looking for, you could have hired it anywhere in town for a lot less than I charge."

"I never considered anything of the sort." But he sounded disappointed.

"How's Mr. Furlong?"

"Dying, although not as precipitately as he was this morning. He's asleep now. He sleeps often, but never for long, and then he has errands for me. For a week now I haven't been in bed long enough to bother with changing into and out of pyjamas." There would be a *Y* in the word the way he used it.

"How's your gout?"

"I'm in considerable discomfort. Thank you for asking. Please report when you have something." He was quiet long enough for me to wonder if he was still on the line. Then he said, "Have something soon."

I cradled the receiver. The string of commercials had come to an end and the *M*A*S*H* rerun hovered back on. It was the episode in which Hawkeye and Trapper John ordered ribs all the way from Chicago. That reminded me of dinner. I went to check on progress.

I wouldn't have ordered it from Korea. The breading on the chicken was like oatmeal and the peas were like nothing in nature. I only buy the things because I like how the courses are arranged. If the rest of the human race could keep the house in one compartment, the office in another, and leave the last for dessert, life would be a Banquet®.

The TV listings had *The Magnificent Ambersons* on Channel 31 at 3:00 A.M. Old movies on regular television were getting to be as rare as glass bottles. I set the alarm for 2:45 and turned in early. I got up with the bell, plugged in the coffee pot, and sat down in front of a $19.95 electro-plated gold necklace on the Home Shopping Network. I checked the selector. It was 31, all right. When it became obvious they weren't going to interrupt the necklace for Orson Welles I turned off the set and went back to bed. Sometimes the peas jump the little partition and spoil the applesauce.

I'd been asleep five minutes when the kid next door started gunning the Roadrunner.

My first sip of coffee six hours later was from a paper cup at the office. I'd left the pot at home percolating all night and the stuff that eventually came out of the spout was what county road crews use to fill potholes. The counter down the street, where I was accustomed to getting carry-out in good insulating Styrofoam, had in a fit of environmental consciousness switched to waxed cardboard, the kind that started to biodegrade on the way upstairs. I had burns on my fingers to match the brand on my arm from yesterday's car-window incident. It could have been worse. I could have had gout.

The mail was a trip down memory lane. The dealership that had sold my Cutlass to its original owner before Kent State had tracked me down to inform me that the car was being recalled to repair a loose nut at the base of the steering column that made the doors fly off at sixty-five miles per hour. If their people decided to go into the detective business

I was through. Two bills I'd sent out for services rendered came back stamped ADDRESSEE UNKNOWN. An eleven-month-old overdue parking ticket had come to the attention of a clerk downtown who spelled *warrant* with one *R*. I filed it under the blotter with the others and slam-dunked everything else. Then I sat back with my eyes closed and waited for my watch to say nine o'clock. That would be as early as I could expect a prime mover like Arsenault to be in his office.

When I woke up shortly before ten I went into the closet, bathed my face, and stood by the fan flapping my damp shirttail while a receptionist put me through. It was another muggy morning, with no relief predicted before the weekend.

"Mr. Arsenault's office. This is Greta."

"Hi, Greta. Hot enough for you?"

"Who's speaking, please?"

"Tell Mr. Arsenault I'm calling for Jay Bell Furlong."

"Isn't he very ill?"

"That's why he isn't making his own calls."

"One moment."

I got violins. It wasn't until the French horns came in that I realized I was listening to "I Want to Hold Your Hand." By then the promised moment was long gone.

"This is Lynn Arsenault. Who is this?"

That No. 3 sandpaper never goes with a voice in its early thirties. He sounded like Mr. Potter in a high school production of *It's a Wonderful Life*.

"Mr. Arsenault, my name is Amos Walker. I'm a licensed private investigator working for Jay Bell Furlong. I wonder if I could have an interview today."

"About what?"

"Lily Talbot."

"I don't know the name."

"I have a photograph of you together."

"I'm afraid I don't know what you're talking about."

"There's a bare chance you don't," I said. "The woman you were photographed with was wearing a different head at the time."

He surprised me by jumping on it. I'd had him pegged for another stall. "I can give you five minutes at eleven o'clock. No more. My calendar's jammed."

I said five minutes would be sufficient and we were through talking to each other.

Allen Park is to Detroit what the interior of Africa was to the British Empire under Victoria: Unexplored Territory, a place everyone has heard of but few know exactly where it is or what goes on there. It's downriver, for one thing, and the peculiar centrifugal force that has been destroying the Motor City since the collapse of the Edsel tends to fling departing residents west, not south. Beyond the spines of the factory stacks its skyline is flat, its surface gridded with broad, empty streets and sutured together with grass-grown railroad tracks leading to and from the calcified Ford River Rouge plant, and when you sit at a stoplight with your windows down you hear the slow, measured heartbeat of life in a nursing home. There are even farms. It seemed a curious location for the headquarters of an expanding architectural firm like Imminent Visions.

But as the man said when the woman's husband asked him what he was doing naked in his wife's bedroom closet, everybody's got to be someplace.

The building was four stories of red brick laid in one-ton sections like giant Legos and sandblasted for that look of genteel old age. It showed just enough of Jay Bell Furlong's prejudice for the horizontal to support the claim of either

Vernon Whiting, Visions' late founder, or Furlong that the other was a thief. With its flat roof and boxed elms it made me think of Beaver Cleaver's elementary school, but then I don't know a groined arch from a ruptured disc.

There was a row of ten diagonally striped parking spaces next to the ramp leading down to an underground garage with a swing-arm gate across the entrance labeled EMPLOYEES ONLY. As I pulled into the only available visitor's slot, the gate opened for an emerald-green Porsche that whipped around the corner and into the street without a sign of a brake light. It's a well-known fact that when you pay $75,000 for an automobile it comes equipped with its own invisible force field.

A construction crew in lightweight blue coveralls and canary-colored hardhats was busy with spades and a pneumatic drill in a barricaded area next to the building, widening an excavation that had been made in the pavement by a yellow backhoe parked nearby. I stopped to ask the foreman, a heavy-shouldered redneck in his fifties, what the project was. His coveralls were black with sweat.

He took a toothpick out of the corner of his mouth as if it were impeding his view and onced me over. I must have looked enough like an employee of the building to talk to. "Problem with the underground cable. Something gnawed through the insulation, probably. Up on the poles it's birds, down here it's ground moles."

"Power?"

"Phone."

"Thank God for cellulars."

"If you don't mind every punk kid with a scanner listening in. You'd be surprised what some turkeys talk about over the fucking public airwaves."

"At least you're working in the shade."

"Just till noon. If we don't finish up by then I'm pulling the crew for a job on the east side of something."

The lobby was done in glazed green-and-white Mexican tile with shiny Bakelite walls and a three-story shaft ending in a skylight. In the center of the room stood a seven-foot granite statue with holes in it on a pedestal three feet high. The sculptor's name was engraved in a brass plate on the pedestal. I didn't recognize it, big surprise. The guard stationed behind the statue was made of the same grade of rock, but without holes, and wore a tan uniform with brown leather patches reading I.V. SECURITY embroidered in red. He shifted his attention from a bank of closed-circuit TV monitors to my ID, found my name on a clipboard, and told me to go to the fourth floor. He gave me a plastic tag with a big numeral 4 to hang on my handkerchief pocket.

Another guard at the elevator, this one female and hewn from softer igneous, checked out the tag and rang for the car. When the doors opened, technology kicked in: A video camera mounted on a heat-sensitive swivel near the ceiling tracked my progress down a hall carpeted in soundproof gray.

Assuming that the late Vernon Whiting had had anything to do with the security in the building, that brief trip laid to rest my curiosity as to who had stolen from whom in the Furlong-Whiting relationship. Crooks buy the best locks.

Lynn Arsenault's name was lettered in gold on a rosewood door near the end of the hall. I opened it on yet another reception room, overgrown with tropical plants in hammered copper pots. The woman who would go with the kidney-shaped desk, coming on sixty with a light blonde wash to cover the gray and glasses with octagonal gold rims, stashed an oversize watering can behind one of the plants and took her post. She had on a tailored suit and a man's silk necktie. "Yes?"

I showed her the ID. "I've got an eleven o'clock with Mr. Arsenault."

"Oh, I'm sorry, Mr. Walker."

"That's okay. I get a new picture taken next month."

"No, I mean Mr. Arsenault had to go out. There's a problem with one of his buildings."

"Can't he find someone else to hold it up?"

"Imminent Visions' designs do not fall down." She tilted her head toward a wall tiled with plaques and framed certificates of merit.

I put away the ID folder. "Where is the building? Maybe I could meet him there."

"He didn't say which building. He took a call. I gathered it couldn't wait. Would you care to reschedule? He has an opening next week."

"I don't."

"I'm very sorry. Normally Mr. Arsenault never misses an appointment."

"Seriously?"

"He's the youngest chief executive officer in the industry. You don't get to be that kind of success without a reputation for keeping commitments."

"You said he took a call. Did you put it through?"

"No, he took it on his private line." She looked at me over the top of her glasses. "Are you asking all these questions as part of an investigation?"

"I'm just stalling. I like the smell of African violets."

Her face brightened. "Do you know much about them?"

"A little. I did an undercover bit behind the counter in a nursery for a week. One of the employees was smuggling hydrangeas out the back door."

"Hydrangeae, actually. Latin plural."

"It was only a week. I had coffee yesterday with a woman who grows dahlias."

She might have sniffed. "Dahlias are just sunflowers with a superiority complex."

"The woman's name is Karen Furlong."

"Oh, yes." She punched her glasses back up her nose. "We've never met. But the name is well known here. Our founder, Mr. Vernon Whiting, used to work with Jay Bell Furlong."

"Did you know Mr. Whiting?"

"I was his secretary for twelve years."

Furlong's name had brought down the temperature. The room was no longer safe for tropical plants.

"I'll call." At the door I looked back. The octagonals were still on me. "Does Arsenault drive a green Porsche?"

She found a smile. "Did he almost run you down? He's a maniac in that thing. We're all worried he'll wrap it around a telephone pole."

In the lobby I returned the plastic tag to the guard at the monitors. "Do they think someone's going to sneak in and steal a building?"

"Hard to fence." He hung up the tag.

I went back out into the heat. The shade was shrinking on the west side of the building and the construction crew was packing up, leaving the excavation open and the underground telephone cable exposed. I only noted it because it's a detective's job to observe and remember.

Eight

"HI, THIS IS NATE Millender. If it's paying work, leave a message. If it's going to cost me, keep trying, you never can tell. Well, you know this shit."

I waited for the beep, introduced myself, and said, "Randy Quarrels says you're the best man in town for the job I've got in mind." I added that I was on an expense account and left my number at the office.

A kid in clown pants and a ball cap back to front, with an electronic beeper clipped to his belt, saw me break the connection and loped toward the telephone. I held up an index finger and dialed the number of the other name I'd gotten from Quarrels. He held up another finger, but hung back. We were standing inside the entrance of a Perry Drugs in downtown Allen Park.

"Well, spit it out."

Here was a voice squeezed from the lungs of someone who went around all hunched over by the chains he had forged in life. Either that or he smoked too much. I put away the Winston I'd been about to light and asked the voice if it belonged to Ulysses Worth.

"Eulisy."

"I'm sorry?"

He gave me the letters. "My mother couldn't spell. That's the closest she got when it came time to fill out the birth certificate. You the guy with the twins?"

"Not so far as I know."

"I'm expecting a guy with twins. He wants their picture taken in matching Red Wings jerseys."

"I'm not the guy. Randy Quarrels says you're the best in the business for what I want."

"What do you want?"

"If I could discuss it over the telephone, we aren't talking about the same business."

"Hey, man, if this is a sting I ain't worth the cost of the wire. You don't get any lower in the food chain than Eulisy Worth."

"I'm strictly private sector. Not a cop. Not a Fed. I'm not with the Klan or Citizens for a Porn-Free America or Sprint. All I want is your time and I'll pay for that."

"This cash? I mean *cash*. Nobody signs nothing."

I still had my half-empty cigarette pack in my hand. I dumped out the butts and crackled it in front of the mouthpiece. "Nothing else quite sounds like C-notes," I said. "When can I come out?"

"Anytime you want, if you don't mind me working while we talk."

"I'm on my way."

The kid with the pager looked up from a display of condoms, but I worked the riser and called my service. "Anything yet from a Nate Millender?"

"No, no messages, Mr. Walker." The girl sounded genuinely apologetic. She was my favorite that week. I thanked her and hung up.

The kid watched me slide the cigarettes back into the pack, then swooped in. He was punching buttons as the door wheezed shut behind me. I figured I'd slowed down the city's drug traffic ten minutes.

Eulisy Worth lived and worked in one of those small white frame houses with a shared driveway and a screened-in front porch, the kind you see on the news whenever a drive-by shooting takes place or an unemployed auto worker barricades himself in with his family and a gun. They are part of the landscape in a city that at one time boasted the highest percentage of private homeowners of any urban center in the United States, and so common they're invisible. This one was on Benson, in case it matters. All the lawns were the color of burned rice. A Dodge minivan with a square of cellophane taped over one window was parked in the driveway.

The screen door was latched. I rapped and waited. After thirty seconds or so I rapped again and pressed my folded handkerchief against the back of my neck. There was evidence the neighborhood had had trees and shade before the city widened the street to drop in a new sewer. Some of the saplings it had planted as an afterthought were still standing. One or two had leaves. Harsh summers and raging winters had beaten the sidings and pavement the same shade of gray.

I rapped a third time. A series of locks and bolts snapped and squeaked on the other side of the door. I hoped the closed windows meant air conditioning inside.

The man who came out to unhook the screen door was small and black and wiry, with a modest flat-top and round wire-rimmed glasses. The prescription was so weak the lenses sent back the light in flat white disks like window glass. He wore a tank top made of cargo netting, Desert Storm camouflage pants with lots of bulging pockets, and square-toed cowboy boots. I liked the look fine except for the moist sheen on his skin. That meant no air conditioning.

"Where are the twins?" He looked past my shoulder. He had gray eyes that darted like silverfish.

"I'm not the guy with the twins. We settled that over the telephone. Walker's the name."

"The guy with the C-notes."

I took out my wallet and showed him the corners of the bills. Not a cigarette pack this time. I'd stopped at the bank on the way.

"Those the new ones? Let me see."

I slid one out and stretched it between my hands.

He squinted. "Ben's off-center."

"That's the idea."

"Sure they ain't queer?"

"I just spend them. I don't ask them about their private life."

"Well, bring 'em in."

He held the screen door while I stepped inside, then searched the street one more time before he hooked it.

"I sure hope that guy shows up with the twins. The Asian market is nuts for twins, the blonder the better."

"You said you were shooting a couple of kids in Red Wings jerseys."

"That was on the phone. For all I knew you was using a cellular. Don't tip nothing over, okay? The equipment's rented."

Someone had punched out a couple of walls and converted the ground floor into a studio. There were reflectors everywhere, a bank of lights on a stand, and a full-size video camera on a professional aluminum frame. There were stacks of three-quarter-inch videotape on the floors and on all the furniture except the bed. It wasn't a bed, really; just a king-size mattress on the floor. A red plush spread had been flung over it, the better to show off the naked female flesh displayed there.

Nudity is deceptive. What looked at first glance to be a pile of writhing bodies turned out to be just two girls in their late teens, one black, the other a pale redhead, lying half entangled on the spread. I could tell my presence was embarrassing them. The black girl yawned and scratched herself under one breast while the redhead applied fresh lipstick from a neon-colored tube.

"Places, ladies," Worth said.

The lipstick went out of sight and the girls swung into a passionate embrace.

"We can talk while I'm shooting." Worth poked a CD into a tabletop player. "The music's just for mood. Someone else'll dub in the oohs and aahs later."

The music was Gilbert and Sullivan.

"I didn't know there was a lesbian pornography market," I said.

"There isn't. And the people I work with prefer to call them 'adult features.'" He had strapped on the camera and was doing a slow schottische around the bed. "Dykes don't rent videos. Straight couples prefer soft-core. The rest of the market is lonely guys—*lots* of lonely guys—and they ain't interested in looking at some other guy's pimply butt. With two women they think they're getting double their money's worth."

"This your day job?"

"Day *and* night. That's how I keep up the payments on this here mansion. Smile, ladies. You're supposed to be having a good time."

The black girl said, "I got a button sticking me in the ass."

"Use it. You're an actress."

"Randy says you're a wizard in the darkroom," I said.

"Best in the Midwest." A mobile made up of metal cutouts of spaceships and sportscars hung from a wire above the mattress. With one hand he set it spinning, then panned up with the camera to catch the motion. Onscreen it would look like a window-shattering climax.

"So why do skinflicks? Excuse me, 'adult features.' "

"Two words," he said. "Cyberspace."

"I think that's one word."

"Who gives a shit? The point is, any fourteen-year-old with a PC can click his mouse and outperform an expert with a house full of copy cameras, air brushes, and developing fluid. You see a movie lately, all them explosions and car crashes? Computer generated. Special-effects guys that were pulling down a million a year five years ago are putting in for food stamps. Still photography got the worst of it. I got downsized right out of my career."

"Bummer."

He stopped to kick out the tape and see how much was left. "You said you had work for me."

"I want a picture of two people together."

"Hire a studio. Or buy a Kodak and do it yourself. It's cheaper."

"The two people I'm talking about aren't that easy to get in the same place at the same time."

"Raise your right leg."

"What?"

"Not you. Linda, is it?"

"Lisa," said the redhead.

"Raise your right leg, Lisa. No, not like that. Like you're pulling on a stocking. That's it. Oh, very nice. Do you dance professionally, Lisa?" He was standing on the mattress now, zooming in on the foot she had pointed at the ceiling.

"Just on the runway. I don't do laps."

"Exactly what kind of picture are we talking about?"

She looked at him. "What?"

"Not you."

"Kind of like what you're shooting now," I said, "only without motion and it doesn't matter if the subjects ever knew each other."

He stepped down to the floor and turned off the camera. His eyeglasses caught the light in blank circles. "How do you know Randy Quarrels?"

"Mutual friend."

"Get dressed, both of you."

"It's only been an hour," the black girl said. "You promised three hours' work."

"I'm out of inspiration. Don't worry, you'll get the full pony."

She stood and stretched. She was my height and it was obvious she worked out. Except for her coloring she reminded me of Quarrels' snow leopard.

"Get a move on. I've seen it before." Worth stooped and jerked a plug out of the wall. Gilbert and Sullivan fell silent, the bank of lights went out with a hiss. Instantly the room seemed less hot.

"Well, shit. This the first time any boy hurried me *into* my clothes." Swishing her hips, the black girl followed the redhead around a curtain slung from a clothesline. Lisa's pale buttocks had less definition than her partner's.

"You too," Worth told me.

"I'm already dressed."

"I mean get out. Randy and I didn't get along, but I never thought he'd tag me for a blackmailer."

"What's the difference to a pornographer?"

"Who're you, Jerry Falwell? I run a legitimate business."

"A legitimate business you won't discuss over the telephone."

"That's just to keep the right-wing nuts off my front

porch. The neighborhood's zoned commercial and I don't use the mails or internet. My stuff sells to the same video stores that carry *The Wizard of Oz*. Okay, it ain't Norman Rockwell. It ain't even Norman Bates. But it's honest work. Last month every tenth tape Aunt Matilda took home was *Hot Cross Nuns*. That was one of mine. It ain't just old men in raincoats anymore."

I tipped my head toward the curtain. "Who did those girls vote for in the last election, Barney the Dinosaur?"

"They're pros. I got releases signed by their mothers. One of *them* appeared in three of my productions before she retired. What do you do for a living, bind Bibles?" Lights flashed off his glasses like bolts from God.

"Throttle down, Fellini. So you're a grindhouse Griffith with ethics. There was only one way to find that out. For the record, I'm trying to trace a frame, not frame one of my own. I'm pretty sure this isn't the place. You'd have to be as good an actor as you are a director."

He let out air. "What work you in?"

I told him. "I've got ID if you need it."

"Why would anyone lie about a thing like that?" He undid the harness and laid the video camera on a spavined sofa loaded with tapes and lingerie.

"Randy and I worked together at the *News* a couple of times," he said. "I was freelancing, doing some stuff for the Sunday magazine. You know, color shots of Denny McLain washing the Caddy and remembering the good old days when he threw strikes for the Tigers and broke legs for Big Vinnie the Camel."

"Not the best use of your talents."

"Talent's what amateurs have. Pros need cash. Sometimes, when a prominent citizen kicks off and his widow has only a picture of him wearing a hat, it's somebody's job to take the hat off in the photo lab. I showed Randy how to do it so even an expert couldn't tell what'd been done. Parlor stuff. He thought I was a genius."

"Are you?"

"I've got a good eye and a steady hand. That's all the genius you need in photography, and now you don't even need that. I ain't doing what I'm doing for fun. One set of tits looks pretty much like all the rest."

"Do you know who took the hat off this one?" I handed him the Talbot-Arsenault picture.

He glanced at it and gave it back. "Not offhand. The girl's head came from another shot."

"Quarrels needed a glass to tell him that."

"That's why he referred you to me. But it's not my racket."

"Whose racket is it?"

"Nate Millender."

"Quarrels mentioned him. He didn't say it was his racket, just that he was capable of this kind of work." I pocketed the picture.

"It's his racket. Or it was. Damn computers are putting everyone out of work, even criminals."

"Not all of them. Who's backing him?"

He took off his glasses and wiped them on his pants. "You're asking plenty for just a peek at Ben Franklin."

"How much?"

The actresses came back from behind the curtain. The black girl had on white shorts, cork sandals, a red handkerchief blouse tied under her breasts, and a white vinyl bag slung over one shoulder. The outfit did more for my libido than her nudity had. The redhead wore an army tunic over a T-shirt and artfully torn Wrangler's. That did nothing for me.

"You said three hours," the black girl said. "That's seventy-five apiece."

"Pay them," said Worth.

I produced my wallet and thumbed out two hundreds. The black girl opened her bag, fished among a pile of wadded-up bills inside, and traded me a fifty. The hundreds went into the bag and she snapped it shut.

Lisa, the redhead, said, "Hey!"

"C'mon. We'll break 'em at the mall."

"Don't look so sad," Worth said when they'd left. "One of them's got a scholarship to Michigan."

"Which one?"

He shrugged and adjusted his glasses. "They all look alike to me. One set of tits."

I watched him tidying up, stacking tapes and coiling cables. He was a one-man production crew. "What else do I get for a hundred and a half?"

"A warning, for one thing. You want to watch yourself with Millender. He does a lot of political work. Those boondogglers play tackle."

"That's worth about a dollar."

He plunked himself down next to the camera, exhausted suddenly. Sweat was fogging his freshly mopped glasses.

"There was a construction bid scandal up in Iroquois Heights a few years back. You know the Heights?"

"Well enough to burn my clothes every time I come back."

"There are crookeder places. There have to be." But he didn't sound convinced. "Anyway, kickback schemes are old stuff here in town, and up there if someone didn't grease all the wheels all the time, the whole damn place would squeak to a stop. But this one wouldn't go away. Did I mention it was an election year?"

"It usually is."

"Bogardus was the name of the city councilman who took the heat. One morning his driver came to his house to pick him up and found his front door open. He went in and there's Councilman Bogardus stretched out on the living room rug with two bullets in his chest. Cops never found the gun. There was a coroner's inquest. You want to hear the verdict?"

I remembered the case. For two weeks it had seemed the reporters would never stop squawking about it. Then they did. A plane crashed, a local beauty queen was crowned, a child's body turned up in a culvert, and Bogardus went to the library files with the pet rock. But I let Eulisy Worth tell it.

"Suicide. Apparently he shot himself twice in the upper thorax, which if you ever tried it you wouldn't call it the easy way out, then hid the gun someplace where two thorough police searches couldn't turn it. All in the sixteen seconds it took his heart to stop pumping. That was raw even for the Heights. You know Royce Grayling?"

"Some kind of dogsbody at city hall. He ran errands for the old mayor."

"Not just the old mayor. He's got free range between Lansing and Toledo. Cops clock him doing ninety in a hospital zone, run his ID, and send him on his way with a polite touch to their visors."

"Your point?"

"Up north they call Grayling Suicide Sam."

"I get it. What's he got to do with Millender?"

"They're tight as hatches. Sailing on Lake St. Clair every weekend, poker at Millender's place Wednesday night. You couldn't blast them apart." He patted the video camera as if it were a big friendly dog. "Worth the hundred and a half?"

"Maybe the best deal I've had all year," I said.

Nine

THAT'S THE THING about the work: Just when you think you've got an uncomplicated little inheritance fraud, it turns into politics and murder.

Either one is bad enough on its own. When you link them up you need six stiff belts and a loaded gun.

So I went back to the office for mine.

I held the number of belts to one and saved the six for the cylinder of the Smith & Wesson I'd been carrying ever since the Detroit Police Academy and I had parted over philosophical differences. I was using hollow points now, a concession to all the heavier stoppers out there. The shiny chrome cases made me feel like the Lone Ranger.

A homicide inspector I knew had tried to interest me in a Sig-Sauer 9mm Automatic, or at least an S&W L-frame. But I'd just gotten the rubber grip of the old Detective Special worn to the shape of my fist, and anyway those jacketed slugs have an annoying habit of greasing straight through their targets when they ought to be staying inside them, doing things. Call me sentimental.

I wiped off the works with an oily rag, squeaked the revolver into its stiff leather holster, and used it to pin down a stack of blank affidavits fluttering in front of the fan while I called the service.

"Yes, Mr. Walker. You have a message from a Mr. Nate Millender. You're to call him back." She made it sound as if I'd heard from the Nobel committee on sleuthing.

I thanked her, clicked off, dialed, and got the bright voice I remembered from the recording.

"How big is the expense account?" Millender asked when he had my name.

"Big enough for the job. It's a big job. When can I come out?"

"I'm shooting in Ann Arbor all day; assignment for *Newsweek*. Say six."

I said six.

I yawned and looked at the calendar, a bank giveaway with a picture of Tahquamenon Falls pounding smoke out of the rocks at its base. I looked at my watch. Then I looked back at the calendar, but it was still June so I looked at my watch again. It was past lunchtime but I wasn't hungry.

I broke out my notebook and started to call the Talbot Gallery. The line was purring when I hung up, snapped the holster onto my belt, and put my jacket on over it. Art galleries are often air-conditioned.

Downtown was more confusing than usual; and there are still gaunt, hollow-eyed delegates in straw hats from the 1980 National Republican Party convention driving around Grand Circus Park with expired out-of-state plates, looking for the way to the airport. The weather had brought out a herd of RVs for the annual shakedown cruise and old men in cataracts were trying to maneuver the brontosaurus-size vehicles around hairpin corners with their blue-haired wives yelling at them from the swivel seat. The curbs were taking a hell of a beating.

Half the street spaces were blocked and the lots and garages were full. I parked in a towaway zone behind a dormant Winnebago and sorted through the collection of plastic signs I keep in the glove compartment. I selected SAFETY INSPECTOR and clipped it to the visor.

The gallery was a walk-in at street level on Congress, a block down from the Penobscot Building, and would rent for roughly what I had earned thus far in my adult life. Its name was etched in discreet block capitals on the glass door. Behind me the door closed against the pressure in a pneumatic tube with all the racket of a manicured hand sliding into a silk-lined pocket.

The first refrigerated puff from inside evaporated the sweat on my skin. Thirty seconds later I wanted to turn up my collar and pull it over my ears. Why they had hung paintings on the walls instead of hams was one for Sotheby's, or maybe Armour Star.

Track lighting glanced shyly off eggshell-colored walls, illuminating canvases in minimal frames and statuary on columns. Photorealism seemed to be on its way back, but there was no discouraging the usual assortment of exploding pigs and warped hunks of plywood with placards reading JUPITER ASCENDANT or something equally helpful. Their prices were neatly processed on three-by-five cards and apparently serious. A stereo system turned so low it might have belonged to the next building played atonal arrangements simulating the tide slapping a beach. It made you want to find the bathroom.

At that hour the place belonged to me and a security guard in a green uniform, who if he hadn't raised a hand to scratch his forehead might have had me looking for his price card. He placed the back of the hand against his mouth, covering a yawn. Daring me to make a break for the door with a Rodin under my coat.

Free-standing partitions divided the exhibits. A woman approached from behind one of them as I was admiring a clay head with its tongue hanging out.

"It's called *The Mortal Thought,*" she said. "Please don't say it looks like someone got hold of a bad burrito."

I looked at her. Something, contempt or amusement, was pulling at the corners of her mouth. It was an interesting mouth, artistically speaking: unfashionably wide in a face with beveled edges. She had brown eyes with short lashes she'd made no attempt to lengthen, a straight nose, and a broad clear forehead. Her hair was brown and hung in crinkled tendrils on either side of the center part. The mouth made sense when you took in the whole face. She would have looked very good next to Jay Bell Furlong's planes and angles. She looked very good standing alone. She didn't look much like her picture, but it had been eight years.

She was tall, of course.

I said, "I was thinking of the last time I saw something like it. It was in Louisiana, when they were still using the gas chamber."

Her lips parted. I'd surprised her. "It's interesting you would say that. It was sculpted in Madrid before the First World War. It represents an execution using the garrote. May I ask what you were doing visiting the gas chamber?"

"It was a business trip. Are you Miss Talbot?"

"No, I'm Jean Sternhagen, her assistant. Miz Talbot's busy in the office. I can help you if there's something specific you want to see." A puzzled line marred the wide brow. She hadn't made up her mind how to take me.

Now I recognized the honey-over-grits dialect of yesterday's brief telephone conversation. She came from one of those states where they're still combing minie balls out of the carpet.

"I need to talk to the boss." I gave her one of my cards.

She pursed her lips over it, excused herself, and swept away. She had on an ivory silk blouse with a calf-length skirt designed for sweeping.

In a little while a woman came my way who was no more than life size, with red hair cut short like a boy's and wearing a black jumpsuit pinched at the waist by a silver belt, the slacks tucked into knee-length black boots. Instead of a riding crop she was carrying my card.

"I know for a fact we haven't been dealing in stolen Picassos." She stopped in front of me and stuck out the pasteboard.

"Keep it," I said. "I couldn't talk the guy into printing just one. You're Lily Talbot?"

She said she was. She gave each syllable its full value. I was betting on one of those elocution tapes you play in the car. The rest of her was just as crisp. She was an interesting example of architecture, from the fine bones of her face to the long legs that whoever had designed her outfit liked to set off. Well, Furlong wouldn't have left his drafting board for anything less; but her lack of stature did surprise me. It must have been true love.

"I need your opinion about a picture," I said.

"I see. Are you representing a collector, or is this for yourself?"

"Neither. At the moment I'm working for Jay Bell Furlong."

A pair of hazel eyes iced over. "Who are you?"

"It's on the card."

"He hired you to find me?"

"He knew where you were. He's kept track of your career. He has a message for you."

"I'm not accepting anything from him. Not even messages."

"It can wait. The picture I wanted to talk about is of you and Lynn Arsenault."

"That bastard."

"Arsenault?"

"Furlong." She touched a corner of the card in her hand with a fingertip, as if testing its sharpness. "I take that back. We're supposed to be charitable toward someone in his condition. He's a fool. How close is he to the end? The media seem impatient."

"Close enough to want to clear the air," I said. "I need a little more than that. Is there someplace we can talk? I think *The Mortal Thought* is listening."

"My interest in Mr. Furlong's condition is purely curiosity. We haven't anything to discuss."

"People who say that usually have plenty."

She glanced toward the guard by the drinking fountain, or maybe it was an exhibit.

"He's big enough," I said. "Your call on whether he can get it done without tipping over statuary."

When she looked back at me she'd made her decision. "How did Jay find you? I wouldn't have thought there was another man like him born in this century."

"I'm the first listing in the book. Under *A* for anachronisms."

She led me through a maze of partitions, kiosks, and *objets d'art,* down a short unfinished corridor not intended for public view, and into a back room nearly as large as the gallery proper. The floor was bare plywood and there were ladders and loose tarpaulins and mops, brooms, and buckets under a skylight that hadn't been cleaned since *Laugh-In.* The turpentine fumes made my eyes burn. Jean Sternhagen caught Miz Talbot's glance from atop one of the ladders. She shoved a cardboard carton into a niche on a supply shelf, climbed down, and went out into the maze without a word.

"It would take more than terminal cancer to affect a mind

like Jay's. He must know it's too late to patch things up."
Lily Talbot leaned back against the table covered with cleaning supplies and stained newspapers and crossed her ankles.

"He still wants to apologize."

"That's all?"

"That's all."

"Tell him I accept."

I waited for the rest. I wanted a cigarette, but the fumes weren't going away.

"It's easy to forgive a person you feel nothing for," she said. "I loved him for a while, and for a long time afterward I hated him, but that passed too. I'm a woman, and I'm supposed to care about a fellow human being in pain. All right, I do. Beyond that the tank's empty."

"Is that why you called him a bastard?"

"That was a knee-jerk reaction from the woman I used to be." She uncrossed her ankles and straightened. "You've delivered your message, and you have my answer. Now I really have a gallery to run."

"He knows the picture's a fake," I said.

"He should have known it then."

"Did you tell him?"

"I would have, had he asked. The question never seemed to have occurred to him. That's what killed us, his readiness to believe he'd been betrayed. I didn't realize it then, but I did a lot of thinking later and I came to the conclusion that he was waiting for something to come along and prove I didn't love him. What it really proved was that he didn't love *me.*"

"That works for everyone but great men and women with rich fathers."

She seemed to realize she was still holding my card. She looked at it. "Funny, it just says 'Investigations.' You left out 'Spiritual Counseling.'"

"No extra charge. What do you know about the picture?"

"I know it wasn't real, of course, but I knew that then. At the time I didn't know the man in it was Lynn Arsenault."

I felt a rush. It might have been the turpentine. "At the time?"

"Last year—longer ago than that, I think—he commissioned some pieces for his new office. He came in person without an appointment or I'd have left it to Jean. I recognized him immediately. If I played by Jay's rules, I'd have told him to shop somewhere else. I won't say I didn't consider it. But it was a big order. I'm not doing well enough yet to afford a set of principles."

"The place looks prosperous."

"Smoke and mirrors. The arts are in eclipse, in case you didn't notice it. Washington's bailing out and so is the public. Culture is the first thing people find they can do without when the squeeze is on. They're just decoration, after all. Talbot Gallery is holding its own, thanks to a little integrity-bending whenever the odd Arsenault comes to call."

"Did he mention the picture?"

"No. I don't think he even knew who I was, apart from someone who could sell him some art. The picture was getting to be a long time ago even then. He might simply have forgotten." She glanced at a tiny watch on a silver strap on her wrist. "I'm expecting a group of Japanese automakers any minute. They want to see the Wyeths. Tell Jay all is forgiven." She held up two fingers in blessing.

"Why not tell him yourself?"

"I should fly to California to ease his guilt?"

"How about driving out to the Airport Marriott?"

"Which airport?"

Somehow the question had sounded less silly when I'd

been the one asking it. "Metro. He's sharing a suite with Stuart Lund."

She turned that over behind her face. Her complexion wasn't as pale as the redhead's in Eulisy Worth's studio. She was getting to that age where even natural red hair looked suspect. "What's Jay hope to gain by convincing the world he's sick?"

"He's sick. You don't get any sicker. He just tweaked the time frame a little. For what it's worth, my instructions don't include telling you any of this, but I don't think a three-word reply to his message is what he hired me to bring back."

"What am I supposed to do, run to his bedside and hold his hand?"

"That's between you and your Wyeths. I'm off the clock." I turned the doorknob.

"Wait."

I waited. She was hugging her upper arms. The place wasn't that cold. The air conditioning stopped at the end of the unfinished corridor.

"The gallery's listed," she said. "So am I. Jay could have sent Windy Lund with the same message. What else are you doing for him?"

"Guess."

She nodded. "Jay wouldn't be Jay if he laid aside pragmatic details for his own mortality. Don't think I haven't wondered who hated me enough to disgrace me. Five years ago I'd have jumped all over Arsenault asking questions. But life goes on. Priorities change."

"Like you said, it was a big order."

She considered her response. "You're not much of a diplomat, are you?"

"It cost me an ambassadorship." I told her good luck with the Japanese and used the doorknob.

Jean Sternhagen was staring at a painting of a cracked water jug when I came out into the gallery. She spoke without turning. "Does that look crooked to you?"

I hung a cigarette off the corner of my lip. "I think it's the jug that's crooked."

"I think so too. I hope I have the courage to tell the artist when he threatens to pull out of the show. Last time he took home everything but the hooks. One of the guests thought the apple in a still life looked like it had a worm."

"Did it?"

"It wasn't an apple. It was a pomegranate."

"You handle the artists as well as the pictures?"

"Lily does all the wheeling and dealing. I fetch and carry and keep the customers warm."

"I guess you wouldn't know anything about the Arsenault sale." I primed the pump. "Executive over at Imminent Visions, an architectural firm."

"Oh, him. We busted our rumps on that deal. Any time a customer's willing to pay full price on an order that size we go the extra mile and a half."

"Full price, no haggling?"

She nodded. "He ordered limited-edition Impressionist prints, reproduced from new plates taken from the original canvases. That runs into money, but we can knock twenty to thirty percent off the purchase price in quantity."

"Like selling in bulk."

"Right. Only we don't call it that in the art world." The wide mouth got wry. "I guess Mr. Arsenault was in a hurry. He bought twenty prints and paid ten thousand dollars. It must be nice to be so rich you don't have to—"

"Jean, why don't you go to lunch? Everything's under control here."

She turned and saw Lily Talbot. Walking noiselessly in

boots on a waxed floor is an art you can't hang in a gallery. Jean's face flushed. "Sure. I was just asking Mr. Walker if he liked *The Mortal Thought*. He was looking at it earlier." Her eyes pleaded.

"I don't," I said. "I didn't like the gas chamber either."

"I'm glad. I keep hoping someone will buy it so I can stop having nightmares about it." She told me good-bye and went out the back.

"I prefer to be present when my employees are being pumped for information." Lily wasn't hugging herself now.

"Don't ride her too hard," I said. "She has to get along with the temperamental types. That means talking."

"Her job's secure. I'm just deciding whether it might be worth breaking a few things to have you thrown out the back door."

"I'm not an architect. For me, pitching two to three thousand dollars down a hole just to save a couple of minutes takes a big hole. Does that kind of thing happen often?"

"A lot of different kinds of people collect art. Some don't like to haggle."

"Rich people."

"It helps when you can afford it."

"Eight years ago I bet he'd have taken the discount."

Her lids narrowed; and she had long feral eyes to begin with. "Tell me something. Does the sun ever rise in your world, or do you see shadows wherever you look?"

"I don't have to look as hard as I used to."

She said the door was in the same place it was when I came in. It was the first thing she'd told me that didn't lead to more questions.

Ten

I LIKED LYNN ARSENAULT. A lot.

I couldn't think of anyone else I'd never met whom I was so crazy about.

Suddenly I was hungry. I washed down a Reuben with a glass of milk downtown and stopped at the telephone to call Imminent Visions. The silver-haired receptionist I'd met earlier apologized and said Mr. Arsenault hadn't yet checked in from whichever building was in crisis. I listened hard, but office acoustics have changed. You can't always hear the rest of the staff snickering in the background.

When I hung up I liked Lynn Arsenault better than Colonel Mustard in the library.

The next call was to my service.

"Yes, Mr. Walker. Mr. Millender called and asked if you could meet him at his boat instead of his house, same time. He's going sailing." She gave me a dock and berth number at the Grosse Pointe Marina.

"Don't hang up," I said. "Do you sail?"

She chuckled. "The last time I was on a boat it capsized when I stepped aboard."

"Clumsy?"

"No, just fat."

I made a note to stop asking personal questions of disembodied voices. I needed to hang on to all the fantasies I had.

I fished out another thirty-five cents and dialed a number I had memorized at the City-County Building. There was a telephone card in my future.

After one ring a voice I recognized came on. Never mind whose.

"This is the tooth fairy," I said.

He paused only long enough to make the connection. "No loose molars today, sorry." But he stayed on the line. I'd sprung him from a jam once involving a female glee club president at Mumford High, which if it had ever come out would have cost him his corner office. The higher he climbed in our democratic society, the more he owed me. Someday he was going to be a powerful enemy.

But not today.

"That's okay, I'm fresh out of quarters. I'm trying to track down a party named Larry Furlong." I spelled it. "Senior citizen, recently retired postmaster. Oakland County maybe, only he isn't listed there."

"Civil servants are public record. Look it up."

"That takes days. My client's in a hurry. The way I see it, your Fed friends outrank mine. They'll know where his Social Security checks are being sent."

"One of the reasons they're my friends is I try not to take advantage of them."

"I see Mumford's number one in its conference," I said.

A drawer banged shut on his end. I thought at first he'd shot himself.

"That gauge is getting low, Walker. You can't run on it forever."

"If the service answers, leave the information with them."
I pegged the receiver politely.

Three and a half hours till Nate Millender. I went back to
the office to clear up old business. The bulb in the reading
lamp in the waiting room had been burned out for a week.

I didn't get to it then. Stuart Lund was sitting on the upholstered bench with his sore foot propped up on the coffee table.

He had on the same gray custom suit or one just like it, cut
skimpy in the shoulders British fashion, with three buttons
and a shallow gorge. He took up all of the bench and most
of the room. When I came in he pointed his cane at the
Casablanca poster in its frame on the wall opposite. "That
looks like an original."

I nodded. "Office-warming present from my wife."

"I wasn't aware you were married."

"Neither was she."

"It would pay your rent for a year if you're ever strapped.
I've represented Mr. Furlong in many negotiations with interior decorators. I've learned things."

"Care to come in?" I shook loose the key to the private bin.

"Thank you, no. I'm just now comfortable. Is this a historic building, by any chance?"

"Just the plumbing. It came over on the *Santa Maria*."

"I thought perhaps there was an ordinance prohibiting the
owner from installing an elevator."

"If you'd called I could have met you at the hotel."

"I needed to get out. I've been cooped up in that suite for
days. I must say this city presents a better appearance than
I'd been led to expect. There seems to be a bit of refurbish-
ing going on."

"The new administration is starting from scratch. The old
one didn't leave much to loot."

"Just like London after the Blitz." He spun the heavy crook of his cane. "Jay had a bad episode last night after I called you. The doctor who came to examine him recognized him, but agreed to keep his presence here a secret provided I hospitalize him as soon as possible."

"How is he now?"

"Better. However, each time he has one of these spells it leaves him—lessened. I think you should accelerate your schedule."

I unlocked and opened the inner door, flipped the keys at my desk, and leaned against the frame facing him. "I'll do what I can. As it is the timetable on this one is burning up all my best contacts."

"You'll be recompensed for the added inconvenience."

"I never change my rates except when I remit them entirely."

He showed his good teeth. "Sherlock Holmes. Surely you didn't expect a born Brit to miss the quotation."

"I'm still hoping to learn from him. I've been busy since we spoke."

"That was my next question."

I gave him what I had, up to my interview with Lily Talbot. I was saving that.

He worried his moustache with a thumbnail. "Who is this Grayling person?"

"Local political fixer, with maybe a little English on it, if you'll pardon the pun. I haven't confirmed that part, but as a general rule you assume the worst. If he's connected with Nate Millender and Millender turns out to be the one who faked the photograph, we're into extra innings. What's Mr. Furlong's interest in politics?"

"He hasn't voted since Roosevelt. He's fond of saying that his rights as an American have cost too many good lives to waste on anyone fool enough to run for public office."

"Yeah, I can't ever find a parking space near the polls either." I fingered out my soggy pack. "I'll let you know if I get anything out of Millender. Right now Lynn Arsenault looks like our best candidate."

"That emergency call he went out on may have been legitimate."

"It may have. I look for shadows."

"I beg your pardon?"

"Just something someone told me today. Also I want to ask him why he dropped ten thousand dollars at Lily Talbot's art gallery last year." I struck a match and watched him over the flame. He'd been scowling at his cane. Now he turned the scowl on me.

"I was there an hour ago." I got the damp tobacco going and shook out the match. Then I gave him the rest of it.

"I specifically instructed you to tell no one that Jay is in Detroit."

"Technically he's not. But a loophole in geography isn't big enough to stick my neck through. It was a judgment call."

"Is *that* what it was."

"I didn't know Mr. Furlong when he had his health. Back then I might have bought into his impassive act. It's got cracks in it now. As much as he wants to know who framed Lily, he wants to square things with her more. The only way to do that is face to face." I blew smoke and fanned it away from him. "If it means anything, I don't think she'll tell anyone. If it doesn't, I'll return the retainer, minus a thousand and change for two days' work and expenses. You'll get a written report so the next op you hire can hit the ground running."

"Do you think she'll see Jay?"

"I'm already in trouble with you for thinking."

He drummed his fingers on that silver crook. He got more mileage out of a cane than anyone since Chaplin. Finally he gripped it, lowered his foot to the floor, and levered himself upright. A spasm of pain swept across his broad soft face like a sheet of hail. It passed quickly and he adjusted his cuffs. The links were gold, with crests inlaid in enamel.

"I can't say I approve of the way you've handled Jay's trust. However, if I were familiar with the correct procedure I wouldn't have needed your services. We'll keep things as they are for now. In future I insist you consult with me before you change the game plan."

"Sometimes things break too fast for that. But I'll keep you posted."

"I can see you're a man who's accustomed to behaving as he pleases."

"Almost never that. But I'm out there, and you're not."

"Well, that's the idea, isn't it."

It was a classy retreat, like at Dunkirk. You had to hand it to them. They'd lost an empire and kept the crease in their pants.

"What do you make of this business with Arsenault?" he asked.

I leaned down and put out the cigarette in the big glass tray on the coffee table. The base was spotless. I was seldom so busy anyone was kept waiting long enough to smoke one down to the butt.

"Lily Talbot thinks it was coincidence," I said, "or she says she does. I don't buy it. However he got to where he is, Arsenault hasn't stayed there by throwing away money. There's a chance he felt guilty about his role in what happened to her and wanted to make amends. He may still feel that way. I hope so. Psychologists say guilt is a useless emotion. They're wrong."

"What do you intend to do?"

"You'll know when I've done it."

"You are insufferable."

"Well, that's the idea, isn't it."

It didn't sound as good coming from me.

His waxy eyes took an impression of mine, then looked away. "Call any hour with news. I don't expect to leave the suite again until it's time to go back to California." He didn't add that he'd be making the trip alone.

I went over and opened the hall door and held it while he limped through. "You should have asked the doctor to give you something for your foot."

"I have medication. Sometimes it's more effective than other times. In any case I hardly need a second opinion to convince me I'm fat." He paused on the threshold. "Oh, two more heirs have arrived. They're on your list: the grand-daughter and her husband, parents of Jay's great-grandchild, Jason. They're staying at the Westin."

"I'll talk to them."

"Nothing there, I suspect. The girl's a child of the sixties and distrusts all things worldly. The trip would be the hus-band's idea. He's a twit."

"That's like a jerk, right?"

The moustache twitched. "I despair of ever mastering the idiom."

When he left I changed the bulb in the lamp and switched on the fan in the office. The pigeon feather was waiting. It fluttered up from the floor, hovered for a moment, consider-ing its options, then drifted down and lighted on the handle of the file drawer I'd been meaning for months to reorga-nize. I plucked off the feather, flicked it out the window, and went to a movie. When you start taking orders from pillow stuffing you might as well be in politics.

Eleven

IT WAS A WEEKNIGHT and a long way from dark, but the cruisers on Jefferson were already clearing their pipes. That stretch of pavement along the river is laid out like a dragstrip. A thing like that can't be expected to pass unnoticed in the town that put America on ethyl. A Jeep C-J towed by a swollen exposed engine chromed to within an inch of its life shrilled past me, throttled down as it drew alongside a black Pontiac crouched on pneumatic risers, and gunned its carburetor. The Pontiac roared in response; the challenge was accepted. Both vehicles lunged forward, flaying rubber from four wheels and etching glistening streaks behind them like goosed snails.

Youth. Someday they'll find a cure.

Farther up, where the river slows and broadens and the avenue changes its name to Lake Shore Drive, things were more peaceful. The Grosse Pointe Police Department is small, but better equipped than some armies in South America.

All the parking spaces at the marina were taken. I blocked a Dodge Ram pickup that looked as if it might be there a while and walked along the dock counting numbers. The waves licked at the pilings in long satiny sheets with sunlight sparking at the edges. Sails flocked the surface like bright birds, a speedboat blatted by, towing a skier in an orange life jacket and a white bikini with a yard of yellow hair fluttering behind. The wind slung an arc of fine sun-smelling spray into my face like a lawn sprinkler. It was a different universe here where grownups played, but not necessarily more peaceful. Michigan has more registered boats than any other state in the union, including Hawaii and California; which makes sense, because it has the longest coastline. The problem, in the Detroit area, is that most of them seem to be berthed on Lake St. Clair.

On nice weekends the scramble for the open water resembles the Jefferson Avenue dragway, with one added attraction, for those who love adventure: At least a third of the people at the tiller don't know one end of their craft from the other or who has the right of way. No minimum age is required to steer a boat through waters crowded with swimmers, skiers, and other vessels. No law demands sobriety on the part of the pilots. The Spanish Armada stood a better chance against the gale.

The berth I was after belonged to a twenty-three-foot sloop, blue as the water, with a teak half-deck up front—I wasn't sure if they called it a forecastle—and brass fittings that snapped back the light. *Mathew Brady* was the name scripted along the bow.

"Walker?"

I looked at the lean length of caramel-colored skin and runner's muscles grinning up at me from the stern.

"Ahoy the boat," I said.

"Call me Nate." He laid aside the line he was coiling and got social. His grip was corded with iron, no surprise; photography is hard physical labor. "Sorry about the change of venue. This is the first chance I've had to get out on the water since Memorial Day."

Millender had on white shorts, a long-peaked fisherman's cap, and nothing else. His teeth were blue-white in a face burned as dark as Eulisy Worth's, only his close-cropped towhead said he hadn't been born with that pigment. He was middle thirties but could pass for twenty.

"You've got a pretty day for it."

"It's a short season, but it's the best in the country. You don't have a hernia or anything like that, do you?"

"Not that I've noticed."

"Good. Pass me that cooler."

It was a blue-and-white plastic Coleman on the dock, big enough to pack a terrier. I hoisted it over the railing and he took it in both hands and lowered it to the deck. It was vein-popping heavy.

"Where are you headed, New Zealand?"

"We're overnighting on Belle Isle. Twelve beers apiece should get us to sunup."

"Who's drinking the other twelve?"

"You know Royce?"

I followed the incline of his head. The man approaching from the other end of the dock was a well-built forty, just under six feet and a hundred and eighty in baggy white ducks, canvas shoes, and a red Windbreaker. The white sun visor he wore shadowed his face. He was carrying a pair of float cushions wedged under his left arm and a picnic hamper in that hand. It was an awkward way to lug those items unless you wanted to keep one hand free.

Much of his weight was in his chest and shoulders, and as he came near I saw that we were fellow campaigners in the war against five o'clock shadow. He hesitated a half-step when he saw me standing by the sloop, but regained momentum smoothly. I might have missed it if I hadn't been briefed on his case and didn't know a thing or two about the species. That studied casual gait is a hallmark of some housecats, and they're the most efficient killers in civilization.

Oh, we were going to get along.

"I bought a roast chicken. I hate sandwiches." He was looking at me.

"Great, we can use it to wash down the beer." Millender reached up and took the hamper. "Royce Grayling, meet Amos Walker."

Grayling nodded, smiling, but his right hand remained at his side. His face was broad with no fat in it and he had a thick brown moustache above a mouth as wide as Jean Sternhagen's but without the humor, although the lips were pulled back to show a full set of good teeth. His eyes were pale. He looked like the young Ernest Hemingway except for those eyes. There was no daylight in them.

"I think we were in the same room once," he said. "A Democratic fundraiser four years ago at the Masonic Temple. I was with the old mayor. You were bodyguarding a city councilman's wife."

"I was guarding her diamonds for the insurance company. Her body just went where the diamonds went. I don't remember meeting you."

"We didn't."

I showed my teeth. "You must be one of those people who never forget a face."

"That's one claim I never made. How would I know if I forgot one? I asked about you."

"I didn't know I looked that interesting."

"You didn't. That's why I asked. It was the first time I'd heard your name."

"But not the last."

"The town isn't that big." He tossed the cushions onto the half-deck and tugged down the elastic hem of his Windbreaker, but not before a tube of shiny brown leather poked out the bottom along his right hipbone, right where I wore mine. I didn't need to see that to know I hadn't wasted the hundred and fifty I'd paid Worth for the dope on Royce Grayling.

Millender got a hand up from his friend—the left one, of course—and bounded onto the dock. In his bare feet he came just above my shoulders. In addition to being strong, photographers are often small. It has something to do with crawling into tight spaces to take pictures of wolf cubs and not banging into black lights in darkrooms.

"What's the job?" he asked me.

I waited while a quartet of chattering femininity in halter tops and briefs passed by on the arms of a couple of lifters in Speedos. Millender's eyes followed appreciatively. Grayling's remained on me.

"Randy Quarrels says you can put Abe Lincoln's head on Marilyn Monroe's body and fool Joe DiMaggio," I said.

"That's the job?"

"That's the basic idea."

"You're an insurance cop?"

"Private."

"Ah. Who's this DiMaggio, a client?"

I looked at Grayling. He rolled his big shoulders. "Notch baby."

I said, "He's the reclusive type. He's willing to pay enough to stay that way."

"I get it. As for instance?"

"I don't guess you have a rate card for this kind of job."

"He's a good guesser," he told Grayling. "What are we talking about, prints or slides or video? Video's big right now, but it costs to edit."

"I'm not interested in video."

"I can cut you a bargain, then. A few years ago, no. The computer's eliminated most of the overhead. All I need is material to work with. I can provide that, too, of course, but—"

"It'll cost. I know. Can you do this?" I showed him the picture of Arsenault and Lily Talbot.

A tanned face got stiff. "Who the hell are you?"

"We established that. How about it?"

"I didn't do that."

"That isn't what I asked."

"I'm not your boy. Try the boys on Michigan Avenue. You'll know them by their big hats and pink suits." He stepped down into the boat. "Let's cast off, Royce. The wind gets cute when the sun goes down."

"Sorry you came all this way," Grayling said.

We stood there a minute guessing each other's weight; the only two characters on the lake wearing jackets because nobody else was wearing a holster.

I said, "The client pays for the gas."

"Well-heeled, is he?"

"Stinking."

"That's the kind to have. I never did understand the pro bono boys. You're worth just what they pay you."

"Sometimes not as much."

He smiled again. His facial expressions were purely hydraulic.

"Do you have a card? Nate might change his mind."

"In a pig's ass. Shake a leg, Royce."

Grayling didn't move. I fished out a card with my left hand and gave it to him. He took it with his left, glanced at it, put it in a pocket, and zipped it up.

"Well, you got out of the heat for a little while."

"I don't mind it so much."

The smile stayed in place. "You know, neither do I."

He busied himself with the lines then and I wasn't there anymore.

The light was changing on my way back down Jefferson, angling just off the horizontal between the buildings downtown. The newer ones sparkled. The older ones, built mostly between the century's turn and Black Friday, gleamed with an old gold light like pre-Prohibition whiskey. These were the neo-classical, Neo-Gothic, Neo-Renaissance Albert Kahn designs that Jay Bell Furlong and his set had ridiculed, then found affection for when they saw what the generation that came after them put up next door. When the last of them fell, imploded in a pile of Italian marble and splinters of mahogany, they would leave holes in the sky like missing constellations.

I stopped for a drink at a hole I knew on Lafayette between the *News* and *Free Press* buildings—both of them Kahn's—looking for faces I recognized and working on not thinking. No help there. The late harvest of communications-school graduates didn't drink, and the crop I'd grown up with were either retired or huddled inside the metal detectors at the Detroit Press Club.

I bombed out on the no-thinking part too. I was beginning to like Nate Millender almost as much as I liked Lynn Arsenault. And I wondered how long it had been since *liked* referred to somebody I wasn't planning to bring down.

When I left the bar, dusk was boating in, towing behind it that brimstone smell of carbon settling and concrete cooling. In a little while the streetlights would blink on and then the headlamps, a set at a time like bats awakening, and the city would turn itself darkside out like a reversible jacket, shaking out the creatures that breathed and bred in its folds. Figuring in a brief stop at my house, by the time I got to Allen Park it would be dark enough for what this one had in mind.

Twelve

NIGHT WORK in the detective business carries its own set of rules.

The first covers wardrobe.

The idea is not to look like one of the Beagle Boys. You can take your inspiration from the movies, put on the black watch cap, matching turtleneck, and skintight trousers, and pose for the cover of *Sneak Thief Quarterly,* but if you do it out in the real world you're going to be arrested as a suspicious person. Especially when everyone else in your zip code is wearing a sport shirt and cotton twill.

I chose a blue short-sleeved sweatshirt, a dark gray nylon jacket to cover my arms, and a new pair of blue jeans, prewashed so I could walk without making as much noise as a sheet of tin. I don't own a ski mask and wasn't about to go shopping for one in June. Leave the burnt cork on the face to Cary Grant. If you're not alert enough to turn your back when headlamps rake around the corner you've got no business breaking the law in the first place. Not to mention the inconvenience of coming up with a good story if the police stop you, minstrel shows being rare these days.

Finally I laced on black high-tops with thick waffled

soles, threw a pair of stiff rubber gloves and bolt-cutters with insulated handles into the trunk, and was off to risk my license for about the thousandth time since Easter. I had a good night for it. The sky was heavily overcast and I couldn't see my feet. I was in great shape as long as I didn't trip over any other burglars.

The street rod next door was parked in the driveway, protected only by a canvas car cover. I hesitated as I pulled out of the garage—it seemed a shame, dressed as I was, not to creep over and cut the starter cable, assuring myself a full night's sleep—but I had a living to earn and put my foot on the gas.

When I got to Imminent Visions I didn't slow down. Much of the metropolitan drug trade takes place in office parking lots after hours, and the places attract police stakeouts. I circled the block for a better look. Lights were on in some of the offices, but there are always some, and in the entrance to the underground garage reserved for employees, the greenish glow of the security lights inside made a pool on the pavement, but the attendant's booth was empty. No marked units were crouched in the likely places. No vehicles, marked or otherwise, were parked in any of the neighboring driveways facing out. It was coming up on nine o'clock by the dial on my dashboard; lunch hour for most cops on the four to midnight.

In and out fast, fingers crossed.

I found a legal space on the street, in the dark middle ground between the lamps on the corners and across from an eight-foot board fence where construction was going on, but not at that hour. The snick when I opened my door sounded like a rifle shot in the still air. I got out and leaned on it until it shut. I kept listening, I wasn't sure for what. The score from *The Pink Panther*, maybe.

After that I moved quickly. I popped up the trunk, pulled on the gloves and a pair of rubbers I kept there in case of sudden weather—the power level would be much lower than Detroit Edison's, but taking chances is for bungie-jumpers and matadors—and reached for the bolt-cutters just as a car turned into the street. I pivoted away from its lamps, blocking the Cutlass's license plate with my body while I pretended to struggle with the spare tire. The car ticked on past without slowing.

I stepped up the pace another notch. The prospect of a cel-lular 911 call knocked ten minutes off my schedule. I took out the cutters, lowered the trunk lid without closing it, and loped toward the visitors' parking lot. There didn't seem to be much use in walking at an unsuspicious pace while in possession of a tool that could get me ninety days at County.

Allen Park is quiet after dark by city standards. Crickets sang, the measured surf of canned laughter coming from someone's television set reached me, perhaps from as far away as Canada across the river. Detroit throbbed in the dis-tance, never entirely silent as long as trucks prowled the in-terstates at night to avoid scales and factories ran around the clock. A fire siren climbed and fell, an ambulance whooped on the downstroke. Someone else's tragedy, as remote as an earthquake in Peru. Call it the night of a thousand apathies.

I'd brought along a pencil flashlight. It stayed in my pocket. There was enough illumination from the security lights to guide me to the area where I'd parked that morn-ing. The telephone crew had erected a nylon tent to protect its excavation from weather and left up its barricades to pro-tect itself from a lawsuit when someone fell in. I stepped be-tween them, found the flap, and ducked inside, letting it fall shut behind me. Now I could use my light.

I found the cable quickly. It was bright orange, and the

crew had inserted a couple of wooden dowels underneath it to lift it free of the earth. I stepped down into the hole, put the penlight between my teeth, and groped for the conduit. The hard rubber gave a little when I squeezed.

That was a break. I was afraid it would turn out to be cased in steel, and I hadn't bothered to bring a hacksaw because the time it would have taken me to saw through it fell outside the margin of safety I had arranged for myself. I had both hands on the bolt-cutters when another pair of headlamps swept across the tent.

I froze.

I was afraid to dive for cover in case the movement was silhouetted against the nylon. The lights stayed on me for a long second. I could feel their heat. My own shadow loomed in front of me like my own guilty conscience. Then it moved. The lights slid the length of the tent and beyond. I heard tires swishing on asphalt, the sound of an engine slowing, idling, and then picking up speed, fading away as it moved off down the street. A driver had chosen the entrance of the lot to turn around in.

No more hesitation now. Whoever it was might have seen something and gone off to report.

The thick conduit was a healthy bite for the cables. I spread the handles all the way, worked the parrot's-beak blades back and forth against the rubber until they bit, planted my feet solidly in the soft earth, and brought the handles together in one clean scissoring jerk.

Conduit and cable parted with a dry cough, blue and white sparks splashed. I stamped out the ones that were still glowing on the ground. I was a vandal, not an arsonist.

Thirteen

LIKE MUMMIFICATION, frigate design, and the lost-wax process, the art of the extortion letter is now a thing of the past.

The computer, as it has done with so many other areas of endeavor, has made the business of shaking down a victim much less messy, while robbing it of most of its charm. No longer must the novice blackmailer waste time combing through an entire newspaper hunting for all the words and letters he needs, encumbered by latex gloves so he can keep his fingerprints at home where they belong. He need merely print out his demands on an accommodating screen and dispatch them through the ether, anonymously and without fear of being traced. No paste, no scissors. No riddled pages of newsprint or scraps of cut-up paper to gather up and throw away where the trash man might find them and report them to the police. No worrying about loose hairs, scales, and other specimens of DNA adhering to the stationery.

On the other hand, there is no romance, either. No jaunty uneven lines or Peter Max-like jumbled fonts or exotic, piratical clashes of characters in Baskerville black and Barnum & Bailey yellow, cavalierly disregarding all the rules of upper and lower case laid down by Strunk and White. Cyberspace has managed to make one of our most popular tools of felony look like a recall letter from General Motors.

I'm a traditionalist. Also I don't own a computer, and even if I had access to one that night and knew how to use it, I had no way of sending my communication to Lynn Arsenault's place of work short of the post office, because some destructive creature of the night had put its telephone lines out of commission. So I did it the old-fashioned way. The result wasn't all that impressive for the above-mentioned effort, but I was proud of the clarity and economy:

$ ten 000 wait 4 mY CALL

I clipped the pasted-over sheet of blank notepaper to the phony photo of Arsenault with Lily Talbot, tipped them into a new envelope fresh from the box, and threw in Nate Millender's Yellow Pages ad, cut from under PHOTOGRAPHERS—FREE-LANCE. I sealed the flap with a sponge dipped in tap water and block-printed LYNN ARSENAULT—PERSONAL & CONFIDENTIAL on the outside with a No. 2 pencil. I'd considered spelling it CONFIDENSHUL, but cuteness can get you nailed.

I scooped the litter into the kitchen wastebasket, dumped a can of tuna between two slices of bread, and washed it down with milk for dinner. Quite a day. I'd pried into people's private affairs, violated a client's confidence, destroyed public property, and framed an extortion. Now I went to bed and slept the sleep of the innocent. I dreamed of waylaying travelers in Sherwood Forest with cobbled-up stickup notes and donating the proceeds to the Errol Flynn Memorial Home for Rakes, Rogues, Rooks, and Rascals for Rent.

After an hour I sat up, wide awake, with a sentence on my lips: " 'Personal and confidential' means 'open now' to a secretary."

I pulled the drawer out of the nightstand and tore loose the little blue-bound notebook I kept taped there. It was an abridged and coded version of the larger one I had locked in the safe at the office. I found the number I wanted there and padded into the living room to dial it.

"Goddamn it, hello."

A young masculine voice I knew, clouded with sleep and maybe something else that was more the business of the DEA than it was mine.

"Bob, this is Walker. Did I get you up?"

"I'm up all the time, friend. Least, I ain't had no complaints. Hee-hee." His fog was lifting. "This where I'm supposed to tell you what time it is?"

"Don't need it. Do you still have that messenger's uniform from your last job?"

"I never had no messenger's job."

"I'm thinking brass buttons and a pillbox hat."

"Oh, *that* uniform. I took it when they canned me for smoking in a supply closet. I was a hop at the Dearborn Hyatt."

"What were you smoking?"

"Tobacco, can you dig it? Every time I bring one of my vices down to the next level, the system lowers its level of tolerance to include me out."

"A uniform's a uniform. Lose the hat."

"What's the job?"

"I need a message delivered."

"Buy a stamp."

"I need it to get there."

"Call FedEx."

"FedEx collects autographs. I need this one delivered to the person whose name is on the envelope, no one else, by someone who doesn't keep records."

"Now?"

"Tomorrow morning at eight. Well, *this* morning. You might have to hang around. He's a cheese, comes in when he feels like it."

"Holy shit, I better get started. I only got seven and a half hours."

"I just wanted to be sure you were available."

"Now you sound like my parole cop. Where we meet, your office?"

"Are you kidding? I don't start work that early."

"Hey, fuck you. Your crib it is. You fix me them eggs with peppers and onions and shit?"

"Do I hear the munchies talking?"

"Fuck you again. I been pissing nothing but clean mountain water for six weeks now."

"One Pancho Villa's Revenge coming up."

"*Up* ain't the direction it generally comes. Be there at seven."

I flipped the receiver at the cradle and went back to bed with my mind clear.

Robert "Hurricane Bob" Lester had played two straight years of a three-night gig at the Chord Progression on Livernois under the billing "The Best Jazz Guitar West of East." When a promoter scouting for a New York record label signed him to back up Art Pepper on ten sides, with the promise of six of his own afterward, Bob went on a bat to celebrate. He dropped acid on top of three lines of cocaine and an indeterminate number of Scotch highballs, became convinced that his right hand had detached itself and was trying to strangle him, and hacked off all his fingers with a hunting knife he carried for protection. Neurosurgeons at Detroit Receiving Hospital managed to sew all but two of them back on, then had to remove everything but the thumb when he developed circulation problems.

All this happened before I met him. His bass player, a friend since childhood who had been left out when Bob signed the record deal, hired me to trace him after he disappeared from the recovery room. I found him in a motel room on Telegraph, working up enough bile to put a slug in his head from a Korean pistol he'd bought from a guy named Slash. After I wrestled it away from him I called in a couple of favors to grease his way past the waiting list at a drug rehab center downtown. The bass player and I were standing out front when he came out, thirty pounds lighter and white-haired at twenty-eight. He hadn't kept a job since, but on the other hand he hadn't shot himself either. I found work for him when I could.

I was up and dressed a few minutes before seven, dusting bits of onion, green pepper, and extra sharp cheddar off my palms into a skillet paved with crackling eggs, when he came to the front door. He was taller than he looked, and much younger. He'd put back on all the weight he'd lost, although he wasn't fat, just beefy, and his white hair was receding straight up the middle. His skin was golden brown and sharply wrinkled, as if it had been tobacco-cured. In his wine-red tunic and matching trousers with a gold stripe up the side he looked like an old man stuck in a menial job.

Perfect.

When I let him in he pointed his nose at the ceiling and inhaled deeply.

"Smell them eggs. Do they make your eyes run?"

"There's no paint left on the ceiling above the stove. You be the judge."

In the kitchen he sat down at the table I'd set and made quick work of six eggs and two cups of coffee. The special mitten he wore on his right hand had a clamp built in that let him grip his fork.

I leaned back on the counter, nursing my first cup. "You working?"

"Got me a part-time. Flag man for the county road." He swept up the last of the omelet with a piece of toast and popped it into his mouth. "We're replacing an overpass railing on the North Lodge. Truck went through it last week."

"I read about that."

"Got to get the cage back up before the local pukes start pitching concrete down on the underpass." He filled a glass from the pitcher of orange juice and drank. "No pulp?"

"When I want to eat an orange I peel one for myself. How's the money?"

"I ain't pricing no Ferraris."

"You said last night you were staying clean. That on the level?"

"I still got the rest of my fingers." He finished his coffee and pushed away his plate. "Good eggs. Next time more onion."

"I was down to half a bag. How well do you know Allen Park?"

"I played a bar there one whole summer."

"The place is on Euclid. Imminent Visions."

"Sounds like a hop joint."

"It's a firm of architects."

"Same thing."

I handed him the envelope and a fifty-dollar bill. "Deliver the envelope. Keep the cash."

He fingered the bill with his good hand. "You can get the job done cheaper."

"If you don't want the work, say so."

"Man, there ain't no word in Ebonics for that." He pocketed the bill. "Thanks, Amos."

I told him to sit still and went for my lightest-weight sportcoat, an unstructured one of raw silk. When I came back I asked him what he was driving.

"Same piece-of-shit Dodge I had two years ago."

"Give me a head start. I want to be there when you go in. Don't forget to lock up when you leave the house."

"Ain't you afraid I'll swipe your TV set and sell it for dope?"

"It wouldn't bring you enough to fill one nostril." I went out.

I smelled a break in the weather. The overcast was stained blue-black and a wind from the east was rattling the burnt-out leaves on the trees along Joseph Campau. When the rains come in summer they come fists first.

Six blocks from my destination I passed an Ameritech truck parked on a corner and two workers in hardhats scowling over a chart they had spread out on the hood. I hoped that meant they were still looking for the trouble along the line.

At Imminent Visions a green Ford Bronco occupied my old space in the visitors' lot, but from where I pulled in two slots down I had a clear view of the tent. Nothing was going on there. I slumped down in the seat for comfort and turned on the radio. The weatherman wasn't reporting rain.

Hurricane Bob Lester's old blue Dart swung into the lot ten minutes later. He double-parked behind the Bronco and went inside, carrying the envelope. He never looked in my direction.

I gave him five minutes to bluff his way past the guard in the lobby. That may have been generous; when he was straight he had a line of patter that was as good as any of his old guitar licks. Ten more to get upstairs and scam the receptionist, and another ten just for fun, unless Arsenault was late. It was Friday and I hoped he was the kind of executive who came in early to clear his desk for the weekend. Much more than that and I'd know Bob was in trouble.

At the end of twenty minutes the Ameritech truck, or its identical twin, rolled right up to the tent and two men got out to inspect the excavation. They were the same pair I'd seen on the corner.

I hate modern technology more than carrots. If they finished splicing the cut cable too soon, I'd risked a vandalism bust for nothing.

Five more minutes crawled past. I had decided to go with Plan B, which was to wish there were a Plan C, when Hurricane Bob came out without the envelope. He walked straight to his car, backed around, and joined the traffic on Euclid, again without tipping me the nod. He left a piece of his tailpipe behind in the driveway.

The rest was waiting.

The whole idea behind planting a burr under a mule's tail is to see where he runs. You can't follow a telephone call even in a souped-up 1970 Cutlass.

I was counting on Lynn Arsenault's reacting to the extortion demand with the same panic that forced him to flee when I'd made an appointment to ask him about the photograph. The theory was that when he tried to call for help and found the telephones dead he wouldn't reach for a cellular and trust the call to the public airwaves. I wanted him to break cover and run to the witchfinder with his fears.

Everyone in this line has something he's best at. Some can stake out Rushmore until Lincoln sneezes. Others can shadow a man on foot for sixty deserted blocks unnoticed, or plant an electronic bug in a woman's wig without her knowing it. With me it's the vehicular tail. The man who taught me the basics said I could follow a Thunderbird from New York to California in a Moscow city bus without detection.

Okay, so it isn't the polio vaccine.

I waited. The clouds took on a purple cast, then black, and still the radio was predicting more of yesterday. Three visitors left the lot, two more pulled in and walked into the building. A secretary or something in a white silk blouse, gray split skirt, and red high heels came out and talked with the telephone workers, who tipped back their hardhats and explained to her the principles of electronics. She nodded understanding, tossed her tawny hair, and clittered back inside. The clouds turned the color of fresh tar. Thunder grumbled. No cars had entered or left the underground garage in half an hour.

The workers struck the tent, rolled and folded it and put it in the back of the truck, and began putting away their tools. I got out of the car and walked down the ramp to the garage entrance.

The attendant in the booth was asleep on his elbow with his mouth open and a thread of spittle glittering off the end of his chin. His visored cap was cocked to one side, showing two inches of shiny pink scalp above a fringe of white hair. He had a flesh-colored lump of hearing aid in one big ear and bifocals with lenses as thick as hockey pucks. I didn't tiptoe on my way past.

The air was fetid, sour with mildew and the dank stench of stale urine and new rubber and old exhaust and concrete that had never quite dried. The atmosphere was oppressive. I walked down the aisle with my mouth open, not so much to avoid the smell as to equalize the pressure inside my head. It was more than just the heat and the stagnant air inside and the storm building outside. I had felt it before, and every time I had come upon something unpleasant.

I found the emerald-green Porsche parked next to the elevator in a space with Arsenault's name embossed on a red metal plaque on the wall in front of it. The vanity plate above the rear bumper read PRED-8-OR.

Somebody had gotten a boot out of that.

The window on the driver's side was starred from a neat round hole in the center. I closed my mouth, shook out my handkerchief, and tried the door handle. It tipped up without resistance and the door came open.

The man behind the wheel didn't fall out right away. He hovered, his head tipped back against the rest, then slid sideways. He turned at the waist in a slow ballet. His shoulder touched the concrete floor first and then his head fell to the side and back, spotting the grainy surface from the hole in his left temple. His feet never left the floorboards.

Fourteen

I LOOKED DOWN AT HIM for a while without moving; trying to siphon off some of the wisdom from those half-open eyes. Now I noticed the one smell that didn't belong in a garage, a mixture of sulphur and saltpeter that stung my nostrils like nettles. It would have hung on longer than usual in the motionless air, but in another few minutes it would be gone entirely.

The expression on Arsenault's face was serene. It belonged in a Renaissance painting. It was the same one he had turned to the camera eight years ago; fleshier now and pinched at the corners of the mouth, but still youthful. Nothing removes stress from one's life like leaving it.

I sat on my heels and touched his skin. It felt warm, but the close air would have preserved his body temperature longer. I wiped off my DNA, then used the handkerchief to mop my palms. Despite that they were as cold as the concrete.

I stood and looked around. From where the shooter had stood I could see the attendant asleep in his booth. Nothing in that. His back was turned, and a small-caliber report in those surroundings would have sounded like someone dropping a pen on the floor. It wouldn't have awakened a man with a hearing disability. It wouldn't even have carried ten yards beyond the entrance, where I had sat in my car listening to the weather report on the radio. The telephone men wouldn't have paid it any attention. Or it might have happened before we got there.

I had a thought.

I was either getting old or the muggy conditions were rusting my reflexes.

Just to prove that wasn't it, I sprang the Detective Special from its clip in a fast-draw. There was no one in view to impress, but the porous rubber grip absorbed perspiration from my hand and the weight of the frame steadied my arm.

There were a dozen more vehicles parked on that level. I inspected them all, jerking open doors that weren't locked and thrusting the gun inside. Nobody was hiding in any of them. I crept up to the fire door by the elevator on the balls of my feet, swung it open by the handle and pivoted, drawing down on a flight of empty steel steps. The heavy door made a lonely sound drifting shut.

Putting away the revolver I went back to the body and frisked it. His suit, gray gabardine with an eggshell silk lining, was made in London. He had an antique Curvex wristwatch worth a couple of thousand on a gold link band and a calfskin wallet full of gold and platinum cards with no compartment for cash. Rich people are always broke. He had an ivory comb, a roll of breath mints, and an unopened package of condoms with a conquistador on the box.

I found one more thing in his breast pocket, an envelope containing a zany-looking paste-up note, a convincing composite photograph, and a clipping from the Yellow Pages. That fixed time of death: somewhere between the morning forecast on WJR and a Ford commercial, with a trained detective sitting fifty feet away. I put the last discovery in my own pocket.

Lynn Arsenault. A sexually responsible young man, with nice hair and sweet-smelling breath. He'd spoken twenty words to me over the telephone.

The geezer in the booth was still sawing logs by the board foot. I could have driven a herd of longhorns past him and never been part of his life. I almost did—go past him, that is, without the beef—but then I remembered the Ameritech workers. They were gone now, but they'd logged in, and they were drilled by the company's PR consultants to keep their eyes and ears open for suspicious activity. If you consider a stranger sitting alone in a car without air conditioning on the hottest day of the year suspicious.

I sighed and rejoined the system.

I separated my ID folder from the honorary Wayne County sheriff's star I used to serve papers and tapped the metal against the glass of the booth.

The snoring changed pitch. The attendant stirred and transferred the weight of his head from his right hand to his left. Then he fell into the old cadence.

I tapped again. He swiped at his face as if a fly were tickling the hairs curling out of his eyebrows. His eyes stayed closed.

I went on tapping until they opened. I watched the pupils contract. His bottom lids were red-rimmed and loose and I could see a sty on one of them the size of a BB.

"What the hell." His voice grated like a rusty flywheel. I could tell right through the glass he needed one of Arsenault's breath mints.

"Rise and shine. It's not Woody Woodpecker." I showed him the buzzer.

His lips moved over the embossed lettering on the

enamel. The corners of his mouth were stained white with Maalox.

I put away the badge. "I'm looking for a car involved in a hit-and-run last Saturday on Seven Mile. Green Porsche, vanity plate Peter Robert Edward David Numeral Eight Oscar Robert. The computer in Lansing kicked out a registration in the name of Lynn Arsenault who works at this address. You got a car here answers that description?"

He worked his lips again, reading the letters I'd given him. Recognition broke the surface like a whale breaching. Then he shoved it back under.

"I don't see no warrant. What kind of a hit-and-run?"

I broke eye contact. Two small color portrait shots of dark-haired boys in Sunday shirts were taped to the glass on the other side of the booth. They were about eight and ten and looked like brothers, if they weren't pictures of the same boy taken two years apart.

"Nine-year-old boy got run over on his bike," I said. "He's critical."

"Oh, shit." He reached for a gold chain inside the collar of his uniform shirt. I like Roman Catholics. Confession comes second-nature to them.

"That's pretty much what his parents said. He's an altar boy at St. Boniface."

"Predator. Pred-eight-or, get it? It's in back by the elevator."

"Show me."

"I ain't supposed to leave the booth."

"Are you supposed to snooze in it?"

"I was resting my eyes."

"On what? Let's go."

He touched the chain again, adjusted his bifocals, and reached for the doorknob.

"Nice-looking grandkids," I said when he came out.

"They're my sons. The oldest starts sixth grade in September."

"What grade is your wife in?"

"That ain't nice." When he stuck out his lower lip he showed a bottom row of nicotine-stained teeth.

"Sorry. I take it back. I take back what I said about your snoozing too. You need all the sleep you can get."

"Her too." He locked up, chuckling, and led the way. He had slits cut in his black Oxfords through which white socks bulged like escaping dough. His wide belt divided his spare tire into duals.

"Get much traffic through here?" I asked.

"Same old. It's restricted to employees. I don't think Mr. Arsenault's your man. He runs the show here, and he's—" He stopped walking. "Mother of God."

I hadn't disturbed Arsenault's position. Corpses are like road maps: You just can't get them back the way they were. The hole in his temple showed and blood had leaked into a round garnet-colored pool on the floor around his head.

"Stay here."

I went over and bent down and made a business of looking for the carotid. His skin seemed to have cooled, but that was just projection; it had only been a few minutes. I straightened.

"Dead. Who's been in here since you came on?"

"Just the regulars."

"Any of them come back out?"

He shook his head. His face was gray. "They never do before lunch."

"They wouldn't get past an alert party like you."

"I got to work the gate," he said. "I wasn't asleep."

"You wouldn't need to work the gate if they came out on foot."

He said nothing. There wasn't anything in it anyway, unless I'd been asleep too. It was just a question someone with the sheriff's department would ask.

"Got a telephone in that booth?"

"I ain't supposed to call out on it."

"You won't have to. Give me the key. Stay here and don't let anyone near the body."

The inside of a cheek got chewed. Then he unclipped the retractable steel case from his belt. "The brass one."

I closed the door and dialed Stuart Lund's suite at the Marriott. After two rings a male switchboard operator came on and told me Mr. Lund had asked not to be disturbed. He asked if he could take a message.

I hung up and dialed 911. The old attendant rapped on the glass.

"Get back to Arsenault," I said through the speaking grid.

"I can hear the elevator and the door to the stairs from here, and there's the entrance. If anybody's going to mess with the body any other way, I ain't equipped to stop 'em. Who you calling?"

"The cops."

"*You're* the cops."

"I mean the locals."

A human voice answered on the eighth ring, some kind of record for the emergency line. I told it what it needed to know and broke the connection. When I came out of the booth the old man's face was a stack of scowls. "I guess I'll have another look at that badge."

I gave him back his keys. "It's a loaner. I'm private."

"What about that hit-and-run? That a loaner too?"

"What say we just tell them what we found and let John Law ask the questions?"

"I ain't holding nothing back."

"I didn't figure you would."

"They might want to know how is it you didn't ask me if that was Mr. Arsenault laying there if you never saw him before."

"Now, why would they ask that?"

"They ain't. I am."

"Well, is it?"

"Too late, Mac." He went inside and banged the door shut. The clear glass separating us might have been lath and plaster for all the attention he paid me after that. He had a lot more bark on him than he looked.

I ignored him back. While I was doing that, he must have broken the rule about not making any calls out, because in ten minutes we were up to our hips in office brass.

There were just two of them, but they made as much noise as a crowd. One was a director of design who looked like an accountant, bald to the ears with a pair of eyeglasses on a chain around his neck and the full spectrum of colored pens in a pocket protector. His companion was a chief accountant who looked like another accountant. They disagreed about which of them had spoken to Arsenault last, they were at odds over whose responsibility it was to speak to the cops, they were not in concurrence that a full-time office security force would have prevented this tragedy from taking place at all. That last appeared to be an old argument.

They both thought the parking attendant, whose name was Gregory, had been hasty about notifying the authorities. Gregory stayed in his booth and didn't say anything until the chief accountant lifted his glasses to peer at me and asked him if I'd been searched for the murder weapon.

"You do it," Gregory said. "I ain't your private police force."

The design director turned his back on all of us. I had the impression he was mad at the chief accountant for getting to be the one who said "murder weapon." Neither of them had paused by the elevator long enough to give the corpse any more than a passing glance.

I winked at Gregory. His face was space for rent.

Fifteen

THE BLONDE who had been talking with the telephone men earlier came clacking out on her high heels, and when she spoke to the two men from the office the question of who called the shots in the boss's absence was answered. The pair withdrew. Tapping her foot waiting for the cops she ignored Gregory, the corpse, and me until I lit a Winston.

"There's no smoking," she said.

I asked if anybody had broken it to the cars.

"The building, the basement, the grounds. It's all a smoke-free environment."

That ended my interest in her.

In the beginning were the uniforms: a sergeant with gray sideburns and sad friendly eyes and a female officer with nothing in her expression but the manual of arms. They went down and looked at the body, but they didn't touch anything. It's really amazing what fear of infection has done to the curiosity of the cop on the beat where two hundred years of department regs failed. They took notes, inspected everybody's ID, asked a few questions, and wrote down the answers in professional shorthand. They spoke politely and if they had opinions they'd left them in their lockers. They could have given a lecture to their brothers and sisters in the big city upriver about where the job started and stopped.

In a little while a gray LeBaron pulled up to the gate and tipped out the plainclothes team. Cops always come in pairs. St. Thomas was black, medium built, and wore glasses in glittering silver frames and a charcoal three-piece suit too heavy for the weather, although he never broke a sweat all the time he was there. His companion, a chalk-faced third-grader named Redburn, had a round fat chin like a baby's and that hungry-eyed look that came from rubbing holes in his gold shield with a cloth soaked in Brasso. He sweated enough for both of them.

Redburn went straight to the body. St. Thomas set up shop near the booth, conferring in turn with the uniforms, the blonde office manager, and then Gregory, the parking attendant. He stood close to each, spoke only in murmurs, and never called over the next candidate before dismissing the last. Then he walked down to the Porsche and stood over its driver, writing in a leather-bound notebook with a Cross pen. I think he used the Palmer Method.

When the police photographer showed up, St. Thomas spent five minutes telling him what he wanted. After the photo session he pulled on a pair of latex gloves and went over the body. His partner recorded the inventory in a dime-store spiral. St. Thomas bagged the items he found in Arsenault's pockets, gave them to Redburn, and crooked a finger at me. I went over.

"Walker, right? What's this about a hit-and-run?"

"Cover story, Lieutenant."

"Sergeant."

"You dress higher. The real story wouldn't have gotten me past the booth."

"Try me."

I left out most of it, and what I gave him wasn't true. It sounded even cheesier than it had in my head. The nut-brown eyes behind the silver frames returned nothing on my investment. When I finished he made no comment, but turned to his partner.

"So our man walked up to the car—there's powder residue on the broken glass, and anyway a twenty-two wouldn't have penetrated beyond a dozen feet—drilled him through the window, and walked away," St. Thomas said. "Who opened the door?"

Redburn pouted at his notes. "The victim, probably. Reflex. Convulsions."

"Maybe. I've had my car two years and I have trouble enough finding the handle in a hurry without a bullet in my head."

"You don't have a Porsche, Sarge."

"Life's a bitch. What made you so interested in Arsenault's car?"

I played with a cigarette. I had a handle on him now. He was one of those come-back-at-you cops.

"I got a glimpse of the car the first time I was here. I wanted a look at the registration. He went from a junior partnership to company prexy in Horatio Alger time, dropped a load at an art gallery in the city on paintings for his office last year. Then there was the car. Either he was the hottest thing in architecture since mortar or he had something on old man Whiting."

"The office manager says Whiting's been dead a couple of years. Did you expect the car to be in his name?"

"I just wondered if they were company wheels or if he bought them out of his salary. And if his salary totaled as much as he spent."

"Whose does? Thorough, aren't you?"

"I don't have a hobby."

"It's a nice car if you like foreign. It couldn't shine the hubcaps on a thirty-nine Cord."

"You a buff?" I lit the cigarette.

"I tinker. That your bomb in the visitors' lot?"

I said it was.

"Cutlass is okay. Those old muscle jobs are mostly over-rated. The Stanley topped two hundred miles per hour in eighteen ninety-eight." He pointed his pen at the corpse. "Who do you like for that?"

"Whoever it is, he's still in the building. Or was when I came in here."

"What makes you think that?"

"I sat in my car for thirty minutes before I decided to take a look. I had the front of the garage in sight the whole time. I'd driven around the building and there was no other way in or out except by the elevator or the fire stairs."

"Why the stakeout?"

"I was early."

St. Thomas caught the eye of the office manager, who was spelling her name for one of the uniforms. She clip-clopped over.

"Everybody in today?" he asked.

"One out sick, two on vacation. The rest all reported in. If you like I'll have a list made." She gave him one of the smiles she'd given the telephone workers.

"That'll help, thanks. Any visitors?"

"Yes. Yes! A messenger to see Mr. Arsenault. I didn't talk to him, but Greta said there was something odd about him."

"Greta?"

"Mr. Arsenault's executive assistant. Secretary, if you want to be old-fashioned."

"What did she find odd about this messenger?"

"It was something about his hand. He wore some kind of contraption on it, she said. A prosthetic device."

"We'll talk to her. Anyone else?"

"No."

St. Thomas glanced at his watch, a plain one with a leather strap. "Slow day."

"Well, he had one other visitor, but he's a regular. Mr. Grayling."

"Royce Grayling?"

She looked at me. She hadn't forgotten the smoking incident.

"Yes. Imminent Visions has a bid in for the contract on a new downtown convention center. Mr. Grayling is employed by the City of Detroit to investigate all bids. Mr. Arsenault keeps—kept—him up to speed on the figures. They met two or three times a week."

"How long did they meet this morning?" I asked.

"They didn't. Mr. Arsenault left unexpectedly. Personal errand, he told Greta. He didn't say when he'd be back. I've been through this." She swept a hand through her stack of hair.

"Again, please." St. Thomas had his notebook open, but he wasn't writing. He might have been checking her story against the record—the number of pages he'd filled with his neat script suggested he'd already entered the uniform team's notes into the hard drive—or he might just have wanted to be holding something. He had what might have been an old nicotine stain on the inside of his right index finger. That was a habit he'd have downloaded a long time ago.

The office manager looked at her nails, coral-painted but pruned short, for the keyboard. "Greta said Mr. Grayling arrived a few minutes after Lynn—Mr. Arsenault—left. He waited about fifteen minutes, then looked at his watch and said he'd be back later and went out. Gregory called just after that to report what had happened."

"Did Grayling come in from the garage or through the suckers' entrance?" I asked.

She glared at me. She had light gray eyes. "Our customers are governments and captains of industry. I'm sure he came in through the main door. The garage is reserved for personnel."

"Yeah, a killer would respect that one."

"Sergeant, is this man connected with your department?"

"No, ma'am, he sure isn't." The silver glasses turned my way. "I've heard of Grayling. Maybe some of the same things you have. The parking guy says nobody came through here since before eight."

"I practically had to blow a bugle before he noticed me."

"The security guard in the lobby will know if Grayling came in the front. We'll check him out either way. You too. I'm not going to bother booking you since you never actually identified yourself as a police officer, but we will notify Wayne County you used a deputy's badge to get past the booth. You might lose it."

"That's okay. It was spoiling the lines of all my suits anyway."

"We'll talk again." His look said he hoped he'd like my next story better.

Redburn said, "Stick around town."

I looked at St. Thomas. "Did he say that?"

"He's new to the division. Color takes time. Remember the sentiment."

I walked out of the garage just as the satellite van from Channel 2 rolled to a stop behind the unmarked LeBaron. A reporter I recognized from television hopped out the passenger's side, pulling on his blazer. He tried to block my path. "Are you with the detectives' division?"

"You're a lot shorter in person." I walked around him. He sprinted after me, slowing as I got to my car, and executed a snippy little turn back to the van as I climbed behind the wheel. City employees don't drive vehicles more than two years old.

I waited for the coroner's wagon to clear the drive, then powered on out. Just as I hit Euclid a sheet of lightning blanked the windshield. The delayed clap shook the car and the hairs on the back of my hand stood on end. Somebody always has to have the last word.

Sixteen

"KEN, HAVE YOU CHECKED OUT the display of classic and antique autos in the Fisher Building lobby?"

"I have, Paul. Most impressive. There's a beautiful old Packard, and a Kaiser, many more I can't identify, I'm no expert, and there's a very old one—I don't know if it's Henry Ford's original quadricycle—"

"I believe it's a replica, Ken."

"Cars have certainly come a long way in a hundred years, haven't they?"

"They have. Although I had a Dodge that never quite made it across Eight Mile Road before breaking down."

The voices on the radio jabbered in that vein a little longer, stretching until the weather reader came on with the hot flash that a stormfront had entered the area. Just then lightning crackled, interrupting the signal. I switched off the knob.

By that time the threat had pretty much passed. When I turned onto Jefferson, five drops thudded the dusty hood, raising brown puffs and leaving marks like tiny crop circles. A big gust batted newspapers and what looked like a folding beach chair across the avenue. It was probably just an advertising supplement.

A thin strip of sunlight appeared to the west and spread like an opening wound. Thunder continued to chortle, but it had lost its stereo effect and seemed to be happening in the northeast. Someone was getting it, Windsor or Chatham.

It was a disappointment, and not just because it meant the heat wave would continue. I like storms. Just about the time we get it into our heads that we're actually capable of destroying nature, one comes along like a burst of rude laughter and blows civilization out like a candle. Lamps turn off, fans stop. Computer screens blip and go black. Businesses shut down until Ma Nature decides to lift her hand. This one was just a playful pass.

Driving along in the widening light I thought about Royce Grayling.

The fifth estate is murder. Those who commit it for personal gain or to feed a habit—food or drugs or plain bloodlust—must be taken into account when you set out to sum up a society. If you ignore them, they float around among the bar codes and pie graphs, messing up the neat lines. But a killer who pushes the button for politicians is altogether more static. He tends to run on the same track throughout his career, taking out treasury clerks with two sets of books and one athletic mouth, police officials who insist on too much pay for too little service under the counter, middle executives who get religion, disgruntled civil servants with a line to the media, media people with a line to disgruntled civil servants, grifters, grafters, hellraisers, and all the rest of that Byzantine chain of private and public liabilities that can flush an intricate and carefully constructed system down the pipes of reform if certain links aren't pried loose and scrapped with as little music as possible. That's why they're called plumbers.

Lynn Arsenault had become one such link. The question was how.

His office manager had said that Imminent Visions had submitted a bid to design a convention center in downtown Detroit; but if the project was somehow connected, icing the CEO during a visit officially related to the project was like drawing a map from the corpse to Grayling's superiors for whoever cared to follow it. Nothing about the man I had met on the dock in Grosse Pointe had said he was clumsy.

True, there was the double reverse to consider. There is always the double reverse. *You know I'm too smart to do such a dumb thing, so it should follow I'm not a suspect.* But if I know that, it won't take me all night to figure you're smart enough to know I know and switch back.

Or more likely, given the linear thinking of cops, reporters, and loose-cannon investigators, I might just jump on the obvious and hang you with it.

And Royce, my man, you're smart enough to know that.

My building was a pressure cooker. The air got hotter and thicker with each flight I climbed. On the third floor—my floor—it had no place else to go but the roof.

I wrenched open the window behind my desk two more inches. It hadn't been raised more than half a foot since Dred Scott, and I overheated myself just enough to balance the minimal effect of the draft that crept in through the space; if anything the humidity was worse than it had been before the storm teaser. Summer's for kids and houseflies.

"One call, Mr. Walker. No name, just a number." It belonged to my contact at the City-County Building, the one with the girlfriend at Mumford High.

It could wait. I called the Marriott, and this time the operator put me through to Stuart Lund.

"I apologize for before," he said. "I didn't sleep well last night."

"I'm not interested. There are complications with the package in Allen Park." Hotel switchboards are like party lines.

He caught on right away. "How complicated?"

"You may be hearing from the cops."

"Did you . . . ?" He was recalling our brass-knuckles conversation in regard to Arsenault.

"No, that was a gag. Someone else got there first."

"Bad?"

"It doesn't get worse. I had to come up with an answer when the cops asked me why I was interested in the package."

"You didn't tell them."

"I didn't, but if I stonewalled they'd have booked me as a material witness. I'm no good to anyone inside. Here's the play. You hired me to clear up this business about stolen designs." I gave him a second to catch up.

He took it. "Stolen designs? Oh, yes. That old matter. Go on."

"Your client is concerned about his good name. He wants to set the record straight before he takes his trip."

"His trip?"

"Before he dies." I had a stranglehold on the receiver.

"That's ludicrous."

"If it made too much sense they'd have hauled me down just for spite. They still might, but it's the best pitch I've got. I want you to check into the Westin."

"Whatever for?"

"Because that's where I told them you're staying. I thought you might not want a gang of dicks poking around the Marriott, pumping your roommate for information."

"Dicks? Oh, quite. I understand. However—"

"Let him stay put. You can hire a nurse to sit with him if you're worried about leaving him alone, but it's just till the cops are through interviewing you. But keep the room at the Westin and check for messages there. Pack a bag for looks and make the reservation in your name."

"I hope I can lie as convincingly as you."

It was too hot to tell a lawyer joke. I said I'd be in touch.

I washed my face and changed shirts. That put back some of the starch, but it wouldn't last long in that room. I broke a fresh pack out of the carton in the file drawer, locked up, and drove down to the Fox Theater, where I bought a ticket to the matinee in order to use the telephone in the air-conditioned lobby. I asked Joe High School what he had for me.

"Larry Furlong," he said. "He retired twelve years ago from the South Lyon Post Office. You'll find him in Beverly Hills."

"Which one, ours or California's?"

"He was a civil servant for forty-six years. Which one do you think?"

I took down the address and telephone number and thanked him.

"Best way to do that is to forget I'm breathing."

The line went dead. I pumped the lever and punched in the number he'd given me.

"Hello?"

A voice a long way from young, coarsened as if from disuse and a little louder than necessary.

"Larry Furlong?"

"What? Don't mumble."

I shouted it. The college-age ticket-taker came out of a standing doze and frowned in my direction.

"Pipe down, for cripe's sake," came the voice. "I ain't deef, just a little hard of. You with Detroit Edison?"

I said I wasn't.

"What?"

I turned my back to the ticket-taker and raised my voice a notch.

"Too bad. I got sixty pounds of prime beef in a freezer that turned into a hall closet an hour ago."

"Is your power out?"

"Isn't yours?"

"No, the storm missed Detroit."

"Lucky you. Had lunch?"

"No, but I'm on a short leash."

"Too bad. I can offer you one hell of a steak dinner. What you selling, son? Generators, I hope. I ought to warn you first, though, I'm on a pension."

"I'm not selling, Mr. Furlong. I'm looking for information. My name is Amos Walker. I'm an investigator."

"I don't need any holes dug. Not till that meat starts to turn, anyway."

"Not excavator, investigator. I'm a private detective." I coiled the telephone cord into a noose.

"Oh. Well, nobody calls me Mr. Furlong these days, and I never did answer to Larry. I've been Buster my whole life. Detective, you said? What'd I do, come up short on petty cash? Took you long enough to count it. I retired two presidents ago."

"It isn't about the post office. I'm working for your brother Jay."

"Isn't he dead yet?"

I was getting tired of answering that one.

"Not yet. It has to do with his will. I'd like to ask you a few questions."

"I don't want any part of it. Give my share to the United Fund."

Something had gone; the folksy tone. It had burned right off, like a coat of cheap paint on a white-hot stove. What was left was bare iron.

I gave him the full rundown, all except Furlong's actual condition and whereabouts. His weak hearing had adjusted to the timber of my voice and I could talk without drowning out the main feature in the auditorium.

When I finished he made a noise like two tree limbs mating. He probably called it laughter.

"So the old buzzard gave up his shot at a pretty young wife just because he thought she was catting around. Well, now he knows what it's like being alone and old. Tell him I'll send flowers, but I won't go to the funeral. I wouldn't even if I didn't have the emphysema." He coughed phlegmily, as if to illustrate the point. "He'll know why. You won't have to draw him any pictures."

"I understand you haven't seen each other in almost fifty years. I guess you don't get along."

"You guess right, son."

I let the silence work on him. Sometimes that's the advantage of using the telephone. Dead air makes some people nervous. Buster Furlong was one of them. Or maybe he just wanted to talk.

"Big-deal architect couldn't be bothered taking care of his own mother when she got old and sick," he said. "Let Buster do that, I got buildings to put up."

"He said that?"

"He didn't have to. Oh, he sent money when he thought about it. I looked after her till it got to be too much, then I put her in a home. Had to. It was just too much for one man. It was a nice enough place if you don't mind being talked to like you're still in rompers. She got confused the last couple of years, thought I was Jay half the time. I let her think it. It was like having the family all together."

There was a series of rattling coughs, followed by a noise like an engine revving up and then an explosion. He'd spat into a handkerchief or something. "I put off getting married till she was out of the house. By that time I was old myself and so was Trudy."

"Your wife?"

"Cancer took her. We had nine years. Would've been twenty if Jay'd pitched in and helped out with Ma. Couple of weeks a year in California might've made all the difference to the old lady. Hell, to me, too, not having to fuss over her for a little while. I bet I hinted at it twenty times in letters till Jay stopped answering them and I gave up writing them. Your parents still living, son?"

"No."

"Just as well. Married?"

"Not now."

"Don't wait too long, that's my advice. One morning you wake up and you're old. I don't recommend it."

"I'll keep that in mind."

"Like hell you will. But you'll remember I said it when it happens."

"I guess you don't know who might have had the picture made up."

"It sure as hell wasn't me. I wouldn't do to him what he did to Ma."

"One last question, Mr. Furlong."

"Buster."

"Does the name Royce Grayling mean anything to you? He's in politics."

"Nope. All I ever knew about politics, or needed to, was

when to take down the picture of the old president and put up the new one. And not to tell jokes about the Kennedys when the Democrats are in office."

I wished him luck with the beef.

"Serves me right for buying more than I'll live to eat."

Another one off the list. I was down to the second and third generations.

I looked at my watch. Just past noon. If Lund had moved quickly and the police had proceeded at their usual drab but efficient clip, he would be entertaining them at the Westin any time now. As soon as I thought of him I put him out of my head. I didn't want to put the whammy on him while he was feeding them the lines I'd written. Superstition has its place in the odds.

I screwed the receiver back into my ear. Unlike the cheesy partitions between the multiplex theaters in the mall, the walls of the grand old Fox were thick enough to absorb sound, but when I leaned against the wall next to the telephone I could feel the vibrations of the space-opera sound-track on the other side.

"Yeah?" Hurricane Bob would never learn the proper way to answer a telephone.

"It's Walker. Did you deliver that message directly to Arsenault?"

He described the dead man down to his gabardine.

"That's him," I said. "You got a place to go to beat the heat?"

He hesitated. "I got an idea you ain't talking about the weather."

"Somebody pumped a slug into Arsenault's head in the company garage right after you left. The cops have your description. I'll stand you to a room if you need it, but it has to be way out of town. You know cops and motels."

"Moths and porchlights. Don't need it. Gandy'll put me up. You know Gandy."

Richard Gandolph was the bass player Bob had neglected to include in his record contract; the man who had hired me to save Bob's life when the music stopped. Gandy and Buster Furlong didn't live in the same world.

"Call me if you need anything," I said. "But don't leave any messages with the service."

"A message is what got me in this hole. But I ain't blaming nobody." A solo guitar was playing low on his end, slow and snarly. It might have been one of his old demo tapes. "Say, man, you didn't, uh—"

"Arsenault? Not my *modus*. I have a poison ring."

"That's cool. Dude was asking to get whacked."

"You had trouble?"

"His door accidentally fell open while his secretary was telling me he was in conference. The *mouth* on him." He broke off for a moment. He was listening to the tape. Then: "You know what? He was in there all by himself. There wasn't nobody to confer with."

"Corporate's a bitch. Is that you I'm hearing?"

"Yeah."

"You okay?"

"Swell as Mel's wells. Hocked my axe last week. Long as it was around I could hear the ghost of my fingers playing it all night. I'd rather listen to the real thing."

"It doesn't come from the fingers, you know."

"I know."

I told him again to call me if anything broke. I hung up, but I kept my hand on the receiver, jingling the change in my pocket. Then I fed in some more coins and started another layer of callus on my index finger.

"Hi, this is Nate Millender. If it's paying work, leave a

message. If it's going to cost me, keep trying, you never can tell. Well, you know this shit."

I took my own advice and didn't leave a message.

I looked at my watch again. It was still just past noon. Some days are like that. Millender couldn't still be out on his boat, because his sailing companion, Royce Grayling, had been in Allen Park bright and early. On assignment, probably. Blissful in his ignorance that he was the only remaining mile of road between me and the witchfinder.

I looked at my watch. Just past noon.

Outside the sky was a clear blue bowl. No shadows to hide in.

At least this time I wouldn't have to go home and change into my burglar clothes.

Seventeen

HOME TO NATE MILLENDER was an apartment on Cadillac Boulevard, not as ritzy as it sounds, but about as far up the scale as you can climb inside the Detroit city limits before you have enough together to get out. It was also his business address.

The building was sandstone, eight stories high with arched windows marching along the top floor like stylized camels and wrought-iron railings erected in front of the basement windows to dishearten the less ambitious burglars. The block to the north was all Queen Anne houses with fresh paint jobs and clipped lawns, narrow gables thrust skyward like aristocratic noses. The block to the south had empty spaces in its rows of brick boxes; crack houses gone the way of Joe Firebug and the wrecking ball. Millender's block was poised between the two neighborhoods like a runner caught off base, trying to decide which direction to run.

Fans whirred in two of the open windows. Air conditioners thrust their boxlike backsides out some of the others. Still others were shut tight, the rooms they belonged to awaiting their next occupants. Vacant apartments are another bellwether of a city in trouble, like empty bleachers at the ballpark. But they weren't boarded up. There was hope.

The foyer smelled of potpourri and clean rubber. A steel-framed glass door with a grid between the thick panes wouldn't budge when I tugged on the handle. I pressed the yellow Bakelite button next to the mailbox with N. MILLENDER lettered on it in soft pencil. The door remained locked. I selected a friendly sounding name higher up. The lock clonked.

The fourth floor was Millender's, paneled in yellow imitation maple with a flocked red carpet in the hallway. I knocked on Millender's door, waited, knocked again. Same no answer.

I took inventory. The celluloid strip in my wallet was out of its class; the molding curled over the edge of the door. I dove for the precision tools.

Nutpicks are best, the kind with curved points like lazy hooks. On jobs like that I carry them in a small paper bag in my jacket pocket along with a cracker and half a dozen walnuts, just in case I'm stopped and searched. I was going on three years on the same walnuts. They would taste like clothespins.

The cheapest lock in creation requires two picks to open: one to hold back the spring-activated shield that protects the tumblers from tampering, the other to tamper. This one wasn't the cheapest and a long way from burglar-proof, but it took me six minutes; my specialty's motor tailing, not breaking and entering. I lost two of those minutes while a round-shouldered woman with a cap of white hair and her escort, a tall, narrow-chested old party wearing a bright cloth cap with a fuzzy ball on top, came hobbling down the hallway. They were leaning on each other and wheezing from the four-flight climb in weather that kills more elderly people than broken hips. I poked the paraphernalia up my sleeve, knocked, and pretended to be waiting for an answer while they made their way past. Finally the old man fished a key ring the size of a bowling ball out of the deep pocket of his slacks, sorted through the items dangling from it with the care of someone selecting his own coffin, and let them into an apartment two doors down. Sixty seconds later I had click.

Millender loved sailing. He had a Maxfield Parrish print of a square-rigger leaning sheets to the wind on a choppy sea framed on the wall facing the door, a regatta trophy standing all alone on the mantel of a false fireplace, brass running lamps mounted on the walls. The living room, which took up most of the floor plan, was dusted and tidy, the furniture arranged at right angles; squared away. In the shallow kitchenette a teabag lay calcifying in an insulated mug with a ketch screen-printed on the side, the way even a fastidious bachelor on a tight schedule might leave it, but the sink and counter gleamed. He had a mariner's love of spotlessness and order.

There was time enough to toss those rooms later. Bedrooms are best for hidden booty.

The bed was a double, made neatly. There was a driftwood lamp on the nightstand, a three-drawer bureau with toilet items laid out on it and a small case full of books on the order of Conrad and C. S. Forester. The only picture was a magazine print in a cheap frame of a pair of satyrs rolling their eyes at each other in a woodland setting.

There was something familiar about the room, but I couldn't stand a quarter on just what it was. It was as if I'd seen it in a dream I'd forgotten.

Not knowing what I was looking for, I looked at everything, including the underside of the mattress and the backs and bottoms of all the drawers. I even pried the top off a plastic container of talcum and poked around inside with the handle of a rattail comb. Just for fun I tasted the powder on the end of a finger. I had him then, if they ever got around to passing a law against cornstarch.

He liked Hawaiian shirts, duck pants, tennis socks, sling-shot underwear, and nude studies. He kept the pictures in a thick envelope under the shirts. They were black-and-whites mostly, eight-by-ten experiments in light and texture with borders, smooth taut skin against rough barnwood and stucco. They ran to a single style, and from the rubbing of the varnished surfaces they seemed to have been taken for Millender's personal use. And they were all male.

There was nothing rampant about them or even obscene according to the Supreme Court. They were just art studies of darkly handsome well-built young men in their prime without clothes. I didn't know any of them from Praxiteles. I put them back.

Millender had gutted a walk-in closet and wired and plumbed it for use as a darkroom. It was just big enough for a double sink and a stainless steel counter holding up some equipment that was new to me since I'd given up developing my own surveillance photos and started going to custom labs. Several negatives clothespinned to the wire hammocked over the sink contained nothing more titillating than a fleet of sailboats cruising fully erect on the flat surface of what might have been Lake St. Clair.

The bathroom was a snooze. Not even any interesting prescription pills in the medicine cabinet. He used Grey Flannel soap.

I went back into the bedroom. It still looked familiar, with something discordant to boot. I stood in the doorway with my hands in my pockets and frisked the place with my eyes. They stopped at the picture of the satyrs.

It had been lithographed from a nineteenth-century original, engraved in that whimsical style the Victorians applied to mythological subjects lest they be accused of sympathy with the lascivious pagans. The nude photographs were kept out of sight; they were not ornaments. It was the only visible testimony to the appetites of the man who slept in that room. Moreover, it was the only decoration in the apartment without a nautical theme.

I went over and took it down off its nail. There was no wall safe behind it, only a rectangular patch of unfaded paint whose size and shape matched the picture. The frame was plastic, the back plain cardboard held in place with bent staples. It was the work of a second to pull it apart. Between the magazine print and the cardboard was an envelope much smaller than the one in the bureau drawer and a savings passbook from the National Bank of Detroit. I slid out a small negative and three photographic prints just over wallet size. They were all the same. A younger, trimmer Lynn Arsenault than the one who was on his way to the Wayne County Morgue lay in bed with a Nate Millender who didn't look a day younger than the one I had met at the Grosse Pointe Marina. Some guys just never age.

Both men were naked. Neither of them looked alarmed by the presence of a camera.

Looking at Arsenault I had that same sense of revisitation I'd felt when I first entered the room. I remembered the envelope in my pocket, the one containing the extortion note I'd had delivered to Arsenault at Imminent Visions and the counterfeit photograph I'd gotten from Jay Bell Furlong. I took out the picture and held it next to one of the prints from inside the frame. It was the same pose. The bed was the same and so was the room. It was the room I was standing in. The only thing different was Arsenault's companion. Millender had been less muscular then, slender rather than lean, with almost no hair on his body. In that position he might have passed for a fairly flat-chested woman, except for his head.

I turned to the passbook and started paging through it. Ichabod Nathan Millender—a better reason than most to go by his middle name—was a man of regular habits when it came to transactions. He never missed a month.

It might have been the job and the extra set of senses that comes with it. It might have been a change in the nearly nonexistent current of air in that shut-up room. More likely I caught a flash of movement in the mirror over the bureau. Whatever it was, I was in motion, diving across the bed and twisting to get my hand on the revolver in its holster, when the room went supernova. Heat scorched my eye sockets, white flame leapt up the walls, melting gaping black holes in them, as if they were plastic. The ceiling bellied and came down on top of me. It was a lot heavier than plastic.

They say you never hear the shot.

As usual, they're wrong.

Eighteen

I WAS EXPERIENCING a midlife crisis.

Some of the old rules still apply. A man towing forty should be steering a desk in a cubicle downtown, or maybe a tractor or a bulldozer in the open air, worrying about his kid getting his driver's license and whether his wife's sudden interest in abdominal crunches is connected with the new young intern she can't stop talking about and if he has enough insurance to get the house out of hock if he blows a major artery at lunch. He's supposed to be developing hemorrhoids, a roll around his trunk, and an affinity for Ban-Lon and Sansabelt on weekends.

He sure isn't supposed to be sprawled on his stomach across the bed in a stranger's apartment, staring glassily at a fat beige spider that had survived the most recent vacuuming and wondering if it would have time to spin a strand from its web to the end of his nose before the morgue wagon came.

Dad was right. I should have taken a civil service test.

The spider wasn't much more than a blur. I was looking at it with my lazy left eye. The right was either an empty socket or caked with blood.

There was quite a lot of blood. I couldn't see it, but I had been careless enough times to know that smell, copper and iron with just a hint of Scotch whisky, just as a dog recognizes its own scent.

I felt detached. It wasn't my blood anymore.

Lying there I was suddenly aware that the bed had changed. It had sprouted wheels and was rolling down a set of steel tracks, clickety-clack, picking up speed on the downgrade with Casey Jones at the controls. Casey was going too fast. I hung on tight as we swooped over the next hill. At the top the coupling came loose. The wheels left the tracks and I was headed into the empty blue bowl of the sky.

I was rescued from falling by a sailboat. The bronze sloop from the trophy on Nate Millender's mantel had sailed off its pedestal, swelling to full size as its canvas filled and tacking around to scoop me up without slowing. Over the Monopoly board of the western neighborhoods we swept, across the jagged business-chart skyline of downtown, splashing down in the Detroit River. Down the river to Lake Erie, through the inlet to Lake Ontario, and along the St. Lawrence Seaway to the North Atlantic, where we had to watch out for U-boats. I smelled the salt air, copper and iron with a hint of Scotch whisky.

I never lost sight of the spider, though. As it shrank in the distance, losing size but gaining detail, it opened its mandibles and said:

"Where's that EMS unit? This guy's going to bleed to death before they get here."

I was curious to know who was on the other end of this arachnoid conversation, since it didn't seem to be directed at me; but I couldn't stay to find out. The curvature of the earth came between us and then the sun set on the water, staining the surface blood red before extinguishing itself beneath the waves. And me with it.

"Bulls got no bench. We'll catch 'em next year."

"Who's *we*? Isiah's gone, we lost Rodman. We got former Pistons scattered all over the NBA. This free-agent shit is ruining the game."

"What if we had Jordan?"

"Hell with Jordan. I don't want no players that bad-mouth Detroit."

"That narrows the field."

"I'd sooner play the guy that waxes the court. I got community pride."

"Hey, this guy's awake."

"I'll get Mrs. Tarnower."

"Wait up."

I never got to see the participants in this pre-game show. I was looking at perforated ceiling tiles and wondering if they were made in Dublin. Tracing a Great Circle route from Newfoundland due east, I should have reached Ireland first. But unless the natives had abandoned Barry Fitzgerald's brogue for the Detroit black dialect, something had gone wrong with my navigation.

On a brighter note, I was seeing with both eyes now. I needed them to count eighty-six holes in the tile directly in my line of sight. I turned my head a micromillimeter to start on the tile next to it and somebody—a Belfast potato-harvester, possibly—hit me with a shovel. A bolt of black lightning arced between my temples and the ceiling vanished behind a purple cloud. I closed my eyes and counted my pulse instead. I got eighty-six to the minute, the same number as the holes in the ceiling tile.

When I opened my eyes I was looking at a pair of glasses

on a female face with a moustache and a mole on the side of its nose. If this was an angel I must have been in the part of heaven reserved for private investigators.

The face in its time disappeared. In a little while I found I could move my head slowly without black lightning. A kid in jeans, Reeboks, and a T-shirt reading I BRAKE FOR NUKES was standing next to the bed monkeying with a clipboard. I peeled my tongue from the roof of my mouth and asked him if he was supposed to be in here. The voice I used had been rejected by Bela Lugosi.

When he grinned, his freckles disappeared into crescents in his cheeks.

"If I'm not, I wish you'd tell the nurse. I've got a softball game to pitch."

"You're a little young for an orderly."

"I guess that's why they made me a doctor."

"And I'm Long John Silver."

"Pleased to make your acquaintance, Mr. Silver. I'm Dr. Ebersole. Got a stethoscope and everything." He picked up the end and waggled it.

"That how they dress for the ER now?"

He glanced down at his teenage chic. "The softball team's looking for a sponsor. We can't afford uniforms."

"I knew you weren't a doctor."

"I didn't say I was one of the rich ones. Hold still, please." He produced a penlight, pried open my eyelids, and shone the beam into the pupils. It pierced through to the back of my skull like a red-hot needle. "This your first concussion?"

"What, today?"

He snapped off the light. "Are you an athlete?"

"No, I just fall down a lot." I moved my eyes around. The noise made my headache worse. "Detroit Receiving, right?"

"How'd you guess? This town has more hospitals than churches and traffic lights."

"I recognized the pallet. Just where was I shot this time?"

" 'This time'?"

"I'd tell you, but I'm saving it for my unauthorized autobiography."

He hung the clipboard on the foot of the bed and hooked his thumbs in his tight pockets, frowning. That made him a doctor.

"I took seventeen stitches in a laceration above your right ear. The skull wasn't fractured, but you're concussed and you lost blood. A lot of blood. I could get more technical, but I was out the day they taught Latin."

"Playing softball."

"I love softball. If I liked medicine half as much I'd be surgeon general by now."

"People would mistake you for a drum major. When do I get sprung?"

"You're lucky to be in a position to ask that question. One of the officers who found you started to call it in as a homicide. You had almost no pulse. There was blood clotted in your right orbit."

"Orbit?"

"Eye socket. He thought it was the exit wound."

"I'm here for the night, huh."

"You don't have the picture, Mr. Walker." He leaned on the bedrail. "When you came in, you had no vital signs. That was twenty-nine hours ago and you've been unconscious ever since. I'd like to keep you two weeks, but we need the bed. There was a gang fight last night on Erskine. The young man on the other side of that curtain had his kidneys crushed by a baseball bat. Next week is graduation, and you know how effective those public-service ads are about not mixing alcohol and gasoline when you've got a brand new sheep-skin and a license to drive. But I'm holding you as long as they'll let me. Cerebral trauma isn't the sniffles."

Twenty-nine hours.

"The pictures," I said.

"I'm sorry?"

"Where are my things?"

"Your clothes and valuables are locked up in that cabinet. You won't be needing them for a while."

It was one of those sheet-metal numbers that open with a sharp look.

"There's a detective waiting outside to talk to you," he said. "I can say you're resting."

"No, the longer they wait the uglier they get."

"Not this one."

"That bad, is he?" I groped for the buttons on the bedrail. The motor hummed and I sat up. My head throbbed in long steady swells. More nautical stuff. Phooey.

Ebersole glanced at the watch on the underside of his wrist. It had a cartoon character on the face. "I can still make the third inning. I'll look in on you tomorrow."

"Personal question."

At the door he turned to grin. "I'll be thirty at the end of August."

"Happy birthday."

The door closed behind him.

A cheesecloth curtain on a rolling rail separated my bed from my neighbor's. I could hear his heart monitor measuring out his life in uncertain blips, the trickle of his damaged kidneys draining down a plastic tube. Dusty-brass daylight crept between vertical blinds on the room's only window.

The right side of my head felt tight and puckered. I reached up and touched a square patch of adhesive and thick cotton and smooth flesh around it where there used to be hair. I made a bet with myself it would grow in even grayer.

"You look like crap."

I had closed my eyes for a moment. I may have dozed. I hadn't heard the door opening.

At first I thought it was the drugs they were feeding me through the tube taped to my arm. Impressions only, to start. A trim waist and legs in a snug black evening dress of some material that ate light, a slit that showed a flash of white thigh when she walked. Bare shoulders and deep cleavage, pearls against skin dusted lightly with freckles. Enormous blue eyes and light brown hair, almost honey-colored but not quite, pushed to one side and free for once of the plastic band that made her look like a cheerleader. Instead she looked like prom night. Saying I looked like crap.

"You don't," I said. "Working undercover, Lieutenant?"

"So to speak?"

I grinned; weakly, I hoped. It didn't take much acting.

She said, "I'm on my way to dinner at Carl's Chop House and then the show at the Fisher. Cops have lives, too. Just thought I'd drop by and see if you were dead yet."

"What time did you draw in the pool?"

Mary Ann Thaler smiled. It wasn't a thing she did often, because her fellow officers in the Detroit Detective Division might not take her seriously. Before she could speak I pointed at her purse, a silver mesh clutch the size of a Montana belt buckle.

"That big enough for the cuffs *and* your departmental piece?"

"Just the gun. I can always tie you up with my pantyhose. Unless there's something you want to tell me."

"I thought you were Felony Homicide."

"I am. You committed the first and almost became a victim of the second."

"Where are your glasses?"

"Contacts. Tortoiseshell rims don't go with pearls. Don't change the subject. Do you always carry walnuts and related utensils?"

"You've been through my personal effects."

"Only dead people have personal effects. How come I never see you eating walnuts?"

"It isn't polite in front of ladies and cops. Who's your date? Has he got a job?"

"Shut up and let me do mine. You're no Jimmy Valentine; you scratched up the lock on your way in. What did you find in Millender's apartment?"

"What did you find on me?"

"Nuts."

Assuming that was a legitimate answer, whoever had shot me had taken the envelope from my pocket. If so he'd also gotten the pictures and the negative I'd found. "Do I get a lawyer?"

"You're not under arrest. All you get is me."

"Off the books?"

She spread her arms. "Where would I be wearing a wire?"

"No comment." I groped for my shirt pocket out of habit. I was wearing a paper robe. "I guess you don't have cigarettes either."

"Don't use 'em. Quit stalling."

"Millender's got a twenty-three-foot sailing sloop to support. He supports it with a keyhole lens. I was after some pictures."

"Homosexual pictures?"

I looked at her for a second. "I don't think they have sex."

"You know what I mean."

"Laughter is the best medicine," I said. "Who said anything about homosexuals?"

"I pulled Millender's sheet. He's got three lewd-and-lascivious beefs in highway rest stops, one conviction, and just finished probation on a federal rap for sending pornography through the mails. He's his own favorite model."

"Sort of like Rembrandt."

"Rembrandt kept his jerkin on. This guy's a state-of-the-art sicko. Who's your client?"

"Excuse me, Lieutenant. I'm having a relapse."

"Impossible. The bullet only hit your head." She tapped a glossy nail against the purse containing her artillery. "Okay, we'll start slow and work our way up to Double Jeopardy. Who shot you?"

"I don't know."

"Was it Millender?"

"I don't know."

"What's the capital of South Dakota?"

"Pierre."

She nodded. "I just wanted to hear you tell the truth once."

"I guessed about Pierre."

"I used to tease John Alderdyce whenever he got his blood up over something you did," she said, "or didn't do, or said, or didn't say, or wouldn't. He told me I should count myself lucky I hadn't tripped over you yet on a case of my own. I'm counting now."

"How is John?"

"Sitting in his inspector's office with his inspector's shoes up on his inspector's desk, dictating a memo to all the other inspectors. You know what I want to be when I grow up?"

"Blonde?"

Her face went blank as a slab. She was all cop in spite of the Dior. "Who shot you?"

"I don't know."

"This hospital has a security floor: One door in and out, wired for alarm, with a guard. No patient release without the signature of the chief of police."

"No, it doesn't."

"It could. The man I'm going out with is on the board of directors."

"And all you want to be is inspector?"

She said nothing.

I made my face haggard. "All I saw was a movement. Not even that. My reflexes were down."

"Brother, they were out of the country. Half an inch to the left and you'd be trying out your stand-up routine on a whole different audience."

"Half an inch to the right and he'd have missed me completely."

"In which case I'd be questioning you as a suspect instead of a victim."

"Unless I just shot the gun out of his hand."

She jumped on it. "His?"

"The general pronoun, Lieutenant. If you're going to go feminist on me there's no hope for this relationship."

"We have a relationship?"

"Mongoose and cobra. Except I'm not feeling especially venomous." I groped at my chest again, then tried the drawer in the bedside table, holding my brains in with my free hand. I found tongue depressors and a package of rubber fingers. Either one would have done, but there was no lighter. I sank back against the mattress. "If this was just a B-and-E with an attempted homicide, you wouldn't be standing here letting the ice melt in your shrimp cocktail. Why the heat?"

Now she was tapping a corner of the silver purse against her teeth. It made my fillings ache worse than my head. She caught the look on my face and stopped.

"I play poker," she said. "When I asked if it was Millender who shot you I was looking for a tell. Either you don't have any or you're just ignorant. When was the last time you saw or spoke to Nate Millender?"

"Yesterday. Well, Thursday. I forgot about the gun lag. He was casting off from the marina in Grosse Pointe."

"That makes you one of the last. His sloop ran aground near Flatrock sometime yesterday. He wasn't in it, but he'd left some of his brains on the sail boom. Or someone's brains if not his. The cops downriver are busy dragging for the rest of him."

Nineteen

SHE WATCHED it sink in. I couldn't decide whether that cop stare was worse with or without glasses.

"Stray booms have killed more sailors than storms at sea," I said. "It could have been an accident."

"Could have. Probably was. When the computer kicks out a sheet like Millender's we look a little harder. When a P.I. named Walker bounces a bullet off his skull in the victim's apartment we break out the microscope." She leaned on the footboard of the bed. Mary Ann Thaler's style was a lot more direct than Sergeant St. Thomas's, but they were both cut from the same bolt of blue serge.

I got the Allen Park detective out of my head in a hurry. When you're in the room with a badge, that police telepathy is as sharp as an earache.

I equivocated. The only thing I needed more than a handful of aspirins and two months in Europe was a little time before Detroit found out about Lynn Arsenault and the common denominator he shared with Nate Millender. That common denominator being me.

"You nailed me, Lieutenant," I said. "I swam out into the middle of Lake St. Clair, brained Millender, dumped him over the side, and swam back to shore and a change of clothes. Except I swim like a headstone."

"That's easily checked. There are other ways you could have done it, including dumping the body somewhere else and smearing hair and gray matter on the boom to make it look like another tragic boating accident. You just gave the sloop a hard shove from some dock and never got your feet wet." She straightened. "Just for now, though, I'm operating on the theory that murder's not your style. Which opens up the probability that you know whose it is and that's why you were shot."

"Harder to make that look accidental."

"It's never easy except in stories. My first day out of uniform, Alderdyce told me the easiest homicides to clear up are the ones somebody tried to make look like something else. A nice clean bullet in the head is a blank wall more often than not. Who shot you?"

"What'd you get from the bullet?"

"We didn't get it. After it grazed you it shattered a window and kept on going. Maybe that's what made him decide not to stick around and put another one in you to grow on. The officers who found you were answering a citizen complaint of a shot fired."

"Just one and they called the cops?"

"Things must be looking up."

Nurse Tarnower came in, if that was the name of the woman who had missed her last electrolysis appointment. She was carrying a tray with a small plastic cup on it and a container of water, also plastic. The recycling frenzy hasn't gotten to hospitals yet.

"I'm afraid you'll have to end your visit. It's time for Mr. Walker's sleeping pill."

"I'll be back later."

"Not before morning. Visiting hours begin at ten."

Thaler dug her badge folder out of her purse. "This man is a witness in a homicide."

"He almost succumbed to one. It's my job to see he still doesn't. You have to leave."

The war of wills ended when I accepted the cup. It contained a white pill half the size of an aspirin.

"How powerful is that thing?" Thaler asked.

"He'll sleep until morning."

I tossed back the cup and took in water through an articulated straw. It tasted like liquid cotton. The lieutenant watched me swallow, then put her hand on the steel broom handle that worked the door.

"I posted a uniform in the hall," she said. "Just in case our friend decides to try for best two out of three."

"What if I say no thanks?"

"This one's on us. Remember that the next time you pay your city income tax."

The back of her dress was scooped down to the waist. She had a tiny crescent-shaped scar on her right shoulderblade where a mole had been removed. Or maybe it was her Marine Corps tattoo.

"Good luck with Mr. Board of Directors."

"Don't need it. It's our fourth date."

The nurse finished punching my pillow out of shape and went out behind her, switching off the light. I caught a glimpse of city blue outside the room, then the door closed. When it latched I opened my fist and flicked the sleeping pill off my palm. The trick takes longer to explain than to perform.

The tubes required a little more effort, but I got free of them and found the catch on the bedrail and swung it down. I tried to hold my head level as I got up. Someone had left the lid off my skull and I was afraid if I tipped it too far this way or that my brains would spill out and I'd have a hell of a time finding them and putting them back. The little blackouts, the second or two of blurred vision that followed, were like refreshing naps.

I felt drained, literally. As predicted, the lock on the cabinet was no match for a smart blow with the heel of a hand; any hand but mine. It took two, covered by loud coughs, before the door sprang open. Then I leaned against the wall and waited for the dizziness to pass before reaching for my clothes.

My wallet, watch, and keys were on the top shelf. My pockets were empty. That broken window hadn't rattled the shooter so much he forgot to frisk me. The holster was still clipped to my belt, but the gun was missing. Time enough to find out who had it, crook or cops, later. I dressed quickly, while I was lucid.

My head was pulsing like a big squishy heart, but most of the blood seemed to have slipped to my feet. I thought about going back and sitting on the edge of the bed until it returned. I took a step in that direction. The sleeping pill I'd ditched crunched under my foot. I lurched past the bed into the bathroom and slapped my face with water. A face carved out of that same water gawked at me from the glass above the sink. Hair stuck up like quills around a big wad of bandages stuck to the side of its head. I wanted to laugh, but the owner of the face might not have gotten the joke. I smoothed down the hairs with water, rasped the back of one hand against a carpet of beard. The sound went straight to the quick of my skull.

Back in the room I peered around the curtain between the beds. My roommate was black, very young but lean-muscled, with tubes in his wrists and nostrils and disappearing under the thin blanket that cloaked him. A transparent breathing mask covered the lower half of his face. His eyes were closed, but his chest moved rhythmically up and down and the green line on the monitor wired to his heart peeped in cadence.

I stepped around the curtain and examined the monitor. It was the only machinery hooked to him, and wasn't life-sustaining. If he needed dialysis for his damaged kidneys it hadn't been diagnosed yet.

I found where the wire plugged into the machine and yanked it out.

The reaction was quieter than anticipated, and none of it came from the patient. The green line went flat, the peeping turned into a high thin whine. He went on sleeping. Any hospital show worthy of its ratings would have had the lights flashing, horns and buzzers sounding, a frantic voice on the P.A., running feet in the corridor. Real life needs a script doctor. I stepped into the bathroom and cracked the door. Nurse Tarnower came in, moving quickly but without noise on rubber heels, jerked open the curtains, glanced at the monitor, and flipped the P.A. switch.

"Code Blue, room three-one-eight."

She might have been calling out a Bingo number; but lack of excitement doesn't mean inefficiency. In less than thirty seconds we had all the drama required. The room filled with personnel of both sexes and all races, a crash wagon, and half the pharmacy. The cop on duty, a pale kid younger even than Dr. Ebersole, with a moustache not nearly as well established as Tarnower's, leaned in through the open door, didn't like his view, and stepped the rest of the way inside, craning to get a look past the whitecoats huddled around the bed. I slipped out of the bathroom and into the hall behind his back. With an exclamation, someone discovered the disconnected plug just as I reached the nurses' station.

"Hey!"

I didn't turn to see if it was the officer calling or a hospital employee. It might not have been directed at me. I was almost to the elevators. I picked up my pace, but I didn't stop to ring. The door to the fire stairs was unlocked.

The bronze light on the street was growing grainy with dusk. The gutters were dry and there was no trace of rain on the pavement. The air was as stale as ever. It hadn't moved all the time I was out of the loop. The city gets the worst of every season.

I kept to the shadows. I didn't expect anyone to put out an APB for a hospital walkaway, or even for a maybe-witness to a possible murder without a citizen complaint attached, but a ghost in yesterday's shirt and last year's sportcoat with a patch on its head just naturally draws passing scout cars. Once, a Tactical Mobile Unit slowed down and I started to put together a story, but then it slid into the curb behind a Subaru stopped at the corner. The girl on the corner, six feet tall in five-inch platforms and a micro-miniskirt, broke off her conversation with the driver, turned, and clip-clopped away double-time; the car took off with a chirp of rubber. The lights and siren came on and the blue-and-white gave chase. I crossed to the opposite side of the street where the shadows were deepest.

Three blocks from the hospital I was drenched in sweat. I couldn't tell if it was the heat. I wasn't even sure it was hot. My knees wobbled and my head banged in delayed tempo behind my heart, like two-handed handball. I stopped and laid my palm against the corner of a building, more to feel the cool granite than to support myself. And the building contained a party store, and the store contained a telephone.

The clerk, a thin young Arab with a pocked face and scars on both cheeks, changed my dollar without taking his eyes off me. He kept one hand out of sight beneath the counter.

I fumbled two coins into the slot and asked the operator to call a taxi company.

"Which one, sir?"

"One with taxis."

"You can dial that number yourself, sir."

"I'm blind." Not a bald lie; the telephone had two receivers, several sets of buttons, and my choice of shelves to lean on with all four elbows.

"One moment, sir."

The dispatcher, one of the broken-windpipe boys, grilled me for a couple of minutes before agreeing to send a cab. Four drivers had been shot at in the city since February, two hit, one killed. Ordering transportation had become a subversive act.

I waited in the doorway until the cab showed, a blue beater on mismatched tires. The driver, black and forty with a cloth cap pulled low over one eye, spent some time fumbling with the city map in the pocket above the sun visor as I got in. When he took his hand down to wheel us away from the curb I saw why. It's illegal in Michigan for cab drivers to carry guns. It's also illegal to drive without wearing a seat belt, and as far as I could tell the car hadn't any.

It was dark out now. I saw his face reflected in the windshield, sea-green in the secondhand light from the dash. He had a couple of dozen figures of Hawaiian dancing girls glued to the ledge, swaying and wiggling as we bumped over the ruts. I couldn't take my eyes off them.

"Man, you looks like you got a early start," he said. "I don't usually picks folks up in your shape this time on a Saturday night."

"I work Sundays."

"Yeah? You some kind of preacher?"

"Our Lady of the Broken Head. I'm the pastor."

"I'm Southern Baptist myself. Well, the wife is, so I am too. She prays so much I don't figure the Lord'll throw any bolts at me or He might hit her. So what happened? Fall off the pulpit?"

"I was shot in somebody's apartment."

"Yeah?"

"Swear to God." I made the sign of the cross. It looked more like a distress signal.

"That's the way I'd go. Hee-hee."

My house was the only one in the block without a light in a window. Saturday night for most of my neighbors meant hot cocoa and Parcheesi. I tipped the driver too much—entertainment tax for the Hawaiian floor show—and let myself in. The rooms had that shut-in smell, but I didn't have the energy to open any windows. I got the bottle down from the cupboard above the sink and filled a glass. I wasn't up to wrestling with an ice cube tray.

The telephone rang and went on ringing. Heading into the living room I barked my shin on a piece of furniture I didn't know I had. Later I found out I'd broken the skin and started bleeding, but against the pain in my head it was just a dull thud and somebody else's injury.

After a short interval the telephone rang again. This time I answered it.

"Where can you have been? I've been calling your office and your house since yesterday afternoon."

For a moment I wondered why Ronald Colman was calling me. I took a drink. The fog burned off.

"Too much story for the telephone, Mr. Lund. Where are you?"

"Back at the Marriott. I stayed at the Westin overnight in case the police wanted to talk to me again. I very much doubt they were satisfied with that ridiculous story you told me to tell them."

"Did they threaten to drag you downtown?"

"No."

"I wouldn't worry about it, then. Cops can't help looking and sounding suspicious; it's chronic, and probably terminal. The story should hold them until they run out of leads. How's Mr. Furlong?"

"Most lively. He ate an enormous breakfast. I begin to think he fares better for my absence. I say, are you all right? You sound badly used."

You had to hand it to the English, despite burning Washington. They had a phrase for everything. "I'll stop by in the morning and report."

He said very good and we wished each other a pleasant night.

After twenty minutes in the easy chair drinking I began to feel a little less like an extra in a George Romero film. That was one advantage of having lost blood; the alcohol didn't take so long to swim upstream. I got up and opened some windows. The super-stocked Plymouth was missing from next door: Cruise Night. With peace in the offing I flipped through the LPs I keep in a wooden crate from the General Beverage Company and put Eartha Kitt on the little tabletop stereo. "I Wanna Be Evil" shook some of the phantoms out of the corners.

The eight-day heirloom clock had run down. I found the key and wound it and set it. The click-clunk was louder than usual in the little silences between bars, as if each tilt of the balance wheel were taking the room further into the clock's past, all the way back to a sawdust-smelling shop in New

England, where European fingers, stained with walnut oil and hindered a little by needles of arthritis that would spread from knuckle to knuckle and eventually force the shop to close, assembled the materials to measure time generations beyond their own.

The headache was in remission and I was seeing single again. I was probably hungry—I.V. fare doesn't last much longer than Chinese—but I didn't feel like eating. Instead I read two chapters of a detective novel I didn't remember buying, about a New York investigator who specialized in child abuse cases. The tough-guy narrator described incidents of abuse with all the detailed slavering rapture of a serial killer recalling past dismemberments. It was the biggest waste of time since leeching and made me want to wash my hands with boric acid.

I gave it up and retired, feeling shot.

Twenty

I WOKE UP THE FIRST TIME around 2:00 A.M. when the kid next door thundered into his parents' driveway, gunned the Roadrunner's mill one last time, and killed the ignition. The noise rammed twin ice picks through my eardrums to the top of my spine.

I rolled out and stumbled into the bathroom, where in the mirror I saw that I'd bled through the bandage. Teeth bared, I peeled away the adhesive and gauze, used a Q-tip dipped in peroxide to clean the yellow-brown ooze from the stitches, and inspected young Dr. Ebersole's needlework. If the scar never healed and the hair didn't grow back I could always start a rock band. Or hire myself out to cure hiccoughs. I applied iodine, and when I climbed back down from the ceiling fixture I put on a fresh patch from the first-aid kit in the medicine cabinet. Then I swallowed a handful of Extra-Strength Bayers and went back to bed.

There's nothing like a little daylight to put a fresh face on your situation.

I had little enough of it because I'd set the alarm to shake me out around dawn. The theory was if Mary Ann Thaler came looking for me she would start as soon as she'd slept off Saturday night on the town, in which case I needed to hit the road early. But a little daylight will do when you're rested and the aching in your head has subsided to a half-pleasant hum. It was good to be in a position to suffer. The dead are immune.

I scrubbed off the animal smell, shaved with two lathers, brushed my hair back from the patch, and dressed, selecting a red sport shirt, tan slacks, argyles, brown belt and shoes, no jacket or tie. It was Sunday after all. While coffee was brewing I fried four eggs and slapped them between two pieces of bread with a slice of cheese. I was hungry now and I knew it. I filled my battered old Thermos, threw everything into a paper sack, and picked up the thick newspaper on my way out the door.

The good news was that when Friday's stormfront passed through it took the cloud cover with it, allowing the sun to come up as red as my shirt and as big as a hula hoop against a sky streaked with salmon and magenta. The bad news was it made the air hotter. The good news after that was the humidity had dropped. The bad news was that didn't matter because I didn't have a car to whisk me from one cool place to another. I can go on in this vein for as long as you'll let me.

At the end of eight blocks I spread out my breakfast on a bus stop bench and pulled apart the paper as I ate. The buses don't run Sundays, but I had time to kill. Even the church traffic wasn't due for two hours. There wasn't a car in motion on the street and the air smelled funny without carcinogens. For that one short stretch of the week, Detroit belonged to me and the merchants setting up in the Farmer's Market.

The newspaper was more of a mess than usual. The *News* and the *Free Press,* formerly the last two hotly competing big-city dailies in the country, had formed a joint operating agreement allowing them to pool their staffs on Sunday. The combined personnel tiptoed around each other like too many hens competing for the attentions of a single rooster. As a result, whatever news found its way into the columns did so by accident and somebody probably caught hell for it. Also there was a newspaper strike on, had been since the Ottoman Empire fell, and most of the bylines were unfamiliar. Not that anyone noticed in the era of CNN.

A piece in the front section reported that there was nothing new to report on the shooting death of Lynn Arsenault, prominent Allen Park architect, and a paragraph back by the obituaries mentioned that a search was under way for freelance photojournalist Nathan Millender, whose abandoned sailboat showed evidence of a possible tragedy. No connection was made between the two incidents.

By the time I got through the funnies, the city was coming to life around me by degrees. An '83 Pontiac held together with masking tape and Bondo stopped for the light and took off with a chatter of lifters, leaving behind a puddle of engine coolant like blue-green urine. The driver had that smoldered-out look of someone on his way home from the last blind pig to close. Two boys not much older than twelve, their Nike high-tops flapping like galoshes on their slender ankles, met in a doorway across the street and completed a business transaction in less time than it takes to describe it. A family of four in stiff blue serge and pressed pink cotton walked past me on their way to the church around the corner. Throw in an auto theft at gunpoint, a WILL WORK FOR FOOD sign, and a citizens' clean-up, fix-up, paint-up committee, and the neighborhood became the drop of teeming water from which an analyst might theorize the existence of a pond called Detroit.

Cruising cabs are scarce on Sunday, even when no one's been taking target practice on the drivers. I caught a break when one stopped at the far corner to let out another group of churchgoers and sprinted over there, carrying my empty Thermos and leaving the newspaper on the bench. One of the boys from the doorway swooped down on the sports section as I got in.

This time my driver was white, sixty pounds overweight, and shared with me his plan for city reform, which sounded a lot like *Mein Kampf* with grease guns and helicopters. I tuned him out and watched the dark dirty blossom of Motown open its petals to the sun.

My car was parked where I had left it Friday; the city towing services were as hard up for manpower as the police department. I paid the cabbie, tipped him a quarter for his political theory, managed not to get my toes run over when he drove away, and laid the ticket I found on my windshield to rest with the others in the glove compartment. I was still two shy of a bench warrant. The motor was slow to turn over after the inactivity and the change in the dew-point, but it caught, and I drove through awakening streets toward the Edsel Ford West and the Airport Marriott. The radio news had nothing new on either Arsenault or Millender.

Stuart Lund had exchanged his gray tailoring for eight yards of light blue summer worsted and tucked a pale silk scarf inside his open shirt collar. Aside from that he looked the same: yellow hair carefully combed, waxen blue eyes, black moustache trimmed neatly into an isosceles triangle. The cane with the heavy silver crook was working as hard to support him as it had during the week. I don't know why I'd expected him to be different. Maybe because I was, and it showed in his face when he opened the door.

"What on earth happened to you?"

"I was shot in the head."

"Be serious. What happened?"

"I don't know why I can't get anyone to believe me. This isn't Mr. Rogers' Neighborhood." I was feeling drained again. "Am I invited?"

"Certainly." He removed his mountain from my path.

The layout didn't seem so big now, but then everything looks smaller when you have come back from the other side. The door to the bedroom was ajar. I kept going and pushed it open the rest of the way. The lawyer lumbered along behind me.

It was nobody's idea of a sickroom. The carpet was deep and wine-colored, the chairs and sofa were overstuffed and upholstered in plush prints, color blowups of rural Michigan in all four seasons hung on the walls. The bed would have slept seven. Its proportions made the man in it seem small and fragile, but he didn't look any less healthy than he had when we'd met. He was sitting up in pale yellow silk pajamas with his knees elevated and a drawing board resting against his thighs. The bend of his back, the set of his angular features, and the swift positive motions of the hand holding the pencil all said he was completely absorbed in his sketch. Seen in profile, his sharp nose and chin made check marks against the bright window.

"One minute," he said without looking up.

I watched a DC-10 landing outside. From this side of the triple-paned window the howl of its engines sounded like a blender in the next room.

Furlong made one last slashing stroke across the paper, then slumped back against the pillows, exhausted. After a moment his eyes opened.

"Thank you for waiting. The energy comes in spurts, like water from a clogged pipe. I never know how long one will last, or how long I'll have to wait before the next. Or if there is a next."

"You're going to need a bigger sheet if you're drawing a portrait of Lund."

Lund hobbled in and dropped into one of the deep chairs. The floor shook. "Having an injury is hardly an excuse to be uncivil. I submit that Jay is suffering a good deal more than either of us, but he has yet to make an insulting remark."

"You're probably right." I dropped into the other chair: three sick men sitting around a thousand-buck-a-night suite. "You are right. I apologize."

He opened the hand holding the cane in a gesture of absolution.

"As for the rest," I said, "I'm not Jay Bell Furlong. If I were I wouldn't have gotten shot."

"Don't be so sure." The architect narrowed his eyes at the paper in front of him. "There. I suppose. Crude stuff without the proper materials, but not too shabby for a man at death's door." He turned the board around and held it up.

The drawing pinned to it was a simple arrangement of horizontal lines, contoured for a three-dimensional effect. It might have been done on a computer, if the computer's circuits were wired into Furlong's brain.

Lund expelled air. "Absolutely lovely, Jay. Your best work."

"Bullshit. Walker? You're the candid one."

"I can't draw a straight line."

"No one has since Leonardo. What does your gut say?"

"Nice. Ranch or country club?"

"Neither. Ha. It's my crypt."

"In that case it's swell."

"For God's sake." Lund looked from one face to the other.

"Mausoleum I suppose is the contemporary term," said

Furlong. "I prefer catafalque, but the imbeciles who take their education from those milk-faced pundits on the tube wouldn't know how to pronounce it. Jay Bell Furlong's last design, also his final resting place. Appropriate?"

Full face now, trying hard not to betray eagerness, a child's plea for praise, he displayed for the first time the signs of decomposition. His ears had begun to turn outward and his teeth showed large and white against his sunken cheeks, the protrusion of his skull. His pajamas hung like tinsel from the bones of his shoulders and slid back from the articulated stalks of his wrists. Cachexia, the oncologists call it. An animated skeleton.

I said, "I didn't peg you for an Ozymandias complex."

His eyebrows lifted, stretching the skin further. "A detective who reads Shelley. I'm impressed."

"Postal screwup. They sent me *The Atlantic* instead of *Guns and Ammo.*"

"Now you're getting as testy as Stuart. You must allow a dying man his prejudices. For the record, I'm not a mono-maniac. And I am. My first choice would be a plain pine box in bare earth. However, cemetery regulations require con-crete vaults, denying us the opportunity of returning to the land, which I might add is a right enjoyed by every other or-ganic thing on the planet."

"There's always cremation."

"Vernon Whiting was cremated. I'd have my ashes scat-tered, but I don't know what they did with his. What if we were to get mixed up? So. Since I'm to be vacuum-sealed for all eternity, I might as well go the whole nine yards, or six feet, or whatever. I've little enough to do with the time left me, and all the buildings this world really needs have al-ready been constructed. All we've done since Eisenhower is repeat ourselves. Why *not* a tomb? Let the world say Furlong was a narcissistic jerk on the grand scale. It will give it something to talk about besides the Super Bowl."

He laid the board facedown beside him on the bed. The speech seemed to have consumed his latest spurt of energy. Beads of sweat glittered on his forehead like condensation on crackle wrap. "Did I hear you say you were almost booked on the same one-way trip?"

"They can burn me if they like. I've smoked since I was seventeen." I shook out a Winston. "Does this suite come with aspirins?"

"Windy? And a glass of water."

"Vodka," I said. "They dissolve quicker in alcohol."

"So does your liver." But Lund was on his feet and lurching toward the bathroom.

The pills, or more likely it was the liquor, started working right away. I emptied the glass to make sure and set it on the floor. That simple movement brought the blood roaring to my head like the ocean in a conch shell. I lit up and poured smoke into it. "I was shot once before. I'm trying to keep it from becoming a habit."

Furlong said, "I take it you know who did it."

"If I knew for sure I'd have sicced the cops on him. Or maybe I wouldn't. The odds say whoever dusted me is the same one who dropped the hammer on Lynn Arsenault. If so it ties the shooter in with the frame on Lily Talbot. Did she ever come around, by the way?"

The architect shook his head. "Did you really think she would?"

"I try not to think. I'm a man of action. That's why I spent twenty-nine hours on my back at Detroit Receiving under the care of a woman who looks like Peter Sellers. Anyway, if I'm right and the gunny knows who ordered the frame, he's no good to us in jail."

"I think you'd better tell me everything. Stuart told me some of it, but I want to hear the works from the contractor on site."

I excused myself and went out to refill my glass. The story took some telling and I was bound to be thirsty by the end.

Twenty-one

PLANES LANDED, planes took off; close enough sometimes to drag their shadows across the window, but eerily without noise. The walls were made of two layers of brick with asbestos and cork sandwiched between. It was like watching a war movie at the drive-in with the speaker turned off.

I went all the way back to what I had learned in Randy Quarrels' studio and continued through Lily Talbot's gallery, the body in the garage, the scene at the dock with Nate Millender and Royce Grayling, my adventures in Millender's apartment, and the brains on the sail boom in his boat. Furlong showed no reaction when I mentioned the ten thousand dollars Arsenault had dropped into the Talbot till last year.

"Do you intend to confront this fellow Grayling?" he asked after a little silence.

I nodded and put out my cigarette. "With a tank if possible. Failing that, with information, when I have it. Starting with some clue as to why a trigger who hires himself out exclusively to local politicians should interest himself in the wedding plans of a famous architect."

"I can't help you there. He would have been in high school the last time I accepted any contract work in Michigan."

"That saves my asking. Up to now Grayling's job has been to prevent answers from reaching the people with the questions. He's not going to open up himself without some kind of pry bar. Also you don't go into lion country without learning everything you can about lions first."

"Are you afraid?"

"Terrified."

That surprised him. "Because of what happened to you?"

"No, killers scare me in general. When you're used to playing by civilization's rules, you work up strategies that don't apply when you come up against someone who doesn't. Touch football and tackle aren't the same game."

"So you're backing out."

"I didn't say that."

"Then I'll say it for all of us." Lund looked up from his sore foot. "Jay, I think you should drop this investigation."

"Oh, you do."

"I do. If anything happens to Walker, it's something you don't need on your conscience at this time."

Furlong looked at me. "He makes sense."

"Lawyers always do."

"What do you suggest?"

I sat back with my drink. "I'm out of choices. I had one in Allen Park and I chose not to come clean with the officers investigating Arsenault's murder. I had another one yesterday and I chose to stonewall my best pipeline into the Detroit Police Department in the Millender investigation. You don't get three. If I go to the cops now I risk losing my license for withholding evidence in two homicides. Also my freedom. That would give Grayling an excellent reason to finish what he started the day before yesterday. So I might as well stay the course. All he can do is kill me."

"You're certain he's the one who shot you?" There was color in the architect's cheeks. He was enjoying a fresh spurt.

"I sure hope so. I can't protect two fronts."

"You're outvoted, Windy."

"That's easy for both of you. I'll be the one to take the heat when Walker's estate sues Furlong's."

"I don't have an estate," I said. "Just a hospital bill."

"Send it to Stuart," said Furlong.

Lund twirled his cane between his fleshy palms. "I can't imagine anyone in these times paying someone a lot of money to keep his homosexuality a secret. But you say this Millender person was blackmailing Arsenault over a photograph of the two of them in bed together."

"I didn't. But Millender had the picture hidden away with a passbook recording monthly deposits of five thousand dollars each for as long as he'd had the book. Good freelance photographers with reputations make money, but not usually so consistently, or in equal amounts. Extortion has its own pattern, like burn marks in arson."

Furlong smiled at his attorney. "You're forgetting you're a liberated faggot, with a rich client who wouldn't care if you made love to hedgehogs as long as you did your job well. Vernon Whiting was a bigot who only started hiring blacks and promoting women when the government threatened to cancel all its construction contracts with Imminent Visions. If he found out Arsenault was a homosexual, he'd have thrown him out the door so hard he'd still be bouncing."

"That doesn't explain why Arsenault would still be paying Millender so long after Whiting's death," I said. "But it explains why, when Millender doctored the picture to break up your engagement to Lily Talbot, Arsenault didn't come forward and expose it as a phony. Whiting was still alive then. And it explains why he paid Millender later."

"To keep him from exposing Arsenault's role in inheritance fraud." Lund frowned. "But he'd have exposed himself as well. And you say Arsenault posed with Millender willingly."

"Exhibitionists come in all persuasions. The risk of getting caught is part of the thrill, but it doesn't mean they want to. That's what makes a mark a mark. As for getting caught himself, Millender had less to lose than Arsenault. He could turn state's evidence."

"So could Arsenault," Lund said.

"Same thing. A freelancer can always find work, no matter how nasty his legal record. Arsenault had partners. Clients. Public con—"

I stopped. The two men's heads came up. They watched me drink off the last of the vodka.

"Well, hell," I said then. "That bullet did some brain damage after all."

"Contracts," Furlong finished. He had his hands on his upraised knees and he was leaning on them. He looked like a gargoyle. "Grayling."

I played with the glass. "It explains plenty, if someone in government had a side deal going with Imminent Visions on a tax-funded project. You don't want Arsenault in a situation where he had to bargain with the authorities. Enter Royce, shooting."

"Kickbacks." Lund chewed his moustache. "That tired old story."

The architect picked up the drawing board and studied his sketch. Then he tore loose the sheet and crumpled it in one hand.

"Say that's why he was killed," he said, "and say Grayling killed Millender to shut him up. We still don't know who hired Millender to fake the picture in the first place. Blank sheet." He tossed the crumple into a corner.

"Not blank," I said. "Smudged. Millender was cagey, or Grayling wouldn't have spent all that time getting chummy with him in order to lure him out onto a big empty body of water where no one could see his death wasn't an accident. So why didn't he scrub that plan when I showed up? I could place him on the scene."

"He shot you later, don't forget," Lund offered.

"I'll try not to. He's got brass or he wouldn't have gone straight to Arsenault's office after killing him, acting as if he'd just arrived for an appointment. That spells pull. If I threw him to the cops now they wouldn't know whether to bust him or salute him. So for the time being I'll keep Royce Grayling for my own." I looked at Lund. "Are you hanging on to that room at the Westin like I said?"

"Yes. That man St. Thomas was most deferential, but I don't think his partner believed a word I said. I had the impression they'll come back."

"Coming back is what cops are best at, after doughnuts. When the routine comes up snake eyes, St. Thomas will check with Los Angeles. When the LAPD drops by Mr. Furlong's hospital room and finds nothing there but smog, he'll be back, minus the deference. Say thirty-six hours. But keep checking for messages in case he jumps procedure. When you talk to him again you might consider telling him some truth." I shrugged, and wished I hadn't. The aspirins were wearing off. "That death-bed wheeze has had its day. It's the will that's bringing in the relatives."

"I'll be fortunate if I don't end up disbarred."

"You're the one who wanted the wraps left on. But I

wouldn't sweat it. You're a lawyer. Mr. Furlong's a legend. Cops got enough to go up against when they go to court without that."

Furlong said, "You're neither of those things."

I tapped the patch on my head. "If they jail me I can always rip out the stitches. The food's better in the infirmary and they change the linen more often."

"Are you as tough as you make out?" The architect was smiling.

"Are you?"

"After all these years I can't say. When does the act become the reality?"

"I wrestle with that one all the time."

"And?"

I spread my hands and stood. The second drink had been a mistake. I put my hand on the back of the chair while the vertigo ran its course. I couldn't tell whether that was the act or the reality. "Thanks for the pills and the chaser. I'll let myself out."

"Where now?" Furlong had slumped back against the headboard.

"I thought I'd swing by the Westin and talk to your granddaughter and her husband."

"I can't believe it was either of them. She's an ideological fool and he's just an idiot. I'm leaving them a generous bequest, but only to keep them from getting their hands on the company."

"You never can tell, as Nate Millender said. I'd hate to stop another bullet only to find out later they were the culprits all along. After that I thought I'd head downtown and soak up some culture."

He opened his eyes. "Lily's gallery?"

"That ten grand of Arsenault's is worse than the headache. It keeps throbbing. Any message?"

"You already delivered it."

"You could call her. She's listed."

"I could."

His tone ended that line.

I didn't trust my balance yet. "As long as I'm butting in," I said.

"I'm listening."

"I talked to Buster."

"Buster?"

"Larry. Your brother."

"I know Larry's my brother. I haven't heard that nickname since before you were born. How is he?"

"Still sore at you."

"Buster never could let a grudge go."

I was steady on my feet now. I found his number in my notebook and went over and wrote it on the pad by the telephone. "Just in case."

His eyes followed my movements, like a dog's. "Windy told me you were once married, Walker. Any children?"

"No."

"Too bad. Mucking around in other people's lives seems to come naturally to you."

"It's my aptitude."

He said nothing. His eyes were closed and after a moment I realized he'd gone to sleep. I shook Stuart Lund's hand and told him again not to bother getting up to see me out.

Walking out the front door into the heat I put on the brakes. A two-hundred-pounder in a buff-and-brown Wayne County sheriff's uniform was standing by the Cutlass where I'd parked it against the curb.

"Sir, is this your car?"

I started to say no, but I had the key in my hand and he'd seen it. I turned it into a noncommittal grunt. I wondered who had put out the call, Thaler in Detroit or St. Thomas in Allen Park.

"This is a fifteen-minute zone," he said. "Loading and unloading only. I was about to have you towed."

I saw the airport division patch on his sleeve then. I thanked him for the warning and got in under the wheel. The keys were slippery in my palm.

Twenty-two

THE TRIP TO THE WESTIN was an unnecessary deposit of carbon into the ozone.

The granddaughter, a second-generation peacenik from Central Casting with horn-rims, one of those all-cotton dresses from India that wrinkle when it rains in Romania, and enough cruelty-free Herbal Essence in her straight black hair to shampoo a woolly mammoth, only wanted her part of the inheritance to outfit an expedition to find a scandal-free Democratic candidate for president; failing that, to save the rainforest. Her husband, a doughy-faced gladhander in plaid slacks and a nylon shirt with crossed golf clubs over the pocket, sold bowling balls. Jay Bell Furlong's towheaded great-grandson spent the whole time I was there shooting Martians on the TV screen. I welcomed them all to the city and left without asking a question.

The door to the Talbot Gallery was locked. A sign on the glass said it was closed Sundays. Leaning against the glass with my hands cupped around my eyes I saw a shadow moving around inside. I rapped and went on rapping until the shadow came my way.

When Jean Sternhagen saw me she flashed her too-wide

smile, pointed at the sign, and mouthed, "We're closed." She looked genuinely apologetic.

I mouthed something elaborate and unintelligible back. She shook her head, puzzle lines on her brow. I recited part of "Jabberwocky" and most of "Louie Louie" while she strained to read my lips. Finally she snapped back the lock and opened the door.

Works every time.

"I just need to talk to Miss Talbot," I said. "Is she around?"

The smile that had started to come back faltered and fell off her face. When that happened the lower half of her beveled countenance collapsed. She was dressed for grunt work in faded jeans worn almost through at one knee and a man's gray shirt with the tail out and the sleeves rolled up to her elbows. "She's at home today. What happened to your head?"

"I was shot."

She took in her breath. "Are you all right?"

"You believe I was shot?"

"Of course. Why would you make up a story like that?"

"Are you married?"

The smile flickered, then stayed on, supporting everything above it. Her mouth made sense then. It was the foundation of her face. "I'm living with someone."

"How big is he?"

"I didn't say it was a he."

"Ah."

"Don't jump to conclusions. I'm staying with Miz Talbot until I find a place near work. The commute from Ann Arbor was killing me, especially in winter."

"You must be pretty good friends."

"Not really. I think she just takes in strays." She reached up and patted her hair in back. She had it tied into a bun, but the corkscrew tendrils still framed her face. "Do you like Southern girls?"

"I was in love with Vivien Leigh."

"She was English."

"No kidding?"

She nodded, wrinkling her nose. "It's still a scandal back home, them Hollywood fellers picking a foreigner over the flowers of the Confederacy. You have the brownest eyes."

"Bambi's were browner. Are you in charge of the gallery's files?"

She stopped fiddling with her hair. "That's a curious question."

"They get curiouser. I wonder if I could get a look at the record of the Arsenault sale."

"Oh! Did you hear? It was the weirdest coincidence, just after you asked about him—Oh," she said again. Her face collapsed. "I forgot you're a detective. Are you investigating the murder?"

I stroked the door frame. "Can we go inside? I feel like a Jehovah's Witness."

"I can't show anyone the files without Miz Talbot's permission."

"Let's go inside. You can call her."

"Why don't you come back tomorrow and ask her yourself?"

I leaned against the frame and looked pale. It wasn't hard.

"Are you sure you're all right?" That antebellum accent came on like Pickett's Charge when she forgot herself.

"I just need a glass of water. Let's go inside."

"There's a counter down the street."

Pickett was back in the barn. I straightened. "I always heard you people were known for your hospitality."

"Yes, and what did it get us? Atlanta burned to the ground and a Pizza Hut in Richmond."

"Tomorrow's too late. I have an impatient client. Can you give me Miss Talbot's address?"

"I'm sure she wouldn't want me to do that." She tapped her fingers on the edge of the door. "She lives in Bloomfield Hills. Forty-four-fifty Bonnymeadow Drive."

"Sounds cushy."

"Better than what I had in Ann Arbor."

"When are you there?"

She'd started to close the door. "Why? I don't have any files you'd be interested in."

"I don't wear a shoulder holster all the time."

She got another smile going on the other side of the plate glass.

Detroit keeps stacking rich suburbs on top of rich suburbs. A long time ago, before the Japanese stopped playing with plastic hula girls and started putting wheels on axles, there was just Grosse Pointe: built slab by marble slab out of materials imported from the same Old World that had spawned the Lelands, Fords, Chryslers, Dodges, and Durants who commissioned the work. When that gate slammed shut, the postwar money built Birmingham: low sprawling brick ranches on green felt lawns, less than five minutes by Mercedes from the nearest beauty parlor and power mower outlet. When the riots came along to drive the third generation farther north and west, Bloomfield Hills sprang up just like its name: bursts of aluminum-sided colonials and four-star restaurants and wallet-size shopping centers, spraying the rolling green country in tints of mauve, pink, ecru, and taupe, the anemic smothered spectrum of the landed gentry. Each new community is more understated than the one that preceded it, the materials and workmanship costlier but less elaborate. The next suburb to follow will be twice as wealthy and damn near invisible.

Lily Talbot's house was modest by local standards, a single-story brickfront with a shallow roof peak and two cozy wings covered with stained cedar siding. Its one showy feature, an entryway made entirely of leaded glass, formed an arch from foundation to eaves with a red oak front door set into it like a ruby in a diamond horseshoe pin. You couldn't admire it in direct sunlight without sacrificing both retinas.

The second time I rang the bell, the gallery owner's voice drifted my way from somewhere behind the house.

"I'm on the deck."

A flagstone path trod deep into the lawn led around back. I passed a bed of blue and red flowers growing in crushed limestone, descended a staircase made of railroad ties studded into a steep grassy slope, and stood at last on a plank platform twenty feet long by fifteen wide, with a twelve-foot fence erected around it for privacy. The construction was new and still smelled of sawn wood and the dope they treat it with to repel weather. Sunlight lay on the planks like a slice of gold warmed by hand.

"Did you bring the sketches?"

She was stretched on her back on a flowered chaise longue in a pale blue bikini bottom and nothing else. She had an athletic build but not masculine, not at all; the long muscles in her arms and legs were sheathed in smooth flesh not too deeply tanned, but not mottled like a redhead's either. It was the first indication I'd had that her short hair had been colored. She had nice breasts: not large, but not so small she'd ever be mistaken for a boy. Her eyes were invisible behind white plastic goggles.

"I hope you won't mind working out here," she said. "It *is* Sunday, and I haven't seen the sun in a week."

"It's the same color it's always been."

She jumped, snatched off the goggles, saw me, and hooked up a towel to cover her upper half. Her face flushed deeply under the tan.

"I thought you were an artist."

"A friendly artist," I said.

"They spend most of their time looking at nudes. They're like doctors."

"I knew I was in the wrong business."

"Would you mind turning your back while I put something on?"

I turned. "Nice deck. Any planes ever land here looking for City Airport?"

"What did you expect, a garret?" Fabric rustled.

"I heard someone say recently the arts are in eclipse."

"You'd be surprised what you can afford when you have no interests apart from work and home. Or rather what debts you're willing to assume. You can turn around now."

She had on a blue silk kimono tied with a sash and cork-soled sandals on her slim bare feet. The outfit didn't make her any more repulsive. My opinion of Furlong's taste kept going up.

"Jean told you where to find me, didn't she?"

"Don't be too hard on her. Whatever you told her before took. She stonewalled me at the gallery."

"We didn't discuss you at all."

"Now I'm hurt."

She glanced at her wrist, but she wasn't wearing a watch. "I'm expecting a sculptor any minute. I'm commissioning a statue for the gallery's tenth anniversary next year. He's Croatian. Strangers make him suspicious."

"We have that emotion in common." I put my hands in my pockets.

"What do you want?"

"A vacation. A comfortable old age. Cable. Answers to some questions. Not necessarily in that order. I guess you heard about Arsenault."

"Did you kill him? Is that how you got that?" She pointed at my bandaged head.

"I fell off my deck." I tapped a Winston out of the pack and put it between my lips, but I didn't light it. "Yeah, I killed him. I didn't like his taste in paintings."

"Neither did I. I'm sick to death of Lautrec and Turner and Monet and Manet."

"I thought they were one guy," I said. "The last two."

"So do the jokers who buy them and hang them in their offices downtown. There are other movements besides Impressionism, but try telling that to our young urban professional bootlickers. Do the police know you're interfering in a homicide investigation?"

"Am I?"

"You didn't come here to cop a peek at my tits."

The cigarette tasted like a tongue depressor. I poked it back into the pack. "I'm no Sherlock," I said. "Neither was Holmes. Any reasonably honest police force can solve the murders that get solved, without help from the bleachers. But the system's a crocodile, with a croc's table manners. While it's busy chewing up leads and alibis and witnesses and clues a lot of little details get stuck between its teeth. Think of me as one of those little birds that walk around inside the crocodile's mouth and pick out the shreds."

"Attractive image."

"It keeps me off chimneys. Anyway, the shred I picked

out this time is a question: Who put Arsenault up to his part in the frame?"

"What makes you think his murder has anything to do with that?"

"No reason, except he spent the eight years since it happened not murdered. Then I came along and wham."

"If I knew who was behind that picture, I'd be living an idle existence as the wife of a millionaire architect. Soon to be a rich widow."

"Looks like you've done okay without him."

"It was a long hard haul, and I made it without any help from anybody. You know something? I'm glad it happened. I'd rather be who I am and unknown than world-famous as Mrs. Jay Bell Furlong."

"That doesn't answer my question."

She had a tall glass on the low table next to the chaise. She picked it up, sipped, made a face, and put it back down. Whatever was in it, the ice cubes had melted and diluted it. "I told you at the gallery everything I know. I'm happy with the way things turned out, but I'm not grateful. If you think I'm shielding the person responsible, you must have me confused with Mother Teresa."

"Not in that outfit. There are hundreds of art galleries listed in the Yellow Pages. When it came time to decorate his office, Arsenault chose yours. Why?"

"The Talbot has a reputation for quality and integrity."

"So does General Motors. But only an idiot pays sticker prices."

"Meaning?"

"Arsenault may have licked his way to the top of the boot, but he didn't stay there by paying the full market amount for art that he could have saved a bundle on buying in bulk; and from someone with good reason to hate his guts, yet. What else did he get for his ten grand?"

She slugged me.

It took me by surprise. I'd braced myself for a good old-fashioned smack, but a full-scale punch to the button is a different movement altogether. I barely managed to turn my head in time to catch it on the ear. It was the side opposite the bandage or I'd have gone down. As it was, a black fish-net drew tight around my eyeballs and I had to rely on instinct over aim when I hooked a foot behind her ankle and pulled. She went down in a burst of blue silk and flashing legs. One sandal went flying. I spread my feet and waited for the worst.

She laughed.

Not a snicker. Not a pep-squad giggle. She rolled half over on her side, drew in her knees, and guffawed like a Teamster. I saw her fillings.

It wasn't hysteria. It was infectious as hell. I caught up with her, leaning on the chaise, and kept up until it looked like we were both going to hurt ourselves. Then I said, "All right, all right," and stuck out a hand.

She grasped it, got her feet under her, and sprang up. She moved so quickly I backpedaled in case she wanted to try for the other ear. But she took back her hand and fumbled for the tie to her kimono, breathing heavily. She looked around for her other sandal.

"It shot over the fence," I said. "Do the Lions know about you?"

"You should've seen the look on your face. I bet you wet your pants." She used a corner of the robe to wipe her eyes. "My father wanted a boy so badly he had the hockey equipment all bought. He showed me how to throw a left hook that kept me a virgin through high school."

"You must've been as popular as Latin."

She laughed again, a short gush, apropos nothing. "Oh, my side. I've been working eighty hours a week getting ready for an anniversary gala that's eighteen months away. I'd hire more help, but the kids I can afford to employ part time all want to be Andy Warhol. They wouldn't touch a broom if I tied a cheeseburger to it. It's just me and Jean. Also I'm waiting for a bank decision on an expansion loan. It was either you or the branch manager. I need that loan."

"You could mug someone."

"Did I hurt your head?"

"Woman's prerogative." I stopped fooling with the bandage and went for that cigarette. "How's your right cross?"

"Not as good as my uppercut, but I won't throw that either. To answer your question, Arsenault wanted twenty prints: Five Lautrecs, three Gauguins, one Monet and one Manet, two Van Goghs—"

"I thought it was Van Gock."

"Two Van *Go*s, four Turners, four Gruns. He didn't ask for anything else and I didn't offer it. I did offer him the standard break on volume. He didn't want to hear about it."

"Which fist did you offer it to him in?"

She took off the other sandal and tossed it after its mate. She was almost short in her bare feet. Standing next to Furlong she would have looked like a young girl. "I could have been more cordial. I wasn't in a financial position to be nasty. And I suppose I had come to the conclusion by then that success on one's own terms is worth more than a wedding spread in *People*. Anyway, my conscience was clear. It still is. Arsenault could have resold the prints the next day for a profit. By now their value has increased ten percent."

"You weren't suspicious?"

"I was curious, but not enough to ask questions that might blow a sale I needed. I've asked them of myself, and I've come up with an answer. I think he came to atone."

"For the picture?"

"For everything. His conscience wasn't clear."

"It came cheap," I said. "He cost you millions."

"That was just a start. If you'd asked me straight out instead of going to Jean behind my back, I'd have told you he asked for estimates to commission high-quality prints to be displayed in all of Imminent Visions' offices nationwide and in its show houses on the West Coast. We were discussing a half-million-dollar order."

"How far did it get?"

"It was still going on when he—died. His secretary was supposed to call me last week with his choices from the catalogue I sent. Obviously she was distracted by her employer's murder."

I flicked ashes on the redwood boards at my feet. "He never brought up your past association?"

"Never. I wasn't going to mention it if he didn't. In retrospect, it was his whole attitude that makes me think he felt guilty. He stammered and seemed unsure of himself. Not at all what you'd expect in a high-powered young shark. I think"—she pulled her robe closer and tightened the sash—"well, now I'm projecting."

"Projecting what?"

"What happened to him, his murder. Projecting it onto his behavior at the gallery. No, damn it, I'm not either. I thought the same thing at the time."

I waited while she took another hit from the watery stuff in her glass.

"All the time he was in the gallery he reminded me of someone who was finally getting around to something he'd been putting off for a long time. It seemed to explain why he didn't want to take time discussing a discount. Like he was cleaning out his desk."

"Getting his affairs in order?"

The doorbell rang. The chimes drifted back toward us like something happening in someone else's life. She tugged down the kimono.

"That will be my sculptor. Will you leave quietly, or do I have to rough you up some more?"

I held up my palms.

"How is Jay?"

I lowered them. "Why don't you ask him yourself? He's still at the Marriott."

"I started to go see him," she said. "I had my car keys in my hand. I didn't use them. I couldn't think of anything to say when I got there."

"That's what hello is for."

"So then he says hello back. Then what?"

"The heat. The Tigers. The flight from California. Who played Dobie Gillis' father. What do I look like, the president of a singles club? Punt."

The doorbell rang again. It was part of her life now. She picked up her towel and folded it.

"This bird thing," she said. "What happens if the crocodile closes its mouth?"

"I was a little slow getting my head out the last time."

Twenty-three

BARRY STACKPOLE WAS WORKING the sabbath at the cable station on Southfield Road, editing videotape with the aid of two monitors in a small room packed with electronic gizmos and strange life forms mutating in the bottoms of polystyrene cups. I found him perched on a turning stool with both hands occupied and a ham-and-cheese sandwich clamped between his teeth.

"Be wiv oo inamint," he said through the ham and cheese.

"A minute's all I need." I transferred a stack of scripts bound with colored construction paper from a plastic scoop chair to the floor and sat down. My back started sweating as soon as it touched the plastic. Most commercial buildings don't run their air conditioners weekends.

Barry had on pleated khaki slacks and an open-weave shirt that showed the lean musculature in his chest. His empty pantsleg dangled off the end of the stump. The prosthesis leaned in a corner, its harness hanging and a blue-and-white-striped Reebok laced on its fiberglass foot.

With a triumphant grunt, he punched a button, snapped a dial, and took the sandwich from his mouth—all but one bite, which he swallowed and chased with whole milk from a tall glass.

"I'm brilliant," he said, leaning back against the console on the other side. "Useless to deny it. What do you think?"

"What do I think of what?" I was looking at freeze-frames on the monitors. The one on the right showed a middle-aged man hemmed in by reporters and camera operators on the steps of the City-County Building. The one on the left showed a different middle-aged man flanked by two men half his age crossing a sidewalk.

"You need to keep up on current local events. Don't you know the guy on the right?"

I looked again at the man on the steps. "Candidate for city gaming commissioner. I saw his picture in the paper this morning."

"Just a second." He clattered some keys on the computer board in front of him. The other monitor zoomed in past the shoulder of the middle-aged man on the sidewalk and closed in on the face of one of the younger men with him. "Now what do you see?"

I looked from one monitor to the other. The family resemblance was hard to miss. "Father and son."

"Uh-uh. The footage on the left is historical, thirty years old. It's the same guy. Look at this." He clattered some more keys. The young man moved out of the frame and I got a closer look at the older man on the sidewalk.

"Sam Lucy. I'll be damned. Hello, Sam. I thought you were dead."

"You know he is. I got this last week from the FBI under Freedom of Information. Sixteen seconds out of four hours shot outside the Flamingo in Vegas, where Lucy attended a summit conference with the heads of the five biggest mob families in America under Johnson. What do you suppose our would-be casino watchdog was doing hanging all over dear old Sammy the Hammer back when the world was young?"

"Conducting his own independent investigation, no doubt."

"Oh, no doubt." He hit two keys simultaneously. Both screens went dark. You wouldn't have known from the way he manipulated his fingers that Barry was missing two. He was luckier than Hurricane Bob Lester, but more sensitive about the condition, and wore a white cotton glove on the injured hand in public. "I got a tip from an old snitch I thought was long dead. He's running a used car lot in Tecumseh and wants me to plug it on the air. What he doesn't know is I'd buy out his stock for something half this good."

"When do you go to air?"

"My producer would want me to wait for the August sweeps, but that's like asking to get scooped. Worse, city council may reject his appointment on whatever grounds, in which case the story turns into a pumpkin. We go tomorrow. This could mean an Emmy *and* a Pulitzer."

"Congratulations."

"I went into mourning when the old mayor stepped down. I thought it was the end of the gravy train for thug-spotters like me. Then the new gang rammed casino gambling through. The station signed me to a new five-year contract the day after the election."

He spun to face me. He had all his hair and it was still sandy. That color never changes until it turns white overnight. He was lucky enough to fit into his old uniform if I hadn't helped him burn it in a stateside ritual. "What's with the head?" he asked. "Trust me, the little light goes off when you slam the refrigerator door."

"This from a man with a metal plate under his scalp." I

leaned forward and placed a paper bag in his lap. Inside the bag were two smaller bags. Inside each of them was a pint bottle of Haig & Haig.

He took a look, then swiveled and stood the package on top of one of the VCRs. "I do like a man who pays his debts. Was Randy Quarrels the photographer you were looking for?"

"No, but he gave me the name of the one who was."

"Anything for me?"

"Not yet."

He smiled his matinee idol's smile. The dynamite charge that had blown him and his car to pieces had denied Hollywood a younger, taller Robert Redford. He was humming. It took me a couple of bars to identify the tune: "Who's Zoomin' Who?"

"Whom," I corrected.

"Dead word. Like *incarnadine*." He went on humming.

"When did I ever hold out on you?"

"Let's see; when was the last time you asked that question?"

"I don't look good on camera, Barry. I come off like a lox."

"We can computer-scramble your face, give you a falsetto."

"I get to be a state-of-the-art Deep Throat?"

He stopped smiling.

"There never was a Deep Throat. Guys like Woodward and Bernstein use that saw to cover up sloppy investigative work. A quote's worthless without a source."

Sore point. I changed the subject. "I may owe you another pint before I leave."

He shook his head. "Spoiling the sponsors with too much good whiskey is counterproductive, and I can't afford to keep the stuff around. Gimme a lead."

"How many mikes does this room have?"

He stretched an arm and threw a knife switch. "Main breaker," he said. "The walls are soundproof."

"You've got to sit on it until I say go."

He waved his good hand.

"Jay Bell Furlong."

"He dead yet?"

"Not yet. And not in California. He's in town."

"I should've guessed. He was taking longer to die than *Saturday Night Live.*"

"He's dying all right, but on his clock." I spelled it out: the job, the Arsenault kill, Nate Millender's disappearance, my shooting in his apartment. I held one thing back for use later. Barry remembered his sandwich and finished it while I spoke.

"You're even luckier than I was," he said over his milk. "How's your vision?"

"I've been seeing single all day."

"Enjoy it while you can." He sucked mustard off his index finger. "This starts to sound like *King Lear.* How big is the inheritance?"

"It can't be small. 'How much' isn't in his vocabulary."

"What's Millender's physical description?"

"Why?"

"Detectives. Jesus. Because I asked."

I ran it for him. He threw the breaker back on and played the computer keyboard with his left hand, boogie-woogie style. The white console was on a swivel. He turned it my way. "That him?"

I stared at the bilious green letters.

FLATROCK 6/16

COMPLAINANT JULIUS MELROSE NO MIDDLE DOB 4/9/60 UN-EMPLOYED 4102 EMPIRE TAYLOR REPORT DECEASED FOUND

WEST BANK DETROIT RIVER 1100 6/15 WELL DEVELOPED
MALE CAUCASIAN BLONDE/BLUE EARLY THIRTIES 5 FEET 5
130 MOLE UPPER LEFT ARM SCAR ONE CENTIMETER RIGHT
FOREHEAD COAGULATED BLOOD BONE SPLINTERS BACK OF
HEAD BELOW CROWN BELLY DISTENDED WHITE SHORTS NO
OTHER CLOTHING

He'd lost his long-billed fisherman's cap, probably when
the sail boom struck him from behind.

I sat back. "You're patched into the police computer?"

"Just the blotter. The stuff on the upper floors has alarms
and tracers hooked up to the access codes. The kid who
empties the wastebaskets here did the hacking for me. He
starts at Redford High this fall."

"You wonder why he'd bother."

"The squeal came over this morning. I took note. You
never know what might connect to the Right and Honorable
Exalted Paterfamilias of Palermo and Vegas. I've been following the Arsenault burn too. The Feds and RICO have
busted up the old gang pretty good, but just when you think
they're six feet under they bounce back up on their pointy
alligator shoes and kick you in the boccie balls."

"Colorful."

"Thank you. I used it last week."

"The boccie balls part is a little much."

"Fuck you. Halberstam loved it."

"If it is Millender—and it sounds like him right down to
the wardrobe—you can count them out this time."

"Could be they're taking on indy work. They've had a
bad decade."

"That's the trouble with you mob watchers. You see guys
in fedoras under every bed. They don't hold exclusive fran-
chise on murder for hire."

"You sound like a man with a hole card."

"I didn't tell you about Millender's close chum," I said. "The light of his last days."

He scratched the end of his stump. "I'm all ears and a yard wide."

"Royce Grayling."

He blinked. Then he beamed all over.

I crossed my legs. "Thought you'd like it."

"God, I love my job. I'd give my remaining leg to keep it forever. Who needs two when you've got floppy disks? R–O–Y–C–E G–R–A–Y–L–I–N–G." He punched each letter on the board as he recited it. "Speak to me, Silicone Valley."

It spoke.

And spoke.

Twenty-four

GRAYLING ROYCE BORN TADEUS ROSCOE GRODNO HAMTRAMCK MI 3/31/49

"Tadeus?" I asked.

Barry grunted. "Hebrew, with a Polish spin. Thaddeus was one of the Twelve Apostles. Saint Jude to you."

"I didn't know you were up on the New Testament."

"I burned my share of candles at St. Boniface when I was twelve."

"He's older than he looks."

"These sons of bitches age on a sliding scale. Most of them ferment twice as fast as the rest of us. The ones that don't must like what they're doing."

"He seemed pretty contented."

"Psychopath," he said. "The world's largest minority."

GRADUATED UNIVERSITY OF DETROIT BA BUSINESS/ROMANCE LANGUAGES 4/10/70 HARVARD UNIVERSITY MA POLITICAL SCIENCE 6/11/76 SERVICE RECORD 101ST AIRBORNE RANGERS VIETNAM 1970–71 CAMBODIA 1972 PURPLE

HEART BEN SUC 9/23/71 PURPLE HEART PHNOM PENH 1/2/72
BRONZE STAR KAMPUCHEA 10/15/72

I said, "I'm surprised we didn't see him over there."
"Who would, in the glare from all that metal?"

CIVILIAN AWARDS AND HONORS FIRST RUNNER UP NATIONAL
PISTOL CHAMPIONSHIP OUTDOOR CONVENTIONAL 1976 FIRST
PLACE STANDARD PISTOL US NRA INTERNATIONAL SHOOTING
CHAMPIONSHIP 1978 TIE FIRST PLACE NATIONAL INDOOR
RIFLE CHAMPIONSHIP 1982 POLISH AMERICAN CITIZEN OF
THE YEAR POLISH CONSTITUTION CELEBRATION BELLE ISLE
DETROIT MI 1986 MARRIED DAWN MARIE ZAEMMLER
6/19/82 DIVORCED 2/10/84 NO CHILDREN

"She probably came out and asked him what he did when
he wasn't competing in shooting matches and kissing Polish
babies," Barry said.
"At least he didn't breed."

EMPLOYMENT SPECIAL CONSULTANT WAYNE COUNTY BOARD OF
SUPERVISORS 1977–81 FIELD AGENT OAKLAND COUNTY PLAN-
NING COMMISSION 1981–83 MANAGER IROQUOIS HEIGHTS CITY
PROSECUTORS OFFICE 1984 CURRENTLY ATTACHED CITY OF DE-
TROIT NO TITLE OR OFFICE DUTIES UNSPECIFIED

An address was listed in Detroit. I asked Barry if that was
still current.
"As of January when I updated the file. He doesn't camp
around as much as he used to. Why should he? He's got a
steady gig."

POLICE RECORD NONE

"Not even a traffic ticket," I said.

"Writing him up would be like asking for permanent assignment to the war zone."

"So far he's cleaner than me."

"Dresses better, too. Would you like to see this month's American Express bill?"

"Not unless he charges his ammunition."

"This file's just for the suckers. Buckle up."

He entered a new code. The details of Royce Grayling's exemplary public life dropped from the screen. The cursor darted to the upper left corner, gunned its motor twice, and towed out a new string of words.

GRAYLING ROYCE A/K/A SUICIDE SAM

I looked at Barry, who gave me his square grin.

"I did the scutwork on this," he said. "There's no program for it at Egghead Software."

The cursor vamped. My pulse kept time with it, thumping in my stitches. After two seconds the file kicked in.

CLEMENTS E EDWARD WAYNE COUNTY TREASURERS OFFICE SHOT TO DEATH VACATION HOME FORD LAKE 11/18/78 WC SHERIFFS OFFICE RULED HUNTING RELATED NO SUSPECTS SEE FILE
INGRAM ADELAID NO MIDDLE COMPTROLLER GILLIAM CONSTRUCTION COMPANY WIXOM MI REPORTED MISSING 2/25/82 CASE OPEN SEE FILE
GALLOWAY IAN MICHAEL OAKLAND COUNTY PLANNING COMMISSIONER DECEASED FARMINGTON HILLS MI HOME 8/1/82 BROKEN VERTEBRAE SEVERED SPINAL CORD OC CORONER RULED DEATH BY MISADVENTURE SEE FILE

"Those stairs are murder," I said.

"Split-level house," said Barry. "Fell about six inches onto a carpet."

BOGARDUS GORDON WALLACE IROQUOIS HEIGHTS MI CITY COUNCILMAN SHOT TO DEATH IROQUOIS HEIGHTS 7/12/84 TWO BULLETS UPPER LEFT THORAX NO WEAPON ON PREMISES IMPLICATED PHOENIX BUILDING & REALTY KICKBACK CONSPIRACY OC CORONER RULED SUICIDE SEE FILE

I said, "Somebody told me about that one."

Barry flicked another key, blanking out the screen. "It stank up the place even in the Heights, not the freshest-smelling six square miles this side of the sulphur works. That's why Grayling left there after less than a year."

"Anything else?"

"Not lately. He's been on his Sunday behavior since coming to the big city."

"Until now."

"Assuming it's not just coincidence that people in delicate positions tend to drop off like moths wherever he lands, the killing's only part of it. The smallest part. Whether by threats or just his own not-inconsiderable presence, he gets things done without leaving a paper trail for the muckrakers to follow. In any democratic government there's always a place for the Graylings."

"What are you, a Communist?"

"I'm an alcoholic. The world's second largest minority."

"How did you pick up on him?"

"I said he never leaves a *paper* trail. The body count is something else. This is all speculation based on the law of averages. He could sue me out of my Dutch leg just for showing you this file."

"What did he do in Nam besides get decorated?"

"Sniper. Westmoreland hung a bronze star on him for picking off a hundred and eighteen Cong and NVA regulars over a thirty-six-hour period."

"What about the Purple Hearts?"

"The first was nothing, a piece of shrapnel in the web of his left hand from an NVA mine that blew his company commander into Reese's Pieces on the road at Ben Suc. That's a maybe; it was raining hard and nobody was around to report what happened but Specialist First Class Grayling. The second one was a bullet in the back."

"Not unusual. I spent my whole tour looking for a skirmish line."

"I Corps wasn't so sure. There was some evidence that it was fired by one of his fellow Rangers; but they'll still be sorting out the fragging incidents from legitimate combat casualties when the next war has come and gone, so the hell with that. Anyway the slug banked off a tree or something and went in all out of shape, plowing up muscle tissue and ligaments. He was laid up in Saigon for six months."

"Any permanent damage?"

"He'll be a little slow turning to his left."

"Good to know."

He killed the monitor.

"Don't let him draw you into a firefight, Amos. He isn't an ape with a shotgun and a comic accent. He's a Washington-class closer. They never leave witnesses."

"He can be taken," I said. "Neglecting to drop the gun at the Bogardus kill was Mickey Mouse. Either he slipped up or he was hot-dogging, telling God and everyone he didn't have to bother making it look like suicide to get a verdict. Either way it's a flaw in the wall."

"He'll tip you over with one hand on his way to his next big hit."

I met his flat sad journalist's eyes. "Just in case you're right, don't buy it when you hear I clocked myself."

"I'd never buy that. You hang on like a weed." He sat back. "You're right about one thing. Grayling was definitely thumbing his nose at the Iroquois Heights City Prosecutor's office. Well, you've met Cecil Fish."

"Fish is a cut-rate corrupter, strictly Kmart. Bribes in the Heights barely pass minimum wage. No wonder Grayling took a powder."

"His pattern's changing," Barry said. "Not counting the Ingram woman, who disappeared somewhere between her house and the bus stop, all of the victims up through Bogardus died at home, in private. No eyewitnesses and very little chance of any. Okay, so maybe Allen Park's another exception. Arsenault buys it at work, in a semiprivate garage where anyone might happen along. A little buzz now and then keeps you from going stale. But then Millender dies in an open craft on one of the busiest stretches of water in North America. If those are Grayling's, he's losing caution. Gone rogue."

"I said it was a flaw."

"That's good for you if it means he's forgotten how to cover his ass; bad for you if you're counting on the standard inhibitions to protect you. He might shoot you at the airport or cut your heart out in Cadillac Square in the middle of the morning rush hour. Mad dogs don't heel."

"It's a thought."

"While you're thinking it, here's another one."

I waited. He'd pulled over his artificial leg by its harness and was tugging up his trousers to strap it on.

"Right now, chances are he's sitting in front of a computer somewhere reading about you."

* * *

It's bothersome not knowing when was the last time you ate.

I remembered vaguely eating a fried-egg sandwich on a bus stop bench, but that was as gone from my system as the precise details. Barry's ham and cheese, which characteristically he had not offered to split with me, had reminded me how empty my stomach was; and with nothing there for my blood to work on it went straight to the gash in my temple. The hammering drowned out the big 455 under the Cutlass's hood. I swung into the first driveway that promised food.

It belonged to a bar and grill, a squat building with an electric sign on the roof and gum wrappers and crumpled cigarette packages growing in a strip of earth with a painted rock border along the path to the front door. I must have driven past the place a hundred times and never noticed it. It had just opened for the day—the Sunday blue laws were in effect—but there were already a half-dozen cars parked in the lot.

Inside was a moist dark cave hollowed out of stucco. The atmosphere was a kind of mulch of sour mash, hot grease, and old nosebleeds. There were booths along the wall with napkin dispensers and laminated menus in clips, but no takers; the regulars, piles of collapsed protoplasm in clothes that made no statement, preferred the stools at the bar. I took one of the booths, inconveniencing the bartender, who made his way over finally to take my order. He was one of those numbers who took a size 6 hat, 32 long jacket, and fifty-inch trousers, shaped like a water balloon.

"Would you have any aspirins?" I asked.

"This ain't no Rexall counter."

"My mistake."

I ate a burger with a thick slice of raw onion to kill the taste of last week's lard, drank two Stroh's to put the snap back into a plate of fries, and watched the lowlights of yesterday's Tigers game on the TV mounted under the ceiling. A round table discussion followed onscreen, involving two ancient athletes, a sportscaster who combed his hair with Valvolene, and a print journalist with an advanced case of the rummy shakes. Ostensibly they were making predictions about the remainder of the season, but since the sound was off they might have been debating the works of Oscar Wilde. When at the end of ten minutes I found myself still watching their lips move, I laid down a couple of bills and headed for the door. One more case like this one and I'd have my own stool.

"Hey!"

I looked at the bartender. He threw me a small bottle.

It was glass with a metal screw-off cap. There were two senile-looking aspirins inside. It must have been twenty years old.

"Are they safe to take?"

The bartender grinned. He had a cleft lip. "What do you care?"

I went back to the table, placed another bill on top of the others, and left.

The aspirins tasted like corn plasters, but they did the trick. Maybe it was the food. The throbbing in my head dulled to a half-pleasant hum, I was ready for the next item on the agenda. I went home to snooze.

Head injuries are counterproductive to detective work. They take the edge off that tickle at the base of the brain that lets you know the sky's about to cave in.

I felt it just as I entered the kitchen through the side door from the garage. My hand was still on the knob. I tore it back open. The hoarse shout came in the same instant.

"Freeze or die!"

Twenty-five

I FROZE. As choices go it was a no-brainer.

Officer Redburn of the Allen Park Police Department looked like a lethal infant behind the oily blue barrel of his 9mm Glock. He was all round eyes and Dennis the Menace cowlick blocking the doorway to the living room. Everything about him said he was scared to his socks.

I couldn't see any way to put a good spin on that combination.

"Cool your jets, Duane. Can't you see the man isn't carrying?"

I looked at Sergeant St. Thomas seated in the breakfast nook. He was wearing the same three-piece suit he'd had on at the scene of Lynn Arsenault's murder. His silver-framed glasses glittered against his blue-black skin. A department-issue .38 Chief's Special revolver lay on the table in front of him with the city seal on the grip. He wasn't in any hurry to pick it up. He would go on not being in a hurry until I did something rash. Then I'd have a .38 slug in me before Redburn squeezed off his automatic. Some things you just know.

There was a moment when nothing moved. I could hear the air in the room. Then the Glock came down.

I relaxed my arms. " 'Freeze or die'?"

"Duane has every episode of *NYPD Blue* on tape. He looks a little like a young Dennis Franz, don't you think?"

"That depends on whether he considers it a compliment."

"With me it was *Dragnet*. The one in black-and-white, not the other. Hats and cigarettes. How about you?"

"M Squad."

The sergeant's forehead wrinkled. "The one with the hippies?"

"That was *Mod Squad*. This one had Lee Marvin."

"He drove that big black Ford with tailfins. I remember. You're older than you look."

"Thanks. Did the deadbolt on the front door give you any trouble?"

"We came in through a window. It was too hot to wait outside."

"I guess it would be stupid to ask if you've got paper."

"The only stupid questions are the ones that don't get asked. Like where all the judges go on Sunday." He drew a thick No. 10 envelope from his inside breast pocket and flipped it onto the table.

I picked it up and slid out the search warrant. "It's not that I don't trust you," I said. "I've been fooled before by brochures from the Fruit of the Month Club."

"I prefer mine canned."

The Latin looked genuine. I stuck the document back in the envelope and returned it. He put it away, rolled over on one hip, and holstered the revolver. He had a nickel-plated automatic in a speed rig under his left arm for stopping heavy trucks.

"Nice neighborhood," he said. "Those senior citizens take good care of their houses. I've got a sure-fire trick to take out that rackety bucket of bolts next door if you care to hear it."

"I already thought of a candy bar."

"I was thinking more along the lines of a rag stuffed in the gas tank and a cigarette lighter. Your way's probably quieter."

"I wish you'd told me you were coming. I'd have made the bed."

"We'd just have unmade it. You keep a neat place for a bachelor. Duane thought you were gay."

"I bet that's the word he used."

"I told him he's never been in the service. We just came from the Marriott," he said.

"I was pretty sure you did. How's Furlong?"

"A class act. He apologized for the runaround and offered to make a substantial contribution to the widows and orphans fund. Most people in his position would've just slipped us each a C-note."

"That's why he's a legend."

"You're under arrest, Walker," he said. "Material witness in a homicide."

Redburn had put up his artillery and produced a pair of handcuffs. "Assume the position."

"Duane, for Christ's sake." The sergeant sounded weary.

I turned around and leaned on my hands against the wall. "You don't waste time. I didn't expect you before tomorrow afternoon."

"I was one of the first ten black patrolmen to break the color line downriver," St. Thomas said. "All that infighting makes you suspicious of everyone. I check stories. Those L.A. cops don't deserve all the bad press they've been getting."

"Burn down one city and they never let you forget."

Redburn finished patting me down, hooked a manacle around my right wrist, jerked it down behind my back, and cuffed the other while I was stumbling for balance. There wasn't anything gentle about it, but the roughness wasn't personal; when you've wrapped a thousand packages for shipping, the thousand and first doesn't rate special handling. He read me my rights.

"I don't suppose there's a way we can settle this here," I said.

"Officer Redburn?"

"No."

"You heard him, Walker. With Duane around I never have to look at the manual. How's your head?"

"The bandage needs changing."

"We'll get it looked at. What happened, by the way?"

"Conception."

"A lot of people make that mistake. That's why Goodyear invented rubber. Let's go. You follow the Tigers? We can listen to the game in the car."

He was standing now, a middle-built professional drifting in the gray channel between his final promotion and retirement, who looked as if he'd forgotten how to be rough, impersonally or otherwise. Plenty of overtime went into achieving that look.

We walked through the living room Indian file, the sergeant in front. His partner brought up the rear with one hand on my arm and the other resting on his Glock. St. Thomas twisted the deadlock and swung the front door wide. Lieutenant Mary Ann Thaler of the Detroit Police Department was standing on the stoop. She had two uniformed officers with her.

"You're under arrest, Walker," she said. "Material witness in a homicide."

Belatedly she realized I wasn't alone. She looked at Redburn first, then at St. Thomas, reacting instinctively to rank.

"Hello?"

Twenty-six

THERE WAS an embarrassed little silence. Being the host, I broke it.

"Lieutenant Thaler," I said, "Sergeant St. Thomas. Officer Redburn, Lieutenant Thaler. Mary Ann, Duane. I don't know Sergeant St. Thomas's Christian name. Am I leaving anybody out?"

I watched the lieutenant's absorbent blue eyes taking it all in behind the brainy-girl glasses. Prom Night was over: She wore her hair in bangs and down to her shoulders with an inward-turning flirt at the ends, no heels, a beige sleeveless cotton top that showed off the gentle definition in her upper arms, and green-and-white-striped culottes. Shorts violated the plainclothes dress code, but she would be the kind who pushed the envelope. She wore a bag on her right shoulder big enough for gun, cuffs, and the Stationary Traffic Unit—no date purse today—with the flap open and her hand resting inside. It would be interesting to see how her fast draw compared with Sergeant St. Thomas's.

She was looking at him. "Flatrock?"

"Allen Park."

"I thought Flatrock was where Millender's body beached."

"Who's Millender?"

"You're not investigating Nate Millender's murder?"

"Never heard of him. We're investigating the murder of Lynn Arsenault."

"Never heard of him."

I said, "I thought you people kept tabs on all the area homicides."

"I told you last night I have a life," she said. "What's this about, Sergeant? I have a warrant." She drew a long fold of paper out of her bag.

"We have one too." He showed her his.

"I have jurisdiction."

"We have Walker."

"I have two armed men."

"I have to sit down," I said.

An open convertible boated down the block trailing Anita Baker from speakers the size of refrigerators. The mood changed.

Thaler said, "Let's all sit down. It's too hot to argue out here."

We went back into the living room. Redburn took off the cuffs on St. Thomas's order and I sat between them on the sofa, kneading blood back into my wrists. Thaler sat in the easy chair, spine straight, knees together, with her hands on the bag in her lap. She looked like the neighbor girl come to interview for babysitter. One of the uniforms pried open a window and switched on the fan. The air stirred resentfully and started circulating.

"Ladies first," said St. Thomas.

"I'm not a lady. I'm a lieutenant with Detroit Felony Homicide."

"I didn't mean it as a putdown. I was just being polite."

Her dimples came out. "Bullshit, Sergeant. This is my beat."

"I'll tell it," I said. "I like co-ed mud wrestling as much as the next guy, but it's my living room and I'm the one who gets to clean the rug."

I laid it out then, everything in its order, starting with the call from Stuart Lund that had gotten me out of bed and into the hotel at the airport. St. Thomas, who had heard most of it from Furlong and Lund, watched me with the unblinking patience of a cat staking out a mousehole; looking for places where the two versions didn't line up. Thaler, female for all her profession and rank, stared at the floor most of the time, making eye contact only when I surprised. Then she glanced away quickly as if I'd caught her at something. It was a good dodge, and so far as I could tell it was all her own. Redburn and the Detroit uniforms were just furniture. I didn't have time for them while two brains, conditioned by training and experience not to accept anything at face value, picked over my monologue behind four panes of prescription glass.

The fan hummed in the silence that rolled down after I finished talking.

The lady from downtown broke it. "I meet more liars in a working day than the average person meets in a lifetime. You may not be the best I ever heard, but, brother, you've sure got the biggest store."

"Are you talking about last night or now?"

"Both. If you're not lying now you're just plain stupid, and stupid is one thing you're not."

"I resent that."

"I didn't mean it as a compliment."

"How was your date?"

"None of your business, and don't change the subject." She tapped her fingers on her bag. "If Royce Grayling killed

Millender and Arsenault, that has nothing to do with your job, which is to find out who smeared this Lily Talbot and got Furlong to call off their engagement. Which means you're interfering in an official homicide investigation for the sake of your own curiosity. How stupid is that?"

"*Two* investigations." St. Thomas was looking at me. "Up until five minutes ago, the messenger who visited Arsenault just before he turned up dead was our best lead, after you. I've had half the squad out looking for him for two days. Now you say he was your plant. Maybe I won't book you after all. Maybe I'll just report you to Ma Bell for vandalizing telephone company equipment and let her do the rest."

"Oh, man." One of the downtown cops shuddered.

Thaler turned over a hand. "You're doing just what John Alderdyce warned me about: using your assignment as an excuse to run out and play Bulldog Drummond. If you even try to deny it, I'll tack obstruction of justice on to the material witness beef."

"Self-analysis isn't a spectator sport," I said. "I'm curious, all right. It's an asset to the job, and you know it. I've got questions about some of the things Grayling did, if he did them, that don't match up with his history. He's taking too many chances and not following up. Until I have answers I won't be able to separate the two killings from my case."

"Maybe I can help," she said. "Millender didn't die on the cruise you saw him off on with Grayling."

I touched my bandage. It was moist. "You've been busy."

"I haven't read Charlie Brown all year; no time. Witnesses saw Millender in good health buying sailing tackle in a specialty store in Grosse Pointe Farms Friday morning. The day after you saw him."

"Positive ID?"

"He was an old customer. He was eating a tomato from a sack he bought at the market next door. When the body washed up we went back with a morgue photo and the clerk made a tentative. Well, you know what a floater looks like."

"Unfortunately."

"We should have a positive from the FBI tomorrow on the prints. So it happened on a different cruise. We'll talk to Grayling, but if he's the heavyweight you say he is he'll have an alibi solid enough to jump on. That careful enough for you?"

"There's still Arsenault," I said, "and witnesses to place him at the scene."

"Witness," St. Thomas put in. "Just one."

I looked at him. He'd removed his glasses and was polishing the lenses with a lawn handkerchief. Most nearsighted people look incomplete and vulnerable when they take them off; with him it was like unsheathing twin steel blades. He didn't stop at the lenses, but went on to wipe off the bows and nosepiece.

"Arsenault's secretary, Mrs.—?" He glanced at Redburn, who paged through his notebook.

"Greta Griswold."

"Good old Detroit name. I'll bet her great-great grandmother served sauerkraut to Cadillac. Apparently she was the only one who saw Grayling at Imminent Visions the day Arsenault was killed. He didn't come past the guard in the lobby."

"What about the security monitors?"

"We've been through every foot of videotape. No Grayling."

"Why did she lie?"

"Damn. I'm glad you thought of that. We'll be sure to ask her, just as soon as we find her." He held the glasses up to the light, squinting, then put them back on. He folded the handkerchief carefully to avoid new creases and returned it to his pocket.

"She powdered?"

"Right after we questioned her the first time. Told the office manager she was too upset to work and asked if she could go home. She went home, all right. She packed everything but the refrigerator and peeled rubber. The squeal's out. She won't run long."

"What about Grayling?"

"Tougher proposition. Nobody in the City-County Building has seen him in a couple of days. Not unusual, we're told. He keeps his office in his glove compartment and spends most of his time on the road. No secretary. His desk is clean. I mean *clean*. There isn't even a pencil in it. We've got a car at his place on Outer Drive."

"He lives in the city?"

Light snapped off the silver frames. "He's a municipal employee, Walker. It's required."

"He can afford to keep a phantom address inside the limits and live in Grosse Pointe."

"Maybe he prefers to hang his hat in the town where he was born."

"Grayling was born here in Hamtramck."

"Right, like you go through Customs when you cross Joseph Campau. It's all Detroit. Tell you something." He leaned back against the arm of the sofa. His underarm pistol gleamed. "I grew up on Riopelle where the rumrunners used to dock. Harbortown they call it now, all six toxic blocks of it with condos made out of warehouses. We used to fish in the river. I made comic book money playing euchre in the B-and-O boxcars on the siding. I'd be a Detroit cop like the lieutenant here if I didn't have a hole in one eardrum. I love every crummy inch of this town. It's home."

"No offense, Sergeant. It's the only urban center in the country where a city address means you can't afford to move out."

"It's a damn shame."

"It's a tragedy. So are two murders. What are you going to do when he comes home, slap the cuffs on him?"

"So far only two people say he's a suspect. One's on the lam and the other's under arrest for lying his ass off. Sorry, Lieutenant."

"Go to hell."

"We'll just talk to him," he said.

"If he lets you," I said.

He sat up. "That means exactly what?"

"Royce Grayling isn't Pittsburgh Phil," I said. "He caps people between lunch with the governor and handball with the mayor. Just you and me sitting here discussing his greatest hits is grounds for a defamation suit. Which he'd win, because he goes fishing with the judge. That doesn't scare me. You've been through my drawers, you know what I'm worth. It wouldn't pay his court costs. The point is he hauls a lot of freight. Don't tell me you're going to grill him like some working stiff who tried to hire an undercover cop to kill his wife. Like the lieutenant said, I'm not stupid."

"So the system stinks. My kid wants to quit school and join the NBA. That stinks too. But I didn't throw up my hands and walk away."

"So you're going to grill Grayling?"

"Maybe just brown him a little, like I did my kid. He starts his junior year in September." He stood. "Saddle up, Duane. We can still catch the late innings. No, put the cuffs away. We got what we wanted."

Mary Ann Thaler said, "You're backing off?"

"He's all yours, Lieutenant. We'll be in touch if Arsenault ties into your floater."

"Wait, I'll walk you out." She got up, slinging the bag over her shoulder.

I looked up at her. "What about me?"

"I almost forgot." She rummaged inside her bag, found what she was looking for, and put it on the coffee table. It was my revolver. I hadn't seen it since Nate Millender's apartment. "When I'm wrong I admit it," she said. "You are stupid."

The front door closed behind all five cops.

Twenty-seven

WHEN THEY WERE GONE I walked through the house, locking doors and checking dark corners for cop eggs. Then I went into the bathroom to cleanse the wound and change dressings.

I tried sleeping, but I was running a slight fever, and as always happened when in that condition I dreamed I was stranded in West Equatorial Africa. This time I was hunting lions. One in particular, a canny old male, had carried off a couple of hundred villagers and left a trail across the veldt like the floor of a slaughterhouse. While I was following it I got that old tickle at the base of my brain that told me I was the one being hunted. I unslung the big-bore Mannlicher from my shoulder, drew back the bolt to inspect the load, slammed it back into the breech, and turned around to face the old graymane just as it sprang. I shouldered the rifle, drew a quick bead between its yellow eyes, and squeezed the trigger.

The shell didn't go off, of course. It never does.

I woke up in a puddle of sweat. My fever had broken. I took a shower, being careful to keep the bandage from getting wet, threw on my cotton robe, and sat down in the living room to watch TV. It was early evening. The ballgame was over—the Tigers had lost, as usual, to the worst team in both leagues—and Channel 4 was running another episode in its series of documentaries marking the one hundredth anniversary of the invention of the automobile.

In 1896, George Baldwin Selden, a fifty-one-year-old tinkerer and backyard inventor who had failed for twenty years to build an internal combustion engine that worked, was granted a patent naming him the sole owner of an unproven invention. In time he fell under the influence of a consortium of investors who employed the patent to extort money from fledgling automobile manufacturers in return for a license to operate. Leland fell into line, as did Chrysler, the brothers Dodge, and twenty or thirty other early moguls whose names have long since disappeared along with their emblems. Henry Ford alone held out, continuing to manufacture his Model T despite a blizzard of summonses, injunctions, and even an advertising campaign warning consumers that the purchase of a Ford included the guarantee of a lawsuit. Henry bore on in the face of additional pressure from legislators, the pro-Selden press, and his fellow automakers, until a federal court ruled in 1911 that no one person or group could claim credit for the gasoline engine. The consortium dissolved, and Selden died eleven years later at the age of seventy-seven, a failure to the finish. But the celebrants had fixed upon the date of his scurrilous patent as an excuse to throw a centennial.

Surf history, stop anywhere, and you'll find someone applying muscle, a lot of someones submitting, someone resisting alone. Henry Ford. Jimmy Hoffa. Jay Bell Furlong. Amos Walker. It promised to be a bizarre-looking Rushmore.

When the show ended I switched off the set, picked up the

Smith & Wesson from the table where Mary Ann Thaler had placed it, swung out the cylinder, dumped the cartridges, and gave it a good cleaning and oiling, wiping off the excess with an old undershirt. Then I loaded it fresh from the box I kept on top of the refrigerator, taking time to wipe each cartridge before thumbing it into the chamber. If I'd thought to do that with the Mannlicher I'd have a lion rug.

I went to bed again at ten, mostly out of boredom, and slept without lions. I awoke in gray darkness, feeling chilled. I got up and shut the window. The floor felt like metal under my feet. Michigan will change its mind just that quickly, breaking off a heat wave for no good reason meteorologically speaking, like snapping a dry stick.

Robed and slippered, I made the circuit, closing windows and turning off fans. The *chee-eek* of a solitary cricket sawing its legs in a corner somewhere grew louder when everything was sealed. I tried counting the number of *chee-eeks* per fifteen seconds and adding thirty-seven. It was a country trick for determining the temperature, taught to me by an old farmer whose city-stricken daughter I'd traced to a crack house on Cass; but I was thinking of too many other things and lost track. Anyway a cricket in the house is supposed to mean good luck. Or a death in the family. I never could keep my folksy aphorisms straight. The girl was dead of an overdose when I'd found her; but that was stuff for another nightmare.

In the kitchen I charged the coffeemaker and set the timer. The digital clock read 4:54. Dawn soon. I switched on the light over the breakfast nook and sat and smoked. I wasn't afraid to go back to sleep. I wasn't afraid of lions or political killers or farmers' dead daughters. I was waiting for the paper.

When it came I almost missed it. The Monday sheet is light after the weekend advertising supplements; it made no more noise than a gypsy moth hurling itself against the screen door. Drops of dew sparkled on the painted concrete stoop in the spreading pink light. The air felt like late fall or early spring. I was actually shivering when I stepped back inside.

I went straight past the sections on Eastern Europe and the Persian Gulf—why try to keep up?—and cracked the obituaries. Funeral arrangements for Lynn Arsenault hadn't appeared Saturday or Sunday, probably waiting for the remains to be released from the morgue. Three days is the usual surfacing time, just like with floaters.

The obituary ran first in alphabetical placement. Unmarried, Lynn Stoddard Arsenault left a sister studying on a cultural exchange program in Beijing and assorted aunts, uncles, and cousins scattered from New Jersey to California. The Rosary and services were to take place Tuesday at Most Blessed Sacrament in Detroit, the Reverend Father Francis X. Ontkean officiating. There was no notice for Millender, but two paragraphs in the City section announced that an unidentified body had been found bobbing against the bank at Flatrock.

I folded the paper and looked at the clock on the coffeemaker. I'd managed to kill twenty-five minutes out of the longest night of my adult life. I ground out my cigarette and went back to bed for the third time in fifteen hours. I might have slept. For sure I was awake two hours later when the alarm went off.

Most Blessed Sacrament is a gaunt old Norman Gothic barn constructed along the lines of Notre Dame de Paris at the distinctly non-Parisian corner of Woodward and Belmont, all spiked towers and clerestories, pointing stubbornly toward heaven in an age embarrassed by faith. I had aired out and pressed the summer lightweight, changed bandages again—steadily downsizing—and was feeling as close to holy as I ever got by the time I entered the rectory. The atmosphere was heavy with burnt wax, cheap furniture oil, and something vaguely reminiscent of a team locker room, the peculiar hormonal scent of the mostly male environment.

"Mr. Walker? I have to say you look like what I'd expect of a private dick. They're always getting hit on the head in movies."

Father Ontkean's strong handshake pulled me into the room. He was in his late twenties, blonde, and wore his hair short on top and long in back like a kid. No body piercing that I could see. He had a deep even tan, pale gray eyes in crisp contrast, and braces on his teeth. He'd sounded older over the telephone. They say you know you're over the hill when doctors, cops, and priests start looking younger. I'd boxed the compass on this case and it was still far from over.

"Thanks for seeing me, Father. I was afraid you'd be too busy."

"The cardinal does most of the administrating. A priest in an archdiocese is like an ensign on an aircraft carrier. My responsibilities aren't exactly crushing."

He wasn't wearing a clerical collar. It wouldn't have gone with his green bowling shirt, faded corduroys, and running shoes without socks, the great equalizing footwear of our time.

His office was more traditional: a leather-topped desk with a steeple chair behind it in front of a tall casement window with the drapes tied back. Dust-motes glittered like brass shavings in the hard bar of light slanting through the leaded panes. The window was tipped open, but the petal fan mounted below the vaulted ceiling was still. Outside it was a comfortable seventy-two degrees Fahrenheit.

He steered me toward a less formal conversation area made up of two chairs and a sofa on a square Oriental rug. I took the sofa while he perched on the edge of one of the chairs with his knees apart and hands suspended between, the way athletes sit on television talk shows. A tiny gold crucifix dangled from a chain around his throat. I found that comforting. If it had turned out to be an ankh I was out of there.

"Your call sounded important," he said. "Were you and Lynn acquainted?" His tone carefully reserved judgment.

"Just over the telephone. You told me he specifically requested you to officiate at his services. Did he make the arrangements himself?"

"Yes, quite some time ago. About the time he converted."

"He converted?"

"Well, returned to the fold. He was raised in the faith, then became a Methodist for business reasons. I understand his late employer had strong feelings about Roman Catholics."

"He seems to have had strong feelings in general. Vernon Whiting's been dead five years. Is that when Arsenault came back?"

"Not that long ago. I was still in divinity school then. Two years, I think; no more than that. I could look it up."

I flicked it away. "Isn't it unusual for a young man in good health to arrange his own funeral?"

"Not really. It's the best way to assure your wishes are honored, and it spares your loved ones the ordeal. Young business tycoons find the organizational aspect particularly appealing."

"So you don't think it had anything to do with the way he died."

"I didn't say that."

I didn't jump on it. "Obviously he trusted you, to ask you to be the one who reads him into heaven. Did he say what made him decide to reconvert?"

"No, and I didn't ask. It isn't Vatican policy to expose tyros to the third degree." He worked his lips over his braces as if he were unfamiliar with them. "We're coming into a delicate area here."

"Confession."

"Yes." He stroked one hand with the other. He had big hands, the hands of a basketball player. Either one would have held enough water to baptize triplets. "There are priests, some of whom have been ordained much longer than I, who hold that the seal of the confessional is broken when the penitent dies. I don't agree with them. Death being merely a transition."

"I think I know one of the things he carried into the booth."

He smiled, showing chrome. "Telling you whether you're getting warm or cold counts as a violation."

"I won't ask you to confirm what he said. I'm more interested in what absolution you offered."

"Are you Catholic, my son?"

"I was raised Episcopalian."

"Non-Catholics often think the role of the confessor is limited to assigning Hail Marys as if he were totaling a bill for services rendered. If it were that simple, there would be standing room only at early Mass. No man is privileged to assure the Lord's forgiveness. The best he can do is provide counsel that may or may not heal one's own sickness of the soul."

"That counsel being?"

"To seek out the injured party and ask for forgiveness there."

"He sought. He didn't ask."

"That's sad. Not surprising. It requires great strength."

"He offered money instead."

He nodded. His face turned toward a large wooden crucifix on the wall above the sofa. "In that case I'm doubly sorry I wasn't present when he passed over."

"If you were, someone else would be sitting in that chair saying the same thing about you."

He turned back. "Perhaps. I can't help feeling responsible for a soul adrift."

"You can't save them all, Father."

"If I could save just one I'd feel that all the effort spent in placing me here wasn't wasted."

There was nothing in that for me. "Even a born-again Catholic has to live in the real world," I said. "Plenty of people would have considered what Arsenault did a kind of expiation."

"They aren't qualified to judge."

"Who is?"

"Only God." He sat back and rested his hands on his knees. "I'll tell you this much. And I've a hunch I'll be confessing that I did. If I considered myself in a position to judge Lynn Arsenault, and if I were to turn all my attention to him from now until Sunday Mass, I could not judge him more harshly than he judged himself. I never met a man so desperate to be cleansed."

"Huh."

He nodded again, as if I'd said something wise. It might just have been something he did on his side of the booth.

I got up. "Thank you, Father."

"I wasn't aware I was any help."

"Our jobs have that much in common. We don't always know."

He worked his lips, then pulled them back and dug at his teeth with a big thumbnail. "You wouldn't be carrying floss, by any chance?"

"Sorry. New braces?"

"The cardinal's idea. Worse than a hair shirt."

"I guess they're a cross you have to bear."

His face went blank. "Go with God, my son."

I took what I had to the office, leaned back in the swivel with my eyes shut, and waited for music.

Not a note.

Not even a hum.

I pulled it apart and looked at the pieces.

One contrite Arsenault, dead in the middle of a campaign to make things right with Lily Talbot for his part in framing her.

One Nate Millender, less than contrite, dead in the middle of the juiciest blackmail scheme since Eve bit the apple.

One stone killer named Grayling, who may or may not have started to show cracks.

Still no music. Laid out like that it was a crystal set with the instructions in Japanese.

And yet when I put it back together a tune began to play.

Not a complete melody. The bridge was missing and the tempo kept changing. But it had a familiar refrain that stayed just out of reach.

I made myself stop listening. Otherwise I'd be all day trying to remember the lyrics.

I went through the Monday morning mail. The Triple-A Detective Mercantile Company of Portland wanted to send me, free for ninety days, a gizmo that looked like a portable electric razor with an earplug attached. *This remarkable technological breakthrough, no larger than a cigarette package, picks up conversations safely and accurately up to six hundred yards away, without batteries or telltale wires.*

The telephone rang while I was trying to read the fine print.

"Four-F Detective Agency," I said. "Slightly larger than a cigarette package and just about as safe. Accuracy costs extra."

"Walker?"

I knew the voice, vaguely. Why it made me smell sun and water was a mystery. Then it wasn't. I put down the circular. "Walker here."

"This is Royce Grayling. Do you remember me?"

"I remember."

"Where can we meet?"

I groped for tobacco. "My office seats two, no waiting."

"Thought you'd never ask."

The door opened from the waiting room and Grayling stepped inside, collapsing the antenna on a cellular telephone receiver with the heel of his hand.

"Silly as hell," he said, pocketing it. "But I'm a slave to gadgets, can't get enough of 'em. Let's jaw."

Twenty-eight

HE WAS DRESSED COMFORTABLY but professionally for a balmy workday, in gray linen slacks, glossy black slip-ons, a blue-and-gray-striped dress shirt, blue silk necktie knotted casually with a dimple below the knot, and an unstructured chambray sportcoat, pale blue and fashionably wrinkled. The coat de-emphasized the power in his chest and shoulders without disguising it. His moustache was dark against his tan, the teeth dazzling in the broad Hemingway grin.

He spun the customer's chair on one leg, straddled it, and folded his arms on the back. As usual he kept his right hand free.

"Good office." He hadn't looked around once. "All business."

"Thanks. I threw out the Louis Quatorze chairs. They clashed with the Rembrandts."

"That's what I mean. You don't junk it up with a lot of phony executive bric-a-brac. I don't use one myself. They cleared one for me downtown but I keep telling them to save the rent and pay me the difference. When you keep an office you get to sitting around in it. I don't spend a whole hell of a lot of time sitting."

"My Uncle Roy had piles too. We shot him finally."

His eyes were dark brown, darker than mine, and he used them on me with that trick he had of absorbing light without reflecting any.

"That's an old one," he said. "Cracking wise to keep the other guy off center while you're thinking about what comes next. You were a cop, right?"

"Stop guessing. You sat somewhere long enough to run my jacket or you wouldn't be here now. Sitting."

He enjoyed that. He enjoyed me. He uncorked the rest of his thousand-candlepower smile to show me just how much. It made me regret leaving my Smith & Wesson in the glove compartment of the Cutlass. It hadn't seemed respectful to carry it into church.

"Okay, you got me," he said. "To begin with, you don't have an Uncle Roy. Vietnam and Cambodia—hey, me, too; but you know that. First Air Cavalry, tough gig. M.P. over here on your second hitch, every week but one of the police training course here in town. You dropped the ball there. It's never a good idea to knock out teeth belonging to sons of prominent politicians. No matter what they try to do to you in the locker room."

"I was younger then. Now I'd choose the gut. Easier on the knuckles."

He went on as if I hadn't interrupted. "Married for a little, which is a bitch as I well know. Junior partner in the present concern until a bullet caught up with the experienced end, leaving you in sole proprietorship. I know where the piece of shit who fired it is living now, in case you're interested."

"Pass."

"Right, revenge is for suckers. With my contacts, the address wasn't too hard to pry loose. I just sort of thought it might come in handy if I needed an in. According to my sources you're not an easy man to trade horses with."

"Depends on the horse."

He reached inside his coat, watching me for a reaction. I didn't give him one. The material was too light to conceal anything more lethal than a handkerchief, and anyway I knew he wore his holster on his hip. He produced a fold of wrinkled paper and spread it out on the desk. I recognized it before I saw the pasted-in letters.

$ ten 000 wait 4 mY CALL

"Sloppy job," I admitted. "They tell me there are better ways of doing it now, but I'm a traditionalist. I don't even watch colorized movies."

"Aren't you going to ask me where I got it?"

"I know where you got it. Your aim isn't what it was in Southeast Asia."

"That was in the open. A moving target in a small room is harder to hit. You aren't doing anything stupid like taping this conversation, are you?"

"What if I am?"

"Well, what do you think?"

I rolled my chair back from the desk and spread my arms. He got up, came around, and opened all the drawers, lifting a stack of insulated mailers in the deep drawer on the left to make sure. The file cabinets were locked, but he checked the cracks for wires leading to hidden microphones. Finally he resumed his position in the customer chair. He hadn't turned his back on me the whole time.

"You could be wearing a wire," he said, "but probably not. You didn't know I was coming. I almost finished the job, you know, in the apartment. It was my first instinct."

"Why didn't you?"

"The pickings were too good. The kitschy note, the racy picture, Millender's ad from the phone book. I figured there had to be more hid out in a safe deposit box or with a lawyer. In the Event of My Death, and blah-blah. Was I right?"

It was my turn. I got out the pack and matches, watching him for a reaction when my hand went to my pocket. Nothing. Well, we'd lamped each other pretty good at the marina. I fired up and blew a jet at the ceiling. "When you ask a question like that, does anybody say no?"

He rolled his shoulders. "You'd be surprised. Anyway I had to ask. I'm pretty straight-on, Walker. The people I work for have to screw themselves through doorways, but that's politics. They see a window, they expect it to be locked. So they get out their jimmies and glass-cutters and suction cups and get to work. Me, I try the window first. And you know what? Three times out of ten it's open."

"You can be too straight-on," I said. "Like not bothering to leave the gun at the scene of a suicide."

"I've heard that story too."

"Like arranging a landlubber's accident for Nate Millender when it was clear just from his décor he was no amateur sailor."

"Most sailing accidents happen to experts," he said. "Ask the Coast Guard."

"I like to think I postponed his accident a day. You're too good a mechanic not to scrub an assignment once a trained detective came along to place you at the scene. Maybe not, though. The lake was pretty crowded that afternoon. Maybe it was a dry run."

"No pun intended." He smiled.

"The next day, after witnesses saw Millender on Belle Isle, buying gear and eating tomatoes, you caught him alone, brained him, slipped him into the water, and launched his sloop. Smearing gray matter on the boom sweetened the pill."

He patted the pocket where he'd stashed his telephone. "I had an emergency meeting in town. I borrowed a car from the curator of the Dossin Museum on the island. An old friend. You can check the time with him."

"Once a body's been floating a couple of days, nobody can determine time of death within twelve hours; plenty of time to scare up forty people of good reputation to testify you were with them when the tragedy took place. That tin soldier's been wound up so many times it runs without a key."

"See, that's what sitting in an office will do to you. Your mind wanders all over the place and brings back any old thing."

"It was a good plan." I used the ashtray. "Complicated enough to seem incredible, but not so tangled you might trip over details. That's why Arsenault was such a disappointment. You took chances. You were seen in the vicinity at the time he was killed. You must have been in a hurry."

"I haven't hurried since I was fourteen. I made mistakes. I don't make them now. I didn't tag Arsenault."

It was the first flat-out denial he'd made. For some reason it disappointed me.

"Arsenault was a lapsed Catholic," I said. "That early guilt training never goes away. Being bled by Millender didn't help him forget. It all came back on him hard enough to drive him back to the Church, where he was advised to take his confession to Lily Talbot and beg forgiveness. When push came to shove he couldn't do it, so he threw money at her, disguised as a business transaction.

"She took it, as who wouldn't? She probably thought she'd earned it. But even a watered-down act of self-abasement on Arsenault's part set off alarm bells. What if he took it a step further and told her who set up the frame that split her and Jay Bell Furlong? She might go straight to Furlong with the information, and that would leave the culprit—we'll call him the witchfinder, just for fun—out in the cold. No bequest. So now Arsenault belongs to the ages."

He wasn't smiling now. He was someone hanging on to a story he didn't care for but wanted to know how it ended.

I went on. "Millender was a footnote: the man who rigged the photograph, a blackmailer who might dip his straw anywhere, a small spill to be wiped up. If you were going to blow off a job quick and dirty, it should have been him. Maybe the assignments came too close together. Busy couple of days for Suicide Sam."

"Mister," he said, "I don't know any Lily Talbot or anything about rigged pictures. Are you talking about the one you had in your pocket?"

"You're letting me down, Royce. We're just two guys talking: no wires or tape recorders. You've been hanging around politicians too long. You're not a straight-on guy anymore." I got rid of some more ash. "Okay, let's hear your version."

"You don't know anything, do you? I mean for real." There was awe in his tone. "When I entered my late good friend Nate Millender's place, found a burglar on the premises, and took action against the rising tide of crime in our fair city, I thought you had some kind of handle. When I frisked you I was sure of it. But you really do work without a net."

I took one last deep drag—it was like drawing a strand of rusty barbed wire down my throat—and punched out the cigarette. My hand wanted to shake but I didn't let it.

"I don't recommend it in your case," I said. "When you

jumped me, the world didn't know Millender was anybody's late anything. The body hadn't been found."

"But his brains had. Don't try to shit a shitter."

I moved a shoulder. "Just staying in practice. For once in my life I don't want the killer. Arsenault was a career snake. Worse, he was an uncommitted one, without the stomach to accept what he was or the guts to change. Millender was a leech. As far as I'm concerned the earth's oxygen supply was wasted on both of them. I just want what I was hired for. Who hung a frame on Lily Talbot?"

"I wish I could help. For once in my life I do. I knew Arsenault from when I worked at county and he made zoning requests. The mayor's shopping around for a new convention center and he tagged me to get a bid from Imminent Visions. Errands are the job most of the time."

"You had an appointment with him the morning he was killed."

"I had a conflict. I tried to cancel, but I couldn't get an answer on the phone."

"It wasn't working; but that's another story. Arsenault's secretary said you kept the appointment."

He ran a finger along his square jaw. "She said that? That makes me very unhappy."

"Is that why she disappeared?"

"Did she." His face was full of thought.

I shifted gears. "Say she's lying, and you're clean on Arsenault. Why Millender? And don't tell me you swung his way. I'll throw you out on your gun."

"Much as I'd like to see you try." The grin was back. "Can I be hypothetical?"

"I wish you were."

"I love you too. Millender liked to take pictures of naked men doing things naked men like to do together; not furrychested specimens like you and me, goes without saying. Suppose somebody who ought to know enough to stay away from cameras unless he's kissing a baby just kind of wandered in front of one in his birthday suit, in the wrong company. Male company. Hey, if they had any brains they wouldn't chase after public office in the first place, right? Hypothetically speaking, remember. It's bad business to judge the people you work for."

"Which one was it? Hypothetically speaking."

"If I told you that I'd just be making more work for myself. And I'm indolent." He tasted the word.

I shook my head.

"Too much coincidence. Why should Arsenault and Millender die within twenty-four hours of each other if there was no connection?"

"If I could answer that, I'd know what the hell we were talking about. I can only give you my side."

"Hypothetically speaking."

"Fuck that, I'm tired of it. We're just two guys talking, like you said. Millender had CANCELED stamped on his forehead the day we started hanging together. These things take time. The cops who bother to backtrack tend to focus on new people and new developments in the deceased's life. You have to establish some kind of norm. Keeps you from being singled out."

"Makes sense."

"Of course it does. I never hurry. But when a private cop comes around asking about Millender's photography, it's time to fill in a date on the stamp."

"What brought you to his apartment later?"

"The party I was working for had bought the negative and all the prints; but Millender's word was all he had on that. I needed to be sure there weren't any more lying around. I almost forgot." Again he went into his pocket. This time he laid Millender's passbook and the negative and prints of Millender and Arsenault on the desk. They looked even more lewd there than they had in the apartment; the passbook no less so than the pictures. "I recognized Arsenault. I thought the shots might come in handy if we wound up doing business with Imminent Visions, but that was before the news broke."

I made no move to pick them up. "What's the catch?"

"Call it professional courtesy."

"Not without choking on it."

He raised a hand. "Whatever. I can't afford to collect junk I don't need. I move a lot."

"Picky neighbors?"

"Candy-ass employers. Sooner or later they get to feeling ashamed of themselves. Keeping me around reminds them of too many things."

"Bummer."

"I'm used to it. And the demand always exceeds the supply."

I let a little silence settle. Then I reached out with my left hand and shuffled the items into a stack. He didn't have to know I was unarmed.

"Okay," I said.

"Okay?"

"We're square for now. You shot me, but you didn't cross the *T*. That puts me in a minority of one, for which I suppose I should show a little gratitude. I'll consider this stuff a bonus." I opened the passbook. "You wonder why Millender bothered working at all."

"Everybody needs a cover." He got up and turned the chair around.

I watched him. "You mean like 'currently attached City of Detroit, no title or office, duties unspecified'?"

"Politics is fuzzy. Good thing, too. There'd be no place for me if it wasn't. You, too, maybe." He stuck out his hand.

I didn't look at it. "Don't tell that one even to your pillow."

He lowered the hand. There was no daylight in his face. The grin was strictly Edison.

"Let's you and me make an effort to stay out of the same room from now on," he said. "I scrape guys like Nate Millender off my heel all the time. You might spoil my appetite."

"Hypothetically speaking."

He shook his head. "Straight on."

"You had your last word," I said. "Now skeedaddle."

His grin hung in the air a moment after he'd left, like the Cheshire Cat's.

In a little while it was replaced by the hard glitter of Sergeant St. Thomas's glasses.

Mondays.

Twenty-nine

TODAY IT WAS A BLUE SUIT, pale salmon shirt, and gay floral print tie, the kind that have bred and multiplied and overrun all the men's departments, stampeding the stripes, dots, and club patterns of old. I'd decided not to shop for ties until the fad blew over; but it seemed to have settled in with all the grim determination of AIDS and the three-button suit. On him it looked all right.

"I just ran into Royce Grayling downstairs," he said. "How'd you manage to smoke him out?"

"I didn't have to. If I sit here long enough every crook and cop in town drifts in with the smog. Did you wrap him up or grill him on the spot?"

"He promised to drop by this afternoon and make a statement."

"Good of him to fit you in. Most of the killers I know are booked up three weeks in advance."

"I didn't draw up the system, Walker. If I did, every cop would be on a five-year contract, subject to renegotiation when his conviction record bumps up above two-fifty."

"How'd you spot him?"

"Detroit Chamber of Commerce faxed us his mug. He's a member." He adjusted his frames. "I wasn't sure it was him downstairs, though, until I got close. I thought he was you."

"Thanks."

"I'm not kidding. Your build and coloring, except his tan's nicer. Even your way of moving, like something you'd see on *Wild Kingdom*. If he shaved off his moustache you could be brothers."

"It's not just the moustache."

"Says you. You both spell more work for me. What did you two find to talk about?"

"Hypothetical situations. Where's your shadow?"

"Shadow? Oh, Redburn. He's got snazzy ideas about taking a day off every few weeks. He's new like I said. Anyway we're not sold as a set." He took the chair Grayling had vacated and rested a manila envelope on his side of the desk. He saw the paste-up on the blotter. "That the note you told me about at your place? Kind of him to bring it back. Are you pressing charges against him, by the way?"

I opened the middle drawer, swept the note inside, and pushed it shut. "Why ask? It isn't your jurisdiction."

"Professionally, I'd just as soon his aim were better. Downriver we like our homicides self-contained: wives and husbands, fathers and families, disgruntled factory workers with pink slips and automatic weapons. We don't need to import mysteries from the big city. I was just being polite." He drummed his fingers on the envelope.

"Your warrants are getting bigger," I said. "You'll need a hand truck for the next one."

"It's not a warrant." He slid it toward the corner, farther out of my reach.

When no explanation was forthcoming, I drew a pencil out of the cup and played with it. I wanted something between my fingers and my throat was raw from smoking a pack since sunup. "Anything yet on the secretary that fingered Grayling? Greta Whatsername?"

"Griswold. We don't know where she is yet, but we know a little more about her. Griswold is her married name. It's old Detroit, like we figured."

"Like you figured."

"I was being modest. When her late husband gave it to her he also gave her U.S. citizenship. The background check stops at Immigration, where she applied for resident status ten years ago under the name Cathlin Margareta Faolin."

"Irish?"

"Sounds like. The folk at Imminent Visions say the brogue came out when she got upset. We're waiting on a callback from Washington for the rest."

"Any make on her car?"

He got out his leatherbound notebook. "She wasn't as flashy as her boss. Blue nineteen-seventy-four Olds eighty-eight. Remember them?"

"Big car. Big trunk."

"Big trunk." He nodded and put away the notebook.

"Think she's in it?"

"The good people of Allen Park don't pay me to think." His eyes shone behind glass. "I'm on my way back from Lieutenant Thaler's office. We've been matching collars and cuffs on our respective homicides. Thought you'd like to know the autopsy results on Millender."

I watched him pull the manila envelope into his lap. "Time of death?"

"Not an exact science, given the circumstances. Forget body temperature. The bloating screws up postmortem lividity and accelerates decomposition. Not the digestive process, though. That stops shortly after death. Still no help, unless you know when the deceased consumed certain items found in the stomach and intestines."

"Tomatoes," I said.

"Thought you'd remember them. He was seen eating one in a store in Grosse Pointe Farms at eight o'clock Friday morning. His stomach stopped digesting it and a few others approximately an hour later. Which means if Lieutenant Thaler, clever woman, nails Grayling with the Detroit murder, he's got an airtight alibi for the one in Allen Park. At the time Arsenault died he was busy killing Millender."

"He said he had a conflict."

"What else did he say?"

I ducked it. "What about vice versa?"

"I sure hope it is vice versa," he said. "Not to wish any fresh headaches on our brothers and sisters here in the big city, but I've got a drug killing and two robbery-murders on my desk besides this one and I'd just as soon tack it on Grayling as anyone so I can think about the others. Let the prosecution worry about swinging an indictment. That's their job, just as running down the bad guys is mine."

"Two killers."

"One's all I'm concerned about. Just thought you'd like to know. Now you owe me."

"I pay my debts sooner or later."

"So does Russia. What did you and Grayling find to talk about?"

I twirled the pencil and holstered it in the cup. "It's not vice versa."

He nodded. "I was pretty sure it wasn't when the Griswold woman rabbited. Did he tell you he's the one who dusted Millender?"

"It's hearsay."

"Like I said, that's the prosecution's wagon. It isn't even

my case. But we're all brothers under the blue. And you're back to withholding information in a homicide."

"Information. Not evidence."

"It's a fuzzy line. Ask the White House." He waited.

"Millender was blackmailing others besides Arsenault. He ran the same homosexual photo scam on a local politician. Enter Royce."

"Exit Nate." He touched his glasses. "What's the politician's name?"

"He didn't say. He didn't say he killed Millender, either. He said it was a hypothetical situation."

"I wondered what that meant."

"The hell you did."

He didn't pursue it. "I'll let Thaler wrestle with the gray area. At least it will tell her where to tighten the screws."

"I'd be grateful if you told her where you got it."

"I'll let you do it. I'm already way ahead on brownie points with Detroit. That homesick I'm not." He picked up the manila envelope and put it in his lap. He made no move to get up.

I bit. "What's in the envelope?"

"Oh, this?" He looked surprised he was holding it. "Pictures of the crime scene in the garage. I dropped off duplicates with Thaler."

"I hate to ask."

"The hell you do." He waited again.

"May I take a peek?"

"Be my guest." He unwound the string and tipped the contents out on to the blotter. I picked up the glistening eight-by-tens and skimmed through them. The body and the blood on the concrete floor looked like cheap Hollywood props in the glare of the flash. Still life with bullet-holes.

"We're lucky in our crime-scene guy," said St. Thomas. "All the really first-rate photographers work for newspapers and magazines. Good second-stringers apply straight to the forensics department in Detroit. Our guy's as good in his way as you say Millender was. He could work anywhere, but he likes what he's doing and he prefers to do it in Allen Park. I'd put his detail work up against anyone's upriver."

I started to return them, then shuffled back to a trunk shot of the corpse. "What's this?"

He leaned forward. I turned the picture his way and pointed at a nearly perfect yellow-brown half-circle the size of a quarter on the concrete near where Arsenault's left arm had come to rest.

He tilted his glasses and squinted through them. Then he sat back. "Blood, or maybe just grease. They look alike when they dry."

"I didn't notice it when I was there."

"Some things show up in the flash that don't under ordinary light."

"It looks like someone drew it with a compass."

"Who knows? Maybe somebody with oil on his hands dropped a coin and somebody picked it up. That's the trouble with real life as opposed to murder mysteries. Most of the time a spot on the floor is just a spot on the floor."

"Is that what you wanted me to see?"

He gave me the cop face. "It's a small police department. Not so small we have to farm out detective work to a one-man agency with a hole in its head."

"Excuse me all to hell."

"Naturally you'll share with us anything you happen to trip over. That's just good citizenship."

"Naturally." I ticked the edge of the photo. "May I borrow this?"

"Any reason I should let you?"

"Call it a reward for good citizenship."

"It's supposed to be its own reward." But he slid the rest of the prints into the envelope and tied the string. Then he stood.

"Thanks, Sergeant."

"We serve and protect."

Thirty

THE GOOD NEWS was I had all the pieces.

The bad news was they belonged to different puzzles.

The worse news was I was getting to hate good news/bad news jokes more than I hate light beer, and the case was full of them.

After Sergeant St. Thomas left I rummaged in the top drawer until I found the Sherlock Holmes magnifying glass my late partner, Dale Leopold, had presented to me the day I joined the firm. It was the size of a hand mirror, heavy as a hammer, with a smooth walnut handle where a pink ribbon had been tied. I had never used it in an investigation. With it in hand I switched on the desk lamp and went over the crime scene picture one more time. That was better, but still not conclusive.

I put the glass back in the drawer and called a number from my notebook.

"Cassandra Photo. Randy Quarrels speaking."

"Quarrels, this is Amos Walker. We met last week." Another life.

"I remember. Any of those names pan out?"

"One did."

"I can guess which one. I read the papers."

"I've got another job for you."

"More names? The city population's going down plenty fast without my help."

"No names. This one calls for your talent. I need a picture blown up but I can't afford to lose a lot of detail."

"The whole picture?"

"Just one part."

"That's a little easier. Got a negative?"

"No."

"That's not so easy."

"If it were easy I'd go to Fotomat."

"Greasy spoon."

"I didn't call to poll your opinion of the competition. Can you do it?"

"I can make a negative from the positive and make an enlargement from the new negative, but you're going to lose something. How much depends on the quality of the print."

"It's a police photo."

"Jesus Christ."

"You might be surprised. This guy's slumming."

"I'll have to see it."

"On my way." I was out the door before the receiver stopped bouncing.

Birmingham looked the same as it had on my last visit; the same as it had always looked since the first grizzled pioneer tacked up the first Neighborhood Watch sign: a patch of expensive sunlight with better police protection than the Oakland County Jail, and a lot less obtrusive. But my perspective had changed.

Today the street was just a street, for all the fresh asphalt and no potholes. The maroon plush staircase leading up from the formal-wear shop was just a set of stairs and the pictures on the walls of the customer area at Cassandra were just patterns trapped in emulsion. Even the snow leopard was just a cat with an attitude.

Randy Quarrels yelled from in back and I flipped up the gate and went behind the counter and then the blue-painted partition. There was a door in back with a red bulb mounted over it. The bulb wasn't lighted. I knocked anyway and got an invitation. The room was a little larger than a walk-in closet and contained a stainless steel double sink, counters, shelves, and a chemical stench that would be there when the building came down. It had none of the state-of-the-art equipment I had seen in Nate Millender's dark room; but Quarrels had more overhead and a scruple or two.

"Got it?" Cassandra's proprietor screwed the cap back on a plastic jug he had half-emptied into one side of the sink and rinsed off his hands in what I assumed was water standing in the other side.

I said I had it. He pulled the chain on a ceiling fixture, dousing us both in harsh unshaded light, took the picture out of the file folder I handed him, and held it up. His mud-colored hair was still gathered into a ponytail and he had squeezed his short thick body into a sweatshirt with the sleeves cut off and jeans soiled and tattered well beyond the fashion standards of Generation X.

"That's what I need a better look at." I indicated the half-circle on the floor by the corpse.

"Good paper. Suburban cops, right?"

"How'd you know?"

"They farm out to custom developers. Detroit uses its own equipment and that cheapshit paper. This stuff gives us a fighting chance at least. You weren't kidding about the photographer."

"What's the verdict?"

"Shut the door and we'll deliberate." He switched on a pink bulb over the sink and jerked the ceiling chain, washing everything in rosy light.

An hour and a half later, poorer by an additional fifty of Jay Bell Furlong's dollars but richer by a high-quality negative, a couple of practice prints, and one reasonably clear suitable-for-framing blowup of a spot on a concrete floor, I swung into the short-term parking lot across from the Airport Marriott. I was past due to report to my client.

What I saw while I was cruising the aisles told me I was going to be later yet.

She only caught my attention because all the slots within easy trotting distance of the hotel entrance were taken. Walking between the rows of cars, fishing in a handbag, she looked like a parking space in the making. By the time she passed me, not looking at me or the Cutlass, I'd placed her.

It might have been the way she carried the handbag once she'd gotten her keys out. She'd carried a watering can the same way, freshening the plants in the reception area outside Lynn Arsenault's office at Imminent Visions. It was enough to make me look again; and two's the limit, dented skull or no.

I'd seen her just once, briefly, when I'd had an appointment with her boss and he'd ducked it. She wasn't wearing the octagonal glasses now and her hair was darker, but someone had told her sometime that tailored suits were becoming to her and the compliment had stuck. Changing one's identity requires a commitment that not every man is prepared to make, and damn few women.

I crept on in the opposite direction, keeping Greta Griswold's straight matronly back in the rearview mirror.

Nobody would have mistaken the yellow Neon she eventually climbed into for the old blue Oldsmobile registered to the former Cathlin Margareta Faolin. The license plate frame that showed when she backed out of the space belonged to Budget Rent-a-Car.

I let her drive to the end of the aisle and out toward the exit, then powered around the end nearest me, down the next aisle, and decelerated in the main traffic lane to avoid catching up to her at the booth. Before Arsenault had inherited her, she had worked for a bigoted, suspicious man for twelve years. She would recognize the same car twice in her mirror.

She paid for her parking, didn't engage the attendant in conversation, didn't take a receipt. I did the same.

I gave her half a long block on Airport Drive, then closed up as we neared the long-term lots and the traffic started to thicken. She never looked around once. We parked a dozen spaces apart in the Green Lot, and while she was wrestling an eggshell suitcase and garment bag to match out of the trunk I threw my coat and tie into the back seat of the Cutlass, put on a pair of dark glasses, and took out the briefcase full of nothing I keep in the trunk for those occasions when I want to look like something other than a snooper on the scent. Airline passengers without luggage stick out like pajamas in church.

We caught the same shuttle bus to the Smith terminal. She took the rear seat by the bags. I sat up front behind the driver. In between us, a white-haired business type in a double-breasted suit and a young black in a ball cap and starter jacket spent the short trip discussing affairs of import.

"Nothing wrong with the Tigers a healthy bullpen wouldn't cure."

"This point I'd settle for a bullpen. They all had AIDS they couldn't be worse than what we got."

"One iron man could do it. You know, an arm that's good for nine innings. You remember Jack Morris?"

"Before my time, man."

"Well, that's what we need. Another Morris."

"Right now I'm just waiting for basketball season. I can't root for no dead men."

I stretched my arms across the back of my seat, half-listening. Thinking about the breaks and how you don't necessarily have to live right to benefit from them. There was hope for the home team yet.

We got out at American, where Greta ignored a skycap who offered to load her bags aboard his cart and carried them herself through the electric doors. She didn't tip the driver, either.

The foot traffic was heavy inside. It was the usual run of corporate nomads augmented by early vacationers, race junkies headed in to catch the Grand Prix on Belle Isle and veteran Detroiters headed out to avoid it. Greta walked past the ticket counter without stopping, paused before the American DEPARTURES monitor—leaning in to read it without her glasses—and went on toward the gates, hauling both pieces of luggage with her. Some people have limitless faith in airline tolerance toward oversize carryons.

That was a hitch. Security was tight that season—a jet had exploded in midair and no one knew the reason, so the continent was crawling with terrorists—and I needed a ticket to get past the checkpoint. I'd hoped to get in line behind her and buy one. The wait wasn't long, but by the time I got away with a roundtrip to Chicago in hand she'd been cleared through the x ray and metal detector. I lost more time showing my ID to the guards and explaining that my briefcase was empty because I was under orders to pick up some affidavits on the other end. The security chief, a tall Masai warrior complete with tribal tattoos on his cheeks, stroked his lower lip with the antenna of his walk-around Motorola, then waved me on. By that time Greta was as gone as Garbo.

I did some detecting. Of the flights listed on the monitor she had stopped to read, the 2:55 to Miami looked most promising; it left in less than an hour, and Miami is the jumping-off point for travelers bound for Argentina and Peru, tropical paradises with the added attraction of having no viable extradition treaty with the United States. The Miami junket was the one most popular with wanted drug-lords, deposed dictators, and secretaries who gave false statements to the police in homicide investigations. In any case it made more sense than the only other cities with flights departing within reasonable waiting time: Kansas City and Pasadena.

I went to the gate indicated. The waiting area was full of everybody but Greta Griswold.

Of the piles of luggage left unattended by optimistic souls off on errands, none contained her suitcase and hanging bag. I checked the nearby cafe and bookshop, glanced in at the magazine stand, then went back and staked out the gate for fifteen minutes, long enough for her to do what needed to be done twice in the ladies' room. When she didn't answer the general boarding announcement I decided to check out the other gates.

There were only seventeen of them stretched out along a concourse longer than the Bataan Death March. I saw honey-mooning couples and sparring old marrieds, unruly children and the creepy Stepford variety, exhausted salesmen in tired pinstripes, high-rollers in yellow socks, nuns and working girls, graying executives and their long-limbed nieces, Mid-western men in floral shirts, Middle Eastern women in saris and veils, briefcase-swinging lawyers, pill-popping aero-

phobes, gaggles of touring seniors with white hair and cocoa
tans, straggles of would-be Amarillo Slims wandering home
from Vegas with their pockets hanging out and poleaxed expressions on their pale faces, stewardesses—excuse me,
flight attendants—towing luggage on leashes, pilots carrying map cases, airport loungers in cowboy hats, teens in
baggy britches improving their minds in the miniature video
arcade, a kindergarten class on a field trip, floor-sitters with
knapsacks, one minor celebrity, women in shoulderpads
with laptops, ten thousand Japanese with cameras, a pair of
drag queens, a lot of people with atrocious taste in reading,
and all the rest of the loose change of humanity that spills
through the vaulted echoing machine-buffed halls of Here to
There. I saw two pockets picked. I didn't see Greta Griswold.

I stood in front of a glass wall, biting the inside of a cheek
and watching a big-bellied 757 take off at a steep angle. I
wondered if she was on it.

Finally I stepped into the brief embarrassment of a bar and
ordered a whiskey sour to match my thoughts. I'd looked in
twice on my way past in both directions and hadn't seen her.
She didn't seem the type; but then she hadn't seemed the type
to ditch a job she'd held for seventeen years and make a dash
for the tall timber either. As I leaned over to set my briefcase
down in front of the bar, I spotted the end of an eggshell-
colored suitcase poking out from behind a square ceiling post
in the corner.

I paid for my drink, picked it up and my case, and walked
over to the hidden booth.

She didn't see me. No one makes eye contact in airports.
A high-profile murder trial in California was grinding away
on the TV screen mounted under the ceiling, but she wasn't
looking at it. She was sitting with her back to the wall,

smoking a filtered True and turning a nearly empty glass around and around in its ring on the laminated tabletop, her eyes on the middle ground between herself and infinity.

She jumped when I set my own glass on the table.

"Can I get you another one, Mrs. Griswold? Just at a glance I'd say gin and bitters. Guessing drinks is one of my hobbies."

She blinked in my direction, squinted. Then she snapped her tongue against her teeth and rummaged through her handbag for the octagonal glasses.

When she had them on she still didn't know me. I realized I was still wearing my dark glasses. I took them off, and when that didn't seem to help I showed her the ID. Then she remembered. Good secretaries retain the names they write down on their employers' appointment calendars.

She slumped back, dragged deeply on her cigarette, and blew a jet at the table. The post-fifty lines in her face showed through the makeup.

"Yes, I will have another." A light brogue came out that I hadn't heard the first time we'd met. "This time ask them to hold the bitters."

Thirty-one

"Yes."

He definitely worked on the accent. Making a single one-syllable word sound British over the telephone takes practice even in England.

"Walker, Mr. Lund. I have something to report."

I had to stick a finger in my ear and raise my voice to blot out the jabber from a gang of French Canadians who had decided to convene near the exit from the Smith terminal. Montreal must be the loudest city north of Dallas.

"Very well." He waited.

"Not over the wire. Not in the suite either. You might want to break it to Mr. Furlong in your own way."

"Is it that bad?"

"Bad is relative. I've found the witchfinder."

"Indeed."

"Where can we meet?"

"I'm expected at the Fisher Building in half an hour. I plan to sublet an office in the tower for the reading of the will and the leaseholder has promised me a tour of the facilities. We could meet in the lobby an hour from now."

"Sounds jake."

"I beg your pardon?"

"The Fisher at four-thirty is satisfactory. How's himself?"

"Not well. I have to help him in and out of bed now. The hotel is sending up a registered nurse. I imagine she'll recommend he check into hospital."

"We'd better talk fast then."

"I fear we had."

I made two more calls against the oo-lah-lahs and got out of there.

Driving back to town on I-94, the Edsel Ford, avoiding flagmen and recently patched potholes mounded over like fresh graves, I thought about dreams and how the subconscious works the swing shift while the rest of the brain is at rest. The one I'd had about hunting lions was a case in point. They're as likely to be behind you as in front. If this kept up I would have to find some way to work snooze time onto the statement I provide clients.

My brief conversation with Greta Griswold in the airport bar had been nothing more than mortar to hold together the foundation I'd built after leaving Cassandra Photo. I'd left her with a pair of county officers, holding a fresh unlit cigarette and contemplating the same gulf of nothing I'd found her staring at when I joined her.

Albert Kahn—like Jay Bell Furlong a legendary architect, but with a twenty-year head start—had left his thumbprints all over the City of Detroit, and although city planners and an army of demolition experts have been working overtime for decades trying to erase them, the soaring, fluted Art Deco lines of his factories, museums, and skyscrapers, all built between the ratification of the Eighteenth Amendment in 1919 and the downfall of the National Industrial Recovery Act in 1935, are likely to remain a part of the metropolitan landscape long after the antiseptic glass towers of the

Less-Is-More crowd have imploded into their basements. The jewel in his crown is the Fisher Building, an L-shaped pile culminating in a twenty-six-story tower commissioned by the seven Fisher brothers of Body by Fisher, across Grand Boulevard from the General Motors Building—another Kahn design resembling a hinged deck of trick playing cards and for many years the largest office building in the world. Rumor had it GM was offering to trade its headquarters to the city for offices in the Renaissance Center on Jefferson, with the RenCen's complex of shops and offices to move into the City-County Building after the bureaucrats vacate. Just what benefit this game of musical chairs held for anyone was a mystery—more space for more council members' relatives, I suppose—but Henry Ford II, who put up the seed money to build the Center, is no Ford at all if he doesn't come back to haunt the General Motors executives who will be scratching up the desks there with the heels of their Guccis.

The Fisher, topped by a glittering cupola covered with gold leaf, houses offices and shops, a plush theater with palatial dressing rooms for the performers, and up at the top the broadcast studios of WJR, one of the most powerful radio stations in the world and among the oldest. I parked in the large monitored lot next to the building, and when I was sure no one was looking I popped open the glove compartment, took out the Smith & Wesson .38, checked the load, and holstered it in the permanent dent behind my right hip. It was concealed well enough when I put my coat on. I bought them long for that purpose.

The brass-framed revolving door sucked me into the lobby with a whoosh. It was an interior arcade, three stories high and lined with pink-veined marble, opening at regular intervals into bookstores, clothing shops, art galleries, and a bank; the world's oldest indoor mall, as exclusive as an audience with George V. My own footsteps whispered back at me from the skylights.

In the spaces between the shops, employees of the Henry Ford Museum in Dearborn had put down black rubber mats and parked antique cars on them, just in case the city's residents and visitors forgot that the one hundredth anniversary of the invention of the automobile was coming up. Tasteful signs erected on free-standing brass pedestals identified the spotless automobiles: included were a 1933 Auburn with curving, cream-colored fenders and chromed exhaust pipes snaking out of ports in the hood like exposed muscles; a white-over-red 1955 Kaiser; a 1928 Cadillac touring car, gunmetal gray with running boards and a spotlight; a 1915 Thomas Flyer, as long as a covered wagon, with a canvas top to complete the illusion; a 1941 Packard with blackout headlamps; and a detailed reproduction of Henry Ford's quadricycle, the backyard invention that predated the Model T, which put America on wheels and the world on the petroleum standard. They gleamed with wax and brass polish and smelled of new rubber and oiled leather.

It was an impressive display, but a historical distortion. The curved-dash Oldsmobile should have been propped up on a jack to represent the condition of the nation's roads in 1900 and there should have been bulletholes in the Prohibition-era Caddy. The farther you go forward, the smoother the path looks behind you.

The security desk stood inside the corner of the L, with a clear view down both ends of the arcade and the corridor that ran between the elevators to the main entrance on Grand. The guard seated behind it was another grayhead in a lightweight blue uniform with balloons of scar tissue over both eyes, a double for Joe Louis in his later years. In another decade or so the natural course of time is going to empty out our store of rent-a-cops. The checked grip of a Ruger Blackhawk pressed into the hard fat around his middle.

"Any way down from the tower except by those elevators?" I jerked a thumb toward the twin banks of brass doors.

He laid a spatulated index finger on a book of crossword puzzles to mark his place and stared down the corridor as if he'd never seen it before.

"Just the stairs," he said finally.

"Know anyone who suffers from gout?"

He thought about that, then nodded. "Me, for one."

"How do you deal with stairs?"

"When there's elevators I don't."

I thanked him and strolled over to stake out the corridor. He watched me, then returned his attention to his puzzle. I wondered if he was going to do me any good.

Doors opened, doors closed. A number of job applicants went up to and came down from interviews, identifiable by their pinstripes and white shirts, both sexes. Those who already had jobs boarded and exited in their shirtsleeves, carrying leather portfolios and cardboard file folders like the one I had under one arm. A local author I recognized from his picture in the *News* and *Free Press* book sections got on, accompanied by a publicist or something in a tailored skirt and jacket and somebody with a portable tape recorder who seemed to be collecting material for a biography; I figured they were on their way up for an interview on the radio. Doors opened, doors closed. None of the elevators stood open for long. People who called Detroit a dead city didn't make it a practice to hang out by the elevators.

Stuart Lund was ten minutes late. He was the last off the elevator and had some trouble fighting his way through a group trying to get on. He was wearing the same gray silk suit he'd had on when we met, with a green club tie and a rusty-orange pocket handkerchief to match the design. He was leaning a little on the cane and it must have been a long ride because the pain of standing showed on his fleshy face. But the waves of yellow hair were in order, the little triangular moustache was trimmed to within a millimeter of its life, and his waxy blue eyes were alert. He spotted me right away.

"I shall never get used to all this hurly-burly at tea time," he said by way of greeting. "Someone should introduce the custom to this country."

"California's spoiled you. Welcome to the Industrial Midwest. How's your foot?"

"It was improving until I left the hotel. How is your head?"

"It was working a little slow until a while ago."

He didn't pry into that. "I don't suppose there's a place in this pretentious barn to sit down."

"There's a coffee shop down in the tunnel."

"And what tunnel might that be?"

It was easier to take him there than to tell him about it. We took the broad open staircase down from the lobby to the sublevel, where a well-lit passage lined with clothing stores, barber shops, and eateries connects the Fisher with General Motors and the New Center Building. It was clean, well-ventilated, and every bit as busy as upstairs.

"Good Lord, I never knew this existed. Does it run all the way under the city?"

"Of course. There's a lake and a pipe organ on the next level down. Then catacombs."

"I find your humor wearying."

"That's okay. I don't get *Monty Python*."

There was a wait for a table. He leaned against the wall next to the blackboard menu on the easel, hooked the cane over a forearm, and mopped his face with a plain handkerchief from his inside breast pocket. It was cool down there, but his collar was damp. "Well, who is it?"

"Who is who?"

"The witchfinder, naturally. The reason I'm not sitting in a comfortable cab right now, on my way back to my comfortable suite and a warm foot bath."

"The case was a little more complicated than I hoped. I thought when I found the party responsible for the fake photograph that broke Mr. Furlong's engagement, I'd have the murderer of Lynn Arsenault and Nate Millender as well. I forgot life isn't that simple."

"You weren't retained to solve any murders at all."

"You can't always pick out the nut without getting a piece of shuck," I said. "Royce Grayling killed Millender. He as much as told me so this morning in my office, not that his confession would hold up in a court of law. It happened Millender was blackmailing Arsenault for his part in the inheritance fraud; a fraud he originally blackmailed Arsenault into with evidence of his homosexuality."

"You forget I'm a homosexual. I don't march in parades, but the world has changed since Oscar Wilde's imprisonment. No one can use my sexual preference to force me to act against my will." He lowered his voice an extra decibel on the phrase *sexual preference*. The buzz in the crowded restaurant would drown out a Buddy Rich solo.

"They might if you worked for Vernon Whiting, and liked your job. Anyway, we're not talking about you. Yet."

I couldn't tell if he heard the last word. Just then our blonde hostess returned and led us to a table for two next to the kitchen. I ordered coffee in a carafe to keep us from being interrupted. Lund said he'd share the carafe.

I lifted my brows. "Not tea?"

"Can't bear it. Sometimes I think that's the reason I left England. You were saying?"

"It looked promising," I said. "But Millender was killed for a different extortion, unrelated to the case. When I started sniffing around, Grayling assumed I was after the goods on that *other* blackmail victim and moved up his timetable on Millender. I should feel guilty for that. I don't. Millender had all the morals of grout mold, and anyway his ticket was punched long before I met him."

Lund started to say something, but our coffee came and he waited until the waitress moved on to deliver the check to another table. "Bit of a coincidence, wouldn't you say? Arsenault and Millender were connected, and Arsenault was in a line of endeavor that brushes frequently with local government. Grayling's employers, if I'm not mistaken."

"Not so coincidental. Blackmailers forget there's only one sure way out from under. Given his penchant for well-set-up victims in delicate circumstances, he was bound to rub up against Grayling or someone like him someday." I tasted my coffee, and dumped in a container of cream to cut the bitter edge. A cellar place is a cellar place. "The cold fact is Grayling couldn't have committed both murders, because they were both committed at almost the same moment. *That's* a coincidence, but only in timing."

I spread open the file folder and handed him the eight-by-ten glossy Sergeant St. Thomas had given me, taken at the murder scene in the garage at Imminent Visions.

He turned it toward the light, scowled. I couldn't read him beyond that. He'd been present at too many litigations. "Arsenault?"

"He didn't take nearly as good a picture as he did eight years ago."

"Why did you want me to see this?"

"When I make a report I don't leave anything out. Here's a closer shot." I gave him one of the blowups Randy Quarrels had made. It was a practice shot.

"Same picture? Odd framing."

"Ignore the corpse. Concentrate on that round spot next to it."

"Blood?"

"More likely grease. There wasn't any blood on the floor until I opened the car door and Arsenault's body fell out. But any garage worthy of the name has streaks and puddles of grease and oil all over. You have to be careful not to track it anywhere."

As I spoke I picked up the best print of the batch and slid it on top of the one he was looking at. This one was much clearer.

"That cane of yours is a valuable antique," I said. "You ought to be more careful where you put it."

His eyes didn't move from the quarter-size circle near Lynn Arsenault's dead arm, the print of the rubber tip of a cane. They were as lifeless as blue candle stumps. They remained that way while he tore all three pictures in half, then in quarters. He went on tearing until he couldn't get the pieces any smaller. Then he turned in his chair and let them flutter to the linoleum between the tables.

Thirty-two

I PLACED THE NEGATIVE and the remaining practice print on his side of the table.

"Tear those too, if you like. The cops have the original negative and can afford to get an even clearer enlargement. Any jury could look at it and match the mark to your cane. From the location, I'd say you leaned on it with your left hand while you used your right to shoot him through the window on the driver's side of his Porsche."

He made no move to pick up the items. "Do you expect me to deny it? Very well. I was with Jay when Arsenault was killed. And I have no motive."

"Furlong might remember whether you were out that morning; sick or well, he's sharper than any ten men his age. Or he might not. I think you said that was one of his bad days. I couldn't get through to you when I called from the garage. When you finally answered the telephone, you'd had time enough to drive to Allen Park and back twice."

"That doesn't prove anything."

"That part's for the cops. So's the motive, but I've got that. You're the witchfinder. You rigged the fake picture scheme to keep Lily Talbot from marrying Furlong and changing his will."

"Ludicrous. His bequest to me is purely honorary. I make more than that in a year on his retainer."

"A retainer that stops the moment he stops breathing. A new one kicks in as soon as you clock in as executor and probate attorney. Given the number of heirs involved—not to mention their temperament—the will could drag on in court for twenty years without a widow in the picture. No one gets anything out of that but the lawyer, you. That has to be the seventh circle of heaven for someone in your profession, a nearly unlimited source of income from a client who can't pester you because he's dead. I can think of the names of a couple of dozen ambulance-chasers who'd kill for a good deal less."

He sipped from his cup. His hand was steady. "If I were your counsel, I'd advise you to keep your voice down. All you have is a snapshot of a stain on a concrete floor. Even if the police manage to match it to my cane there's nothing to prove I was in the garage at the time of the murder. I could sue you for everything you own."

"Be my guest."

"You say that merely because what you own isn't worth much. But you're forgetting your reputation as a detective. When I'm through with you, you won't even have a livelihood."

I said, "The cops have Greta Griswold."

He spilled coffee on his hand. He yelped, slammed down the cup, and wound his handkerchief around the burn. One or two of the diners seated nearby looked at him, then dove back into their conversations.

"And who might she be?" he asked then.

"You might want to put ice on that," I said. "Hot coffee can raise blisters. I turned her over to the sheriff's deputies at the airport. I'd tailed her from the Marriott, where you gave her cash to lam to Pasadena. She has friends there. She told me everything. Now she's telling the cops."

"What sort of lies did she tell?"

"She's not good at them. She knows that; it's why she ran. *You* know that, or you wouldn't have bankrolled her flight. But then you know her better than anyone."

"I never heard the name before this moment."

"That's a lie, but you did know her better as Cathlin Faolin. She went back to her maiden name after you stopped living together as man and wife in England."

He wound the handkerchief tighter and said nothing. The flesh on the back of his hand bulged as white as the fabric.

"Some marriages involving a homosexual partner last a long time." Since he hadn't touched the picture and negative, I returned them to the folder and closed it. "Yours wasn't one of those, although technically you're still married. She didn't know that at the time. You told her the divorce was final, and being a solicitor you were able to rig up documents for her to sign that satisfied her. It wasn't until after she emigrated to America, married again, became a widow, and took a job at Imminent Visions, that you told her she was a bigamist. That meant she was never legally married to a United States citizen and could have been deported. That was your leverage."

I shook my head. "Poor old Nate Millender thought he was hot stuff as a blackmailer, but he wasn't a patch on you. You got Greta to help you kill Arsenault by threatening to report her to the State Department if she refused. She didn't much like him, and she has bad memories of Northern Ireland. It didn't take her long to make the decision.

"Her car had a big trunk," I went on. "Still, it must have been a snug fit for a man your size. No wonder your gout's worse. She smuggled you into the garage past the parking attendant, let you out to wait for Arsenault to come down, and smuggled you back out in the trunk afterward. That's where you were hiding all the time the cops were searching the building for suspicious persons. Simple enough to work. But you complicated things when you forced Greta to tell the cops Royce Grayling was on the premises at the time of the murder. How long did you think that would hold up, when neither the security guard in the lobby nor any of the video cameras scattered throughout the building saw him?"

"He had an appointment! He—" He clamped his jaw shut. Pain spasmed his heavy features. He unwound the handkerchief from his hand, reached inside his coat, and brought out a plastic prescription bottle. He shook out two pills, swallowed them, and washed them down with coffee.

I nodded. His slip should have made me tingle. Instead I felt saturated and old. My head hurt.

"You have the right to remain silent, Counselor," I said. "Yeah, Grayling had an appointment to see Arsenault that morning. You knew who he was and what he was from what I'd told you. When you learned from Greta he was expected, you got the bright idea to set him up to take the fall for Arsenault. Only you couldn't know that Grayling tried to call and cancel. The telephones weren't working that morning, thanks to me, and Greta couldn't warn you. She can't remember now what scheme you'd cooked up with her to get Arsenault to go out to his car at the time Grayling was expected, but that doesn't matter. She didn't get a chance to use it. I smoked him out first.

"When he came down to the garage where you were waiting, you assumed Grayling was in position for the frame and went ahead with the kill. Greta nailed Grayling for the cops even though he never showed, not knowing what else to do without you on hand to advise her. That was the blunder, the X factor you didn't allow for. It turned her into a fugitive; something she wasn't any better at than she was at improvising a more acceptable lie. These things happen when you don't take time to plan."

I glanced at my watch. "She'll have made her statement by now. It will include how you panicked when I told you Arsenault was ready to crack, and decided to take him down before Furlong found out he was sheltering a fat snake in his bosom and dropped you from the will."

"There's no reason to be insulting." Lund drew a deep breath and let it out. The pills were taking effect. "You don't know how much of that sort of thing I've had to put up with from Jay all these years. I was just his great waddling eunuch. Good enough to be trusted with his financial and legal affairs because I was too hound-dog loyal ever to consider cheating him, but certainly not his equal; not on a level with the immortal embalmed genius, resting as he was on his half-century-old laurels.

"None of this is evidence," he said. "I'm not confessing to any murders, or even inheritance fraud. I'm just telling you what I'd like to have done. There's no law against that, here or in my native country."

I spread open my coat to show him I wasn't wearing a wire. My shirt was lightweight and he could see through to my undershirt. He shrugged his rounded shoulders.

"First he threw me the bone of custodianship. My years of loyalty entitled me to far more. Then he threatened to take it away by marrying a woman who wasn't even born when he made his last significant contribution to his field. He was flaunting his wealth and status—yes, and his heterosexuality—and expecting me to accept it without comment. No, not even that. He never thought about me at all. I was just another design on his drafting board: drawn, built, filed, and forgotten along with all his other creations. Well, this was one design that thought for itself."

"How'd you find Millender?"

"You mean, if I did find him. I told you I'm not confessing to anything. Call it serendipity. I met him in one of those gay singles clubs that were so popular before the plague came along and closed them. The affair didn't last, but when I found out how he made his money, and that Lynn Arsenault of Imminent Visions was one of his photographic subjects, I started planning. Greta was already in place, a bit of luck. She'd been a legal secretary with my firm in England for four years, and answered the telephone in the Detroit office of Furlong, Belder, and Associates after coming to this country. I arranged that, for old times' sake. She was grateful, since employment helped her obtain a visa."

"Is that why she agreed to apply for a job with Vernon Whiting?"

"Partly. The position also paid better and she had more responsibility. At the time it was just a ploy to ingratiate myself further with Jay. The inside information she supplied enabled me to make a number of suggestions that helped Furlong and Belder remain competitive. That was one more of the many services I performed that Jay took for granted."

"He wasn't the only one. Greta must have had a lot on the ball to remain with Imminent Visions this long. Along the way she managed to hand you Lynn Arsenault on a silver tray. Twice. She doesn't owe you a damn thing."

"She always was an accommodating girl." He played with the prescription bottle, rolling it back and forth between his great soft palms.

"You must have thought you had God in a box when Grayling capped Nate Millender. Sooner or later he would have put the squeeze on you the way he did Arsenault and others, and Greta might not have been able to help. It's sort of too bad that's the very thing that keeps you from pinning Grayling to the murder in Allen Park."

"Timing is important. Right now I need as much time as I can get." He returned the bottle to his pocket. When his hand came back out it was wrapped around the butt of a small nickel-plated automatic.

Both my hands were on the table, resting on top of the file folder. The .38 was on my hip. I could have gone for it, possibly even had him cold before he could squeeze the trigger of the .22 he had used on Lynn Arsenault. I had all the experience in the world over him when it came to getting a gun out into the air and firing it.

I didn't move. "No good, Windy. I called the Detroit and Allen Park Police Departments after I called you. They've had plenty of time to seal all the exits."

"I'll take my chances. Keep your hands on the table." He rose. He had the pistol in his right hand, clamped against his side. The great bulk of his body concealed it from the other diners as he picked up his cane. "Awfully un-British of me to stick you with the check, old man. But I'm an American now. I ought to start acting like one. If you try to follow me I'll shoot, and I can't answer for my aim. Some innocent people might get hurt."

I said, "I'll just stay here and finish my coffee. It's been a long day, even for Monday."

"Do tell Jay I said good-bye. I'm fond of the old boy even if he did treat me like an old fat dog." He withdrew into a hungry throng of men and women in business suits being led to their tables, swiveling a little to keep me in his field of fire until the crowd closed in behind him. Then he moved swiftly, not leaning on the cane now. His foot wasn't bothering him nearly as much as he'd let on.

I was still sitting there drinking coffee when I heard the first shot. It was loud and deep and came from a much bigger bore than Stuart Lund's .22.

Thirty-three

THERE WERE TWO MORE SHOTS, fired a split-second behind
the first. By then I was up and moving.

When I reached the entrance to the coffee shop, the crowd
was closing back in after scattering for cover. Someone said
something about 911. I saw Stuart Lund's silver-crooked
cane lying on the waxed floor. Then I saw Lund, sprawled a
few feet away with Sergeant St. Thomas of the Allen Park
Police Department on his knees supporting the attorney's
head. Three separate stains were spreading across the fat
man's white dress shirt. His automatic lay on the floor at his
side. The waxy blue eyes were already beginning to lose
their sheen.

St. Thomas looked up at me. "It was Grayling. He took
off that way before I could get my gun out." He pointed
down the tunnel toward the stairs to the Fisher Building.

Just then there was another shot.

"That's Redburn," he said. "I posted him by the stairs."

I started that way. My revolver was in my hand. I didn't
remember drawing it.

"Walker."

I looked back at the sergeant just in time to catch his

badge folder against my chest. I tucked it into my outside breast pocket on the run with the shield hanging out.

Officer Redburn was leaning against the wall in the stairwell, gripping his right arm with his left hand. Blood and splinters of bone poked out between his fingers. His Glock dangled at the end of the shattered arm. His round face was blank with pain and shock.

I bounded up the steps. At the top the wall exploded next to my head. I retreated a step, flattening against the wall. Running footsteps echoed away across the lobby. I flicked bits of Italian marble from my right eye and resumed pursuit.

The guard at the security desk was just getting up from his seat, staring in the direction of the parking lot. I ran that way.

"Police! Stop or I'll shoot!"

I stopped. The revolving door at the end of the arcade was still turning behind a figure spread-eagled against the light. I saw shapely legs beneath a skirt an inch too short for regulations. There was nothing between us but a row of antique automobiles.

"Me, Lieutenant," I called out. "Amos Walker."

"Walker? Where'd you get the shield?" Mary Ann Thaler lowered her service piece.

At that moment Royce Grayling stepped out from between the gleaming Packard and the canvas-topped Thomas Flyer and fired at the Felony Homicide lieutenant.

She had fast reflexes. At the first flash of movement she hit the floor and rolled toward the wall. Grayling's slug struck sparks off the revolving door frame. The door spun. In the same instant he swung my way.

He'll be a little slow turning to his left, Barry Stackpole had said. That second Purple Heart.

I took aim like an old-time duelist, offering a narrow sideways target as I sighted down my right arm stretched out at shoulder level. Taking my time. Fill the lungs halfway and hold it. Slow and steady pressure on the trigger. The echo of the .38 joined the others walloping between the marble walls.

Grayling disappeared behind the Packard.

There was an echo-filled pause. A squad of uniforms barreled through the revolving door. Thaler, up on one knee in the corner with an elbow propped on her raised thigh and her pistol pointing at the skylight, shouted at them to seek cover. They spread out along both walls.

"That you, Walker?"

It was Grayling's voice. I crouched behind the Ford quadricycle, resting my gun arm across one of the solid-rubber tires, as big as a bicycle wheel. As far as cover went it was as flimsy as a baby carriage.

"That depends on whether you're hit," I called out.

"What if I'm not?"

"Then you're a liar too. You weren't the only sharpshooter in the Asian theater."

"I've been hit before. Twice. I'm hard to bring down." He was breathing heavily, but he might have been faking.

"No medals this time, Royce," I said. "You blew your sweet cover."

"I guess I don't like being set up. Not for an amateur job anyway."

"How'd you know we were here?"

"You called downtown for backup. I've got friends downtown, remember?"

"Not anymore."

"Yeah, well. I was getting tired of this place anyway. No night life."

Another chunk of marble burst near the parking-lot exit. One of the uniforms drew back quickly. He'd been inching closer along the wall. Grayling still had the instincts of a jungle guerrilla.

I said, "Give it up, Royce. You need medical attention, and you're spoiling a landmark besides."

"I never much liked it. I'm a Furlong man myself." He laughed, coughed. It sounded genuine. He hadn't long if I'd made a lung shot. If he didn't move soon he'd drown in his own blood.

Unless he was faking.

I tested him.

"They told me you were a pro. Gunning down a man in front of a couple of dozen witnesses is kid stuff."

"Witnesses are a joke."

"I don't hear the cops laughing. You shot one of those too."

"You fight dirty, Walker. These cops didn't know that."

I opened my mouth to reply.

Something growled.

It sounded like the MGM lion in those acoustics.

Another growl, and then another, ragged and prolonged. An engine caught. There was a drumroll of pistons and then the long black Packard began to move.

Gears groaned. Blue exhaust hazed the air. All the time he'd kept me talking he'd been busy hot-wiring the primitive starter.

The car had been parked at an angle, facing out from the wall. Now it was rolling my way up the arcade, a big beetle-backed sedan nearly as long as a bus, with windwings and blackout headlamps squinted like dragon's eyes, picking up speed. The door on the passenger's side flapped shut, but I couldn't see Grayling through the windshield. He'd be stretched across the front seat, turning the steering wheel from the bottom with his other hand on the foot pedal.

A gun barked at the end of the arcade. The Packard's rear window and windshield collapsed in triangular shards of nonshatterproof glass. The car was moving faster now, headed for the lobby. He would have to make a tricky right turn to make the main entrance, but once he'd done that and smashed through to the street there was nothing to stop him as long as he had gas in the tank.

I made a quick reconnaissance.

Henry Ford was a simple man. His quadricycle was operated by only two levers, a tall one with a smooth cylindrical handle for steering and a straight one that came up to the driver's knees. That would be the brake.

I changed hands on my revolver, grasped the handle of the brake, and shoved it forward.

The fragile little car began to roll, but not nearly fast enough; the Packard was almost on top of me. I laid the .38 on the floorboards, got a hold of the footboard and the back of the seat, and heaved. The vehicle lurched out into the middle of the corridor and the big sedan rammed into its side.

But the Packard didn't stop.

Its weight and momentum carried the little Ford sideways for ten feet, its solid rubber tires screeching on the highly polished floor. But Grayling was unable to work the clutch and the throttle with just one hand; the engine coughed and died. The juggernaut rolled to a halt.

The door on the driver's side flew open. Grayling, gathering his feet beneath him, leaned out and drew down on me with a blue-barreled nine-millimeter automatic in his right hand.

My gun was on the floor of the quadricycle. I backpedaled, but the wall stopped me. There was no place to go.

The report was louder than any of the others. I jumped, but not from the impact; a splatter of Royce Grayling's blood had stung my left eye.

For an agonizing moment he hung there, one knee on the Packard's mohair seat, one foot on the floorboards, a shin braced against the steering column. His mouth was working, but nothing was coming out except blood, a lot of it. The entire front of his striped shirt was stained red, but it was the fresher wound that was giving him the most trouble, the great gaping hole where his throat had been. Then his eyes rolled over white and he fell forward. His automatic bounced off the running board and clattered to the floor.

The aging guard from the security desk stood in the middle of the corridor just this side of the elevators. His feet were spread and he had his arms stretched out in front of him, at the end of which smoked the shiny long-barreled Ruger Blackhawk I'd seen in his hip holster.

Thirty-four

A FUEL-GUZZLING JET venerable enough to have starred in Chet Huntley's coach lounge commercial in 1972 bellied in over the tarmac, touched down with a shriek of rubber, and taxied toward the gates with beads of rain glittering like perspiration on its red-and-white metal skin. The sky had been weeping over the metropolitan area since before dawn, lowering the temperature another ten degrees and putting paid to the hot spell, at least until the next front came through or the fan in my office gave up the ghost. Burning cigarettes with the rest of the lepers in the designated area, I rested my feet on my overnight bag and hoped for a craft built sometime in the present decade. Flying is one of those activities best left to children and that class of adults who are content to let other people make decisions regarding their survival, like Szechuan chefs.

I'd read up on the latest developments in the Fisher Building demolition derby and turkey shoot, in the loose sections of newspaper laying around the waiting area; why anyone bothered to buy one in an airport was a mystery I wasn't paid to solve. There was nothing I hadn't known already, not counting errors and embellishments. *USA Today* had run a honey of a picture of the wreckage on its front page. When a 1941 Packard runs into an 1896 Ford, it's national news. My name didn't appear in the caption.

I sensed Lily Talbot before I saw her. Walking down the concourse, she turned heads male and female in a kind of personal telegraphy, like an infrared beam tripping breakers. It wasn't a question of beauty, although she possessed that quality, common enough in the age of liposuction, silicone, collagen, rhinoplasty, and broadening tastes. It was a combination of looks, attitude, and carriage.

She beat watching the traffic on the runway. Her long pleated skirt, trailing scarf, and boots with three-inch heels drew attention to her unconventional disregard for current fashion, and her short red hair to her long classic skull, like something found among the porcelains in an Egyptian tomb. She walked with her back straight but not rigid, her chin raised but not upthrust, and she maintained a lively artist's interest in her surroundings that set her apart from the job lot of attractive women who stared through people and things as if they didn't exist in their dimension. I was on my feet before I thought about getting up.

We touched hands. She smiled noncommittally and said something that evaporated in the air. We adjourned to an uninhabited corner by an unused gate, where I ditched my filter in an ashcan. She smelled lightly of lilac. An uncomplicated scent for a complex character.

"I wasn't sure you'd get my message," I said. "Jean Sternhagen said you were out of town."

"An art auction in Toledo. When I called in she told me what you told her and I drove right up. You made quite an impression on her."

"Chicks dig a bandage."

She looked around. "Where is he?"

"Boarding. His kind of passenger gets on early."

"You're going along?"

"He paid for my ticket yesterday and hired me to escort him. After what happened he changed his mind about staying in Detroit. L.A.'s his home now. I was just waiting for you."

"But you couldn't be sure I was coming."

"People generally do, in the end. Guilt is a waste of time, but it's stronger than love or hate when it comes to making people do things they don't want to."

"I never said I didn't. The world isn't that cut-and-dried."

"Sure it is."

"I find that surprising, coming from you."

"The world's black and white, good and bad, no matter what you hear. The people who say it isn't have already chosen black."

"You seem pretty sure of your philosophy."

"It's a philosophy."

"Could I see him?"

"I'll ask."

I went over and talked with the clerk at the counter, an unbruised twenty under all the varnish and peroxide. When I got back, Lily was looking out the window. A Tinkertown train was hauling baggage around the tail section of the plane parked at the gate.

"She's checking," I said. "Just in case you smuggled an atomic device past security."

"Thank you." She leaned a shoulder against the glass. "I was too busy framing bids to follow the news. Bids I never got to enter because of your message. Jean's information was sketchy and the car radio had it all garbled. What happened?"

I told her. It was still fresh because I'd gone over it several times for the cops and again for Furlong. I was typing it all up in the office for whoever cared to read it when I got the call from Henry Ford Hospital, where he'd checked in after leaving the Marriott. When the airline called later to report that all the arrangements had been made I'd just had time to call Jean Sternhagen, throw a change of clothes and a razor into the bag, and drive out to catch the 1:28 nonstop to LAX. Then the flight was delayed two hours because of twisters in Oklahoma and Kansas.

"So Royce Grayling's dead," she said when I finished.

"He was DOA at Detroit Receiving, but that's just for the blotter. The cops pulled a dead man out of the Packard."

"Are you in trouble with the law?"

"The answer to that question is always yes. But not as much as I was a couple of days ago. I called Sergeant St. Thomas in Allen Park and Lieutenant Thaler in Detroit and gave them the whole story before I met with Stuart Lund. I had a hunch he'd cut and run. I needed the backup. Two homicides solved for two departments in one afternoon is worth some points. Not that you'd know it from the way they interrogated me."

She said nothing. I moved a shoulder.

"It's a job. It's not as pretty as running an art gallery."

"I still don't understand why Grayling shot Stuart."

"Professional pride. He had a lot of it. Enough anyway to cowboy the job when he learned from his plant at Detroit Police Headquarters that I was meeting with the man who tried to frame him for that bald-faced murder in Allen Park. He still might have gotten away with it, but there were twice as many cops on hand as he expected."

"How is Stuart?"

"Still in a coma at Receiving last time I checked. He won't be much good for anything even if he comes out of it, and I doubt he will. One of Grayling's slugs severed his spinal column. Getting yourself paralyzed from the neck down is a hell of a way to cure a bad case of gout."

"Poor Windy."

"It would've been a short run even without Grayling. His wife was talking, and Rio de Janeiro has all the lawyers it needs. Anyway, Poor Windy was a killer and a corrupter. He tried to ruin your life."

"He didn't ruin it."

"That wasn't his fault."

She looked away, toward the crowded gate area. "Three dead, and one might as well be. All over a broken engagement eight years old."

"Engagements get broken every day without people getting killed. Furlong's estate is worth millions. It all comes down to greed. Sooner or later everything does."

She looked at me. "Do you really believe that?"

"I do today. My head hurts and I hate to fly."

"It wasn't greed. It was love. Stuart loved Jay, don't you see that?" Her slightly Oriental eyes were dry and clear.

"He knew Furlong was straight."

"That isn't what I'm talking about and you know it. Or maybe you don't. Jay didn't. He could be remarkably blind for an artist; even I knew that in the short time we were together. But he wasn't always that way. He trusted Stuart with a secret he wouldn't even share with me until he was absolutely certain we were going to spend our lives together."

"You mean the fact that he really did steal one of Vernon Whiting's designs when they worked together?"

"He told *you*?"

"No. I figured it out when he said he thought Whiting had put you up to seduce him. He'd only have considered that if he thought Whiting had a good reason to want revenge."

"It was an act of desperation, when Jay was overworked and blocked and not thinking straight. He regretted it the rest of his life. It put a bitterness in him, right at the core. I think that bitterness would have broken us up in the end. That's the ironic part. The fake picture was unnecessary.

"It wasn't a homosexual thing, Stuart's love for Jay," she went on, "although Stuart himself might have thought it was. When two people share a vision for years they develop a bond much stronger than sexual attraction. When one or the other breaks that bond, anything can happen. The money was just an excuse. Scar tissue over a broken heart. What do you think of that?"

"I think you should take Jean Sternhagen out to dinner before she smashes a Monet over your head."

She stared at me.

"Or a Manet," I finished.

After a second she smiled.

Airport security approached in the person of a bearded party in black-rimmed glasses and a blue serge suit cut badly over his shoulder rig. He was carrying a Motorola and had a gold ring in one ear. "Mr. Walker?"

"Miss Talbot." I indicated her. "She wants to see Mr. Furlong."

Just then the clerk at the counter got on the P.A. and announced general boarding.

"There's my ride." I offered my hand.

Lily Talbot took it. "Thanks. For trying. I guess that makes two blind artists you've known."

I said good-bye. Security took charge and she accompanied him through a door he opened with a computerized ID card, on out to where the cargo-handlers were getting ready to load Jay Bell Furlong's coffin aboard the plane.

More
Loren D. Estleman!

Please turn this page
for a
bonus excerpt
from

THE HOURS OF
THE VIRGIN

a new
Mysterious Press hardcover
available at
bookstores everywhere.

I spotted Merlin Gilly standing against the empty space where the Hotel LaSalle had stood two minutes earlier. It was a bum trade.

The hotel had been a going concern in July 1930, when Jerry Buckley signed off his radio broadcast at midnight, went down to the lobby to meet a woman, and was met instead by three men in silk suits who shot him eleven times. They never identified the woman and they never found the shooters, but the memorial service on Belle Isle lit up the sky on both sides of the Canadian border. That was when

Detroit was run by the Irish, who thought a wake was better than a trial any day.

In the decades since, the LaSalle had hit all the landings on the slippery back stairs of modern history: residential hotel, home for the aged, crack house, and blackened shell in the biggest ghost town this side of Sarajevo. Pigeons sailed in through the missing windowpanes and cartwheeled back out on a contact high from the angel dust blowing about inside. The time had come to end its suffering.

The new mayor, dapper in a borsalino hat, tan Chesterfield with gray suede patches on the lapels, and gray kid gloves, said a few words on the order of Detroit rising from its ashes, then squashed down the red button on a remote control the size of a pocket Webster's. Following a shuddery pause, the joints of the scabby old girders blew out, starting at the cigar stand and walking up toward the presidential suite. Beneath the concussions there was a long, silvery tinkle of several tons of rose-tinted mirrors collapsing inside, but for a moment after the final charge went off everything was silent. It appeared as if the construction methods of the turn of the last century were more than a match for the high-tech demolitions of the millennium. But it was just mortal shock. All eighteen stories slid into the foundation in a single sheet, like a magician's velvet cloth. Dust—marble and mahogany, gold leaf and leaded glass, horsehair plaster and cut crystal, and worm-eaten Florentine tessellate—rolled out from the bottom and settled over the galoshes of the TV reporters, car-crash buffs, police officers, and pickpockets watching from outside the yellow tape.

When it was over, they applauded, whistled and cheered, as if the relic were making way for a school or a free clinic. A casino was going in next year, or the year after that if the Japanese held out. Until then it would be just another vacant lot in a city with more empty spaces in its skyline than a goaltender's grin.

Snow covered the ground. The old mayor was in Intensive Care once again, corrupted finally to his vital organs; the spot in front of Henry Ford Hospital where the local news crews shot their stand-ups was beginning to look like a buzzard aviary. His legacy was everywhere. New York and Orlando had placed campaign contributions as carefully as the dynamite men had laid their charges, clearing space in the moral landscape for legalized gambling. The police were beefing up the Domestic Violence Unit for the statistical upsurge once the rent money started disappearing into slot machines. Two new stadiums we didn't need were going in downtown, J. L. Hudson's department store was next in line for destruction, and a couple of dozen long-established businesses were packing their inventories to make room for the chains.

They called it Renaissance. I called it opportunity; but then no one comes to me with work when he's happy.

"Walker! Amos Walker!"

Merlin was shouting and waving, in case I missed the overcoat. I'd have been nobody's idea of a detective if I had. It was a shaggy gray-brown tent that reached to his ankles, heavy enough for a Siberian sleigh ride. The species it belonged to wouldn't have any use for it in the Smithsonian. What it was doing wrapped around somebody like Merlin Gilly went with some story I was probably going to hear.

Pretending I hadn't noticed him wasn't an option. The mayor's white stretch limousine was sliding away through the slush and the crowd was breaking up, off in search of something else to watch fall down. Merlin was heading my way across the flow, dipping in and out among the Carhartts and London Fogs like furry flotsam. Very soon he was standing in front of me, adjusting the big coat and patting down the hairs that had managed to work their way loose from the mousse, as black and shiny as fresh asphalt. He was black Irish, swarthy and small-boned, and taller than he appeared from a distance, although he had the jerky nervous mannerisms and bantam bounce of a born runt.

4

"Best show in town, am I right?" he said by way of greeting. "Boom! Whoosh! The city's missing a bet. They ought to sell tickets."

"I was just waiting to cross the street."

"You can do that anytime. Motor City, phooey. The Wings ought to practice on Woodward at rush hour."

"Hello, Merlin. What'd you do, skin every rat in your building?"

"Rat? Oh, this?" He shrugged the coat up and down across his shoulders, as if that would improve the fit. He could have turned around inside it and brought a friend. "Pine marten, the genuine article. Go ahead, feel it." He held up a sleeve with manicured fingers sticking out of it. His hands were pink and shiny, like a doll's. He never bent them except to grab a glass or a buck.

I kept mine in my pockets. "I better not. I might startle it."

He felt it himself with his other hand. "It's warm, all right. I wish I could pull it up over my ears." They were as red as banker's dye.

"You should have had them kill the cub, too. Then you'd have a hat."

"Aw. You ain't one of them. I seen you eat steak blood rare. You ever see a picture of one of these in the woods? They're better off on my back."

"I bet you're going to tell me how it got there."

5

"Over drinks, boy, over drinks. A little premium's what I need to cuddle up with. You know a pump near here? I'm kind of off my lot." He almost never got above Corktown.

"If you mean a bar, there's one around the corner."

"There always is." He beamed. "And this town's got more corners than the country's got Kennedys. Let's go bob for olives."

We went around the corner. I didn't have an appointment with anything but the magazines in my office, and they'd been waiting since Desert Storm. Anyway, Merlin was a man with a mission. This was an accidental meeting the way the Hotel LaSalle had fallen down without help.

The bar was a cigar lounge now. Before that it had been a brew pub, and before that just a bar. They'd torn up six strata of linoleum to find the original oak planks—oiled golden yellow and no more than an inch and a half wide—replaced the slippery red vinyl with brown imitation leather, installed a back-bar, paneled the walls, and hung them with rusty advertising signs. Then they'd gone over everything with steel wool and paint remover to make it look old. A cloud of blue Havana smoke hung just under the pressed tin ceiling, but it was last night's exhaust. That time of the morning was reserved for veteran drinkers. Later the young legal sharks from downtown would glide in wearing their Armanis

6

and Donna Karans, firing up Montecristos with gold lighters, talking too loud and slurping Arctic gin from glass funnels, like William Powell and Myrna Loy. By then the reinforcements would be out. Just now the bar was under the sole command of a heavily made-up blonde in tuxedo pants and a man's white dress shirt with a red bow tie, who came over to our booth and took my order for a screwdriver. I was fighting the flu and thought the vitamin C would help. The vodka was just there to help me forget I was drinking orange juice. She turned to Merlin, and the glitter in his eye told me to sit back and shake a smoke out of the pack. He was experimenting again.

"I got something new," he told her. "How's your game?"

She glanced back at the clock, ringed in green neon with a picture of the Rat Pack on the face, and let out some air. "Good enough, I guess. It's early yet."

"You might want to write it down."

"Just jump right in. I'll holler if I get lost."

"Start out with a rocks glass. Mix two ounces Gordon's gin, two ounces creme de cacao"—he pronounced it *cocoa*—"two ounces black coffee. Everything's two ounces, got that?"

She nodded. "*Hot* coffee?"

"Cold if you got it. Throw in ice if you ain't, but

7

don't do a *Titanic* on the son of a bitch. One thing more. A teaspoon of blackstrap molasses."

"Molasses?"

"Most important part. Well, except for the gin." He sat back, beaming. "I call it the Bubonic Plague."

She rolled her eyes and left.

"Still searching for the perfect drink?" I lit a Winston.

"Not no more. I come up with it ten days ago at the Erin, fifteen minutes before closing. That's how I got this coat. Tommy McCarty bet me I couldn't invent a drink before the lights come up that wouldn't send everyone in the joint running to the crapper. He went home wearing that moldy old Harris tweed I bought in Ecorse."

"Congratulations. You shafted your best friend and made the *Bartender's Guide* all in one shot."

"Tommy stopped being my best friend when he voted for Bush."

The barmaid returned and set down my screwdriver and a rocks glass containing a dead black liquid. "Can I interest either of you in a cigar?"

I shook my head. Merlin produced a slim box from an inside breast pocket and stripped off the cellophane. "I got my own, angel cake. Why send thirty bucks to Castro when I can burn ten boxes of Grenadiers for the same price?" He speared a slim green cigar between his lips and leaned over while she lit it with a wooden match as long as a swizzle stick. The stench reminded me I needed to get my brakes relined. When we were alone, he blew a ring at the ceiling and slid his glass my way. "Go ahead, take a hit."

I put out my cigarette in a glass ashtray with a picture of General Grant in the base and sipped. "Not bad." I pushed the drink back across the table. "A little sweet."

"That's the molasses." He looked at the cigar in profile. It was an excuse to admire the half-carat diamond on his pinky. You never knew when Merlin was eating catfood or hauling his wallet around on a hand truck; his suits always fit, even if the coat didn't, and the shine on his cordovans would attract low-flying aircraft. I'd inherited him from Dale Leopold, my late partner. A long time ago, when the Irish were in charge, he had run interference between Mayor Cavanagh and the local building trade. These days he hung around the Erin Go Bar in Corktown, peddling dirt in election years, swapping war stories, and living off a succession of women who thought he could do with a little reforming.

I drank some of my screwdriver and put it down. It tasted like a Bubonic Plague. "Whatever it is, Merlin, it better not cost too much. I haven't had a client in a week."

He stuck a hurt look on his face. It was all skull,

bad skin plastered over the cheekstraps and eyesockets. "Dale should of taught you respect. The two of us was like that." The pair of fingers he held up were exactly the same length.

"His dying words? 'Don't give Merlin Gilly the time of day if you expect to get it back.'"

"Dying words my ass. He was dead on arrival at the pavement."

I shrugged out of my belted coat. The sight of him in all that fur overheated me, but he hadn't broken a sweat. If he ever did it would come out pure Gordon's gin. "Paper says snow," I said. "I've got a throbbing rib says the same thing. A bullet splintered it eighteen years ago last November."

"Who cares? I got something will cost you an easy fifty."

"I don't have any easy fifties. What can I get for a sweaty sawbuck?"

He filled his mouth with smoke and let it roll out. A complacent Merlin Gilly is harder to look at than a C-section. I folded two twenties and a ten into a tight rectangle and walked it across the back of my hand. That fascinated and irritated him. Parlor tricks weren't in his repertoire.

"Guy downtown needs a good detective. They're all busy so I thought of you."

"Jail or Holding?"

"DIA."

I walked the bills back the other way. "DIA to me stands for the Detroit Institute of Arts. What's it stand for to you?"

"Same thing. You think I ain't got no culture? I gaped at a Van Gogh there once." He pronounced both *g*'s.

"Forget it, Merl. Where would you fence it?"

He thought about getting mad, then let it blow. "This is about missing property. There's a ten percent finder's fee, might run ten grand."

"Stolen painting?"

"A book, if you can believe it. I mean, with the liberry right across the street, where you can borrow one free gratis and nobody chases you. Crime's gone to hell in this town."

"When did you ever borrow a book?"

He pushed back his chair. "I come up here to do you a turn, you insult me. I guess I'm leaving."

"You're still sitting." But I stood the fifty on its end within his reach. He scooted up his chair and stuck the rectangle in the pocket with the cigars.

"His name's Harold Boyette. He's got him a private line." He gave me a number from memory. I pulled out my notebook and scribbled. "Some kind of old book expert," he said. "I guess there's a living in it. I'm a people person myself."

"Uh-huh. All dead presidents." I put away the notebook.

"Hey, if I started paying taxes now, Uncle Sam would have a stroke."

"Who's your source?"

"Cost you another fifty."

I moved a shoulder and drank orange juice and vodka. "I never knew you to take the short money when there was more than a hundred to be made."

"Aw, you know my contacts. All they know about books is the point spread in Cincinnati." He glanced at the clock, pressed out his Grenadier, and picked up his drink. "I'm due at the Erin. Get this?" He cocked an elbow toward the check the barmaid had left.

"Why should today be any different? Got a date?"

He grinned. His teeth were his only good feature and he took care of them. "Auto money. She thinks I look like Johnny Depp."

I played with my glass.

"I never figured you for screwdrivers," he said.

"I'm fighting a bug."

"That ain't the way to do it. You need hot Vernor's and Smirnoff's, half and half."

"What do you call it?"

He finished his Bubonic Plague and set it down, gently and with pity. "You only get to name one drink. Everybody knows that."

PRIME CRIME FROM
<u>DONALD E. WESTLAKE</u>

AVAILABLE WHEREVER WARNER BOOKS ARE SOLD

1010